Death at the Tidal Mill

Sandrine Perrot - Brittany Mystery Series
Book 5

Christophe Villain

Celebration by the Rance

A thunderstorm front swept over the Emerald Coast, and the loud pattering of rain on the skylights awakened Sandrine. It was early in the morning, and she forced herself to stay in bed but it was hard to fall asleep again. Her body felt tired, but too many unpleasant thoughts whirled around her mind, keeping her awake. She had taken a few days off and would resume her duties at the Saint-Malo police station today, which she hadn't entered since the investigations in Bécherel. She wondered what to expect after the eventful days of the past week. Probably nothing good. First, a coffee, then the world would look friendlier.

She didn't want to wake Léon and carefully pushed aside the duvet. The jogging bottoms and hoodie hanging over a chair would have to do for the moment. She could dress for work later.

In the kitchen, which was open to the living room, she frothed milk and poured a double espresso into it. The rain had passed and she went into the garden, a bowl of café au lait in one hand and a warm blanket in the other. Drops fell from the trees, and the grass of the lawn was wet under her bare feet. A

fresh breeze, making her shiver, rustled through the leaves of the
bushes at the edge of her property. With a thread-worn towel,
she half-dried one of the loungers before sitting down and wrapping the fleece blanket around her legs. The bowl warmed her
hands pleasantly, and she sipped the hot coffee. Sandrine loved
the garden behind the former sheepfold, which had been
converted into an apartment, and enjoyed the view of the vast
bay of Mont-Saint-Michel. On the opposite side of the bay, the
edge of the rising sun appeared over the coast of Normandy.
The clouds glowed in a soft pink, eliciting a smile from her. She
breathed in the sea air, carrying the spicy scent of pine. It was
her favourite time of day when the small towns along the
Emerald Coast slowly woke up, and the first boats set sail.

Léon came down the stairs and made a coffee for himself.
He had come home late from the Équinoxe and stayed
overnight. Sandrine turned to him as he stepped onto the
terrace.

"Why are you up so early? You hardly slept."

"I wanted to see you before you went to work." He leaned
over and kissed her.

"I'm not leaving for a while," she said. "We have plenty of
time for a leisurely breakfast. Sit down, I'll see if there's anything
in the fridge."

"Oh, I'll take care of that." He waved it off.

"As you wish."

Léon took over the kitchen in her tiny house when he was
visiting, and she didn't resist. He loved conjuring up something
delicious and spoiling her, while she saw cooking as a tedious
chore. In that respect, they complemented each other perfectly.

"What about you? When will you be off work today?"

Sandrine looked up at him. He usually didn't ask but took
her unpredictable working hours with stoic calmness.

"I'm not tied up with any current case that could keep me at the station. With the many overtime hours I've accumulated, there's nothing stopping me from being home by early afternoon. Anything planned?" *Perhaps a surprise outing?* He had been talking more often lately about wanting to show her more of Brittany. A free weekend was perfect for that. According to the weather forecast, it would be warm and dry, suitable for a motorcycle trip along the coast.

"As a matter of fact, we do," he said, sitting down next to her. Sandrine had a feeling he wasn't talking about a romantic candlelit dinner and a good wine.

"And what would that be?"

"We've been invited somewhere."

She looked at him questioningly, waiting for him to continue. She didn't have many acquaintances who would spontaneously invite them out.

"By Lilou and her boyfriend, Alain Nebot."

Lilou Lanvers trained with her and Léon at the same martial arts studio, but Sandrine never expected a private invitation from her. They weren't that close.

"From her and her boyfriend ... she has a boyfriend? I always thought ... never mind. What kind of event are we invited to?"

"Alain is hosting a small party tonight. It's not far from here. The two of them own an old mill by the Rance."

"Tonight? And we're getting an invitation just now?"

"Of course not. I'm sorry, but our lives have been quite hectic lately, and I forgot to mention it. My mind was elsewhere."

She placed her hand on his forearm and gently stroked it. After the raid and the drug discovery in his office, he could have easily lost his club; even a prison sentence had been within the realms of possibility. At least those accusations had proven baseless.

"No problem. Tell Lilou I'm looking forward to it."

"Thank you. I was afraid I'd have to cancel or go alone."

"Why should you have all the fun?"

Whether it would actually be fun remained to be seen. She was sceptical because she and Lilou didn't necessarily share the same sense of humour.

"Right, I'll go to the kitchen and throw something in the pan," he said, getting up. His relief at her acceptance was clearly visible.

"I'm looking forward to it," she assured him.

On his way back into Sandrine's cottage, he stopped and turned to her.

"I'll pick you up this afternoon and bring a tent. Do you have a sleeping bag?"

"A what?" She straightened up and looked at him, bewildered.

"A sleeping bag. It can get quite chilly at night."

"We're sleeping in a tent?"

"Of course. A lot of people will be coming, and Alain needs to accommodate everyone somehow."

"Why don't we just drive back home in the evening and sleep in a cozy and comfortable bed?"

"Are you not adventurous?"

Sandrine blew out her breath between her lips. Actually, her job fulfilled her appetite for adventure completely.

"Of course. Spending a night in a tent will surely be memorable," she fibbed, not wanting to disappoint him. He seemed excited about the party. It couldn't be worse than a night in the car during surveillance. Except for the stones and roots under the sleeping mat or the rain dripping through the tent fabric. *I must remember to bring mosquito repellent.*

"Don't worry, I'll bring a second sleeping bag for you. Otherwise, we'll hardly need anything. I'll take care of it for us." He smiled contentedly and went back inside Sandrine's tiny house.

She sighed softly. The past few weeks had been stressful; she would have preferred a lazy weekend inside the comfort of her own four walls. She had grown up in Paris; camping in the great outdoors was not among her preferred childhood memories.

* * *

Sandrine entered the open-plan space where her workstation was located. Inès Boni waved to her from her glassed-in office at the end of the room. Brigadier Chief de Police Adel Azarou swivelled his office chair and looked at her. As usual, he was slightly overdressed for the job. If it became necessary to climb into a dumpster again, she would gladly let him take the lead in his hand-sewn leather shoes and beige polo shirt. The thought brought a smile to her face. But it faded when she saw Renard Dubois sitting at his desk. The seat opposite him was empty. Brigadier Poutin, whom one rarely saw without Dubois, had been placed on leave. He had admitted to planting drugs on Léon during a raid at the Équinoxe. At the very least, the officer faced an internal investigation, and if things went poorly for him, possibly charges for fabricating evidence. Despite everything he had done to her and Léon, she felt sorry for the man who had spent his entire working life in the police force, even more so for Dubois, who had lost his longtime partner and friend. She nodded to the brigadier and sat down next to Adel.

"Matisse wants to speak to you to finalise the deployment of personnel and vacation planning," he greeted her. "Don't forget, I submitted my vacation request weeks ago."

"It probably won't be urgent." She wasn't exactly looking forward to the conversation with her boss. Administrative work bored her immensely, and she didn't envy him for his job, which mostly kept him in the office.

"It's utterly quiet in Saint-Malo at the moment. The criminals are on vacation, which suits me just fine."

"I hope it stays that way," she said. The unfinished paperwork piling up on her desk would likely take her a full week to tackle.

"Surely it will. The holidays are coming soon, then the crime rate will further drop, except for the petty thefts." He rested his forearms on the desk and leaned forward slightly.

"Any plans for the weekend?"

"We're invited to a party where we'll be spending the night in a tent."

He looked at her bewildered. "That sounds like the kind of fun you love," he said sarcastically.

"Mock me all you want. I'm a city girl. How should I know what to bring for camping?"

"Bonjour," greeted Inès. The office manager placed several document folders on Adel's desk. "It sounds like Sandrine is invited to Alain Nebot's party." Since their return from Bécherel, they had decided to switch to informal address. Yet, it didn't quite roll off the young woman's tongue smoothly. The slight hesitation was hard to miss.

"You know him?"

"Of course. He's renovating a tidal mill on the Rance. It used to belong to the Château de Tréchet."

"The former tidal mill?" Adel seemed surprised.

"Exactly. Why?"

He looked at Sandrine. "Then you'll see my sister, Jamila. She's there with her class. Practical history lessons or something. We didn't have that kind of thing at my old school. I'd pitch the tent far away from the gang if you want to get any sleep. Jamila has been completely overexcited for a week now." She knew the young woman from the Papillon Rouge creperie in the old town, where she worked after school.

"Léon hinted that it's a larger party, but I didn't expect a school class. Makes sense, since Lilou is a history teacher at the high school." She remembered the lump of iron the woman had shown her a while ago. It came from a historic blast furnace they had built and operated with her students. She was always good for a surprise.

Adel leaned back and massaged his neck thoughtfully. "Geneviève will be there too. She's into anything related to the Middle Ages, and she's preparing an exhibition in the former farmhouse that belongs to the Château de Tréchet, just a few minutes' walk from the mill."

"Then maybe we'll meet. Surely she'll want to take you along."

"It's unlikely. I'm on duty today. And besides, I hardly look like I care about a night in a tent, do I?"

"As if I do?"

Adel looked at her for a while. "Boots, leather pants, gloves, and a helmet. It does look somewhat rustic. What do you think, Inès?"

"Should I ride a motorcycle in a dress and high heels?"

"I'm sure Sandrine will somehow survive a camping trip," said Inès. "Léon will surely ensure a pleasant overnight stay. The main thing is that the tent is waterproof, in case it rains again. But now I have to go; I actually have work to do, unlike some people. Don't forget your expense reports, or there won't be any money."

Sandrine looked at her intently, but she couldn't tell if the casual remark about Léon was meant to be suggestive or not. Judging by the grin on Adel's face, it probably was.

"I'll go see Matisse now, and then I'll tackle the paperwork," she decided, standing up. She was back to the daily grind.

* * *

Léon picked her up in Cancale late in the afternoon. The way to the mill led south past Saint-Malo, and they crossed the Rance at the tidal power station. Shortly thereafter, they turned onto the country road that followed the course of the river southward.

"We go in here."

He turned onto a dirt road, and Sandrine was glad Léon had taken the SUV. His Karmann-Ghia would have definitely gotten stuck in the potholes and deep ruts, hastily filled with gravel. *My Citroën 2CV would have easily handled the path.* On the one hand, she was proud of her car, but on the other, she was glad not to have to wash it after driving on the muddy road. About a few hundred metres farther, a single-storey building appeared between the trees of a small wooded area, with several cars parked in front of it.

"There's an asphalt road leading to the château and the farmhouse, but we can't park well there, and the space in front of the mill is limited. Alain asked me to park the car here and walk the rest of the way. Luckily, it's not too far."

"Looks like an ancient stable or barn," said Sandrine, getting out. It reminded her of the cottage she lived in in Cancale. Only this one was abandoned and left to decay. Ivy had overgrown the wall of rough stones. If there were any windows, they couldn't be seen under the dense vegetation. The roof had collapsed in places, the rest covered with a layer of moss.

"The sheepfold belongs to the Château de Tréchet, but farming was abandoned decades ago. Today, only the owner lives there. A quirky guy who sold the mill to Alain and Lilou. It was in a sorry state, just like the sheepfold. I'm curious to see what they've made of it."

"Looks like someone wants to restore the building." Sandrine pointed to a stack of lumber piled up at the edge of the parking lot.

"You should ask Lilou; she'll know what the owner intends."
Léon retrieved a round, flat package from the trunk.

"What's that for?"

"That's our tent."

"It looks like it's going to be quite cozy," she said, eyeing the small package sceptically. "I haven't set up something like this since school."

"You don't have to. The tent sets up all by itself." Léon beamed at her with a broad smile.

"Says who?"

"The salesman in the store I bought it from. All I have to do is take it out of the case, toss it up, and it unfolds. Perfect."

"How intriguing."

"You'll see, it'll be a real adventure, even for a city kid like you. We've got everything: sleeping bags, mats, a camping lantern, and plenty of snacks."

She retrieved her backpack from the trunk, threw it on her back and took the two sleeping mats, while he carried a collapsible crate filled with their gear.

"Let's go before all the best camping spots are taken. A clear view of the river would be nice."

"That should be doable," Léon promised.

A narrow dirt path led from the parking lot through the wooded area to the mill. After a short walk, they reached an open area between the forest and the Rance. The tide had significantly raised the river level, and sailboats drifted lazily by. Teenagers stood on the shore, waving to the sailors. It must be the school class Adel had mentioned. She looked for Jamila, but couldn't spot her.

A single-storey building made of grey stones with a rectangular annex stood at the end of a wall that curved in a wide arc, framing part of the riverbank and forming a retention basin, similar to the tidal pool at Saint-Malo beach. The dam was interrupted along the outer wall of the house, and a water wheel slowly turned in the flowing waters of the Rance.

"Is this the mill Lilou and her boyfriend renovated?" she asked Léon, who set down a crate.

"Yes. They restored it true to every detail. Except for the foundation, everything was rotten, and the two of them put in a lot of work and certainly a tidy sum of money. But now it's a real gem. There aren't many tidal mills like this left in Brittany. Upstream is the Moulin du Prat, which is open to visitors."

"Living directly by the water must be very pleasant in summer. Perhaps a bit too damp and chilly in winter."

"They haven't moved in yet, if they even plan to. Alain mainly works in the mill."

"He's a miller?" She found it hard to imagine a need for freshly ground grain.

"No. Look at the annex."

Sandrine examined the outside corner of the house, which was attached at a right angle to the main building. The windows were dark, but smoke billowed from the chimney. It was too warm to turn on the heating.

"He's a blacksmith and uses the annex as a workshop," Léon explained.

"Can one make a living from that?" He had piqued her curiosity; she had never met a blacksmith before. Lilou wouldn't want her to ask about her finances, it was too private, but Léon knew the two of them well.

"I think so. Alain specialises in historical weapons and armour, which he crafts using traditional techniques: swords, daggers, pikes and axes. All things that can be used to kill."

She didn't miss his searching gaze and answered the unspoken question. "The pistol is at home in the safe, where it belongs. We're here to celebrate with people, not to hunt down criminals."

"I didn't assume otherwise," Léon replied, a tad too quickly to sound completely sincere.

At the mill they met Lilou, who was talking to an older man who wore a moss-green tweed jacket, a matching cap and tall rubber boots, and leaned on a silver-handled walking stick with both hands. His snowy white hair brushed his shoulders, making his slender face appear even more gaunt. Sandrine estimated him to be in his late sixties.

"There you are. Just in time for dinner," Lilou said, turning back to the man. "Sandrine and Léon, friends of mine."

"Pleased to meet you," he said, extending a hand. His grip was surprisingly firm, as was the gaze of his grey-blue eyes, which studied Sandrine intently. "Alexandre de Tréchet," he introduced himself.

"Alexandre owns the château." Lilou gestured towards the edge of the forest. A three-storey mansion rose above the tree-tops. At its centre was a square tower, from which two identical wings extended. Small windows pierced the roof of dark slate.

"A splendid estate with an excellent view of the Rance," Léon said, impressed.

"An old family property that requires far too much work. The children have moved out, and I only occupy a few rooms there now. The rest remains empty for most of the year." He glanced at Lilou and smiled at her. "While they were renovating the mill, Lilou and Alain lived in the château; they often kept me company and helped with some pending repairs. Without the two of them, I would have surely sold the Château de Tréchet long ago."

Sandrine nodded thoughtfully. An estate of this size and with direct riverfront must be worth a fortune. Renting an apartment in a comparable house was certainly beyond the financial means of a teacher.

"We enjoy helping at the château." Lilou brushed it off. "But now come along, someone needs to take care of all the food our guests brought, and you both look hungry."

Sandrine gave Léon a quick glance. He hadn't mentioned any meal contributions, but he nodded reassuringly and tapped a huge plastic container in the crate he was carrying. So, he had taken care of it.

"Wonderful that life has returned here. In recent years, the area has become increasingly lonely." Alexandre de Tréchet looked out over the mill and the guests gathered for the celebration.

Sandrine guessed there must be about a hundred people plus Lilou's school class. Probably more people than she even knew in Brittany. *So this is what people around here call a small party.*

Several men surrounded an oversized swing grill slowly turning over a charcoal fire. A few steps away stood a smoker that reminded them of a tipped-over elongated barrel. Grey smoke rose into the sky from a side-protruding chimney pipe.

"That smells absolutely fantastic." Léon smiled with a mix of admiration for the cook and anticipation of the food. "I'll put the salad we brought to the buffet."

Lilou waved to a man with broad shoulders who towered over most of the guests by at least a hand's breadth. He set aside the grill tongs, took off the sturdy leather apron, and approached them.

"Sandrine, this is Alain," she introduced him, running her fingers through her millimetre-short bright red hair. If it weren't so absurd, Sandrine might have thought the otherwise confident woman seemed nervous introducing her friend. She offered him a hand, which he shook firmly.

"Pleasure to finally meet you, Sandrine. Lilou often speaks of you," he said. He wasn't particularly formal, but he was so friendly it felt natural.

"Really?" she said, surprised, before she could think about how it would sound.

"But of course, you often train together. I hear you're a tough opponent."

"That's flattering. In reality, she easily kicks my butt," Sandrine tried to joke. Occasionally, she helped out as a sparring partner. In a real match, she wouldn't have lasted three rounds against the wiry woman who regularly competed for the Breton championships.

"That's not what I heard."

"Hello, Alain." Léon came back from the buffet, chewing on a piece of baguette with butter and ham. He gave the man a hearty slap on his broad shoulders. "When I last saw the mill, it was hardly more than a ruin. You've created a real miracle."

"Thank you. It was hard work, but in the end, the mill turned out exactly as we imagined," he said, looking at Lilou who nodded in agreement, and put an arm around her shoulders.

"You probably want to take a look at the workshop." Enthusiasm that made it impossible to refuse the offer flickered in his eyes. The man seemed to love his work with all his heart.

"Of course," Léon assured, without hesitation. "I only know the old forge."

"Then follow me."

Alain led them to the annex. The massive door was locked, and Léon looked at him questioningly.

"Just show them," Lilou urged gently. She seemed to know what her boyfriend had in mind.

"I couldn't resist installing a medieval lock," he said, reaching for an overhanging wooden beam and pulling out an oddly shaped object.

"Of course it's not real protection, but no one steals anything here anyway."

"I have my doubts. You surely have some valuable things in there." A slightly cynical tone crept into Léon's voice.

"You're from the police. Tell me if it's safe." Alain handed Sandrine the key, which looked more like a multiple right-angled bent rod with a handle. Curiously, she took it.

"In any case, it won't fit in a trouser pocket."

Alain laughed. "It's not meant to," he replied.

"Men's toys," Lilou muttered under her breath.

Sandrine noticed a finger-thick borehole above the handle on the massive wooden door. "So that must be the keyhole," she remarked. She turned the key and slowly inserted it through the opening until two of the bends were through. "Now the tip should be facing the door from the inside," she murmured, noticing Alain's approving nod from the corner of her eye. She pulled the key towards her until it met resistance. "Must be a movable bolt," she thought aloud, carefully manoeuvring the tip over the wood. "Got it," she said as she found the notch in the bolt. She pulled the handle towards her until she was sure the key was securely seated in the recess and turned it. The bolt resisted briefly, then slid aside and the door swung open.

"That was faster than most have managed so far. Impressive. I'm sure you learn that kind of thing in the police," Alain remarked.

"Or from burglars," Sandrine joked and stepped aside.

She saw Léon smiling. He had learned quite a bit about her family lately. Just recently, she had picked the lock of his club's door and deactivated the alarm system with a few quick moves when he had forgotten his key in the office. As a result, he had installed a more modern system.

Alain opened the door and turned on the overhead light. The interior of the workshop was more spacious than it appeared from the outside. A brick forge stood in the centre of the room directly under the chimney. Within reach was an anvil, and on the walls hung hammers, pliers, chisels and other tools a blacksmith needed for his work.

"What's that?" Sandrine walked over to a smooth wooden log that hung rotatable in a metal frame. A heavy iron hammer was attached to the head, and below was an anvil.

"That's a replica of a tilt hammer from the late Middle Ages," Alain explained, tapping on the wood. "The log is also called a helm. It's movable, suspended on a rocker, and is operated by a wooden camshaft driven by the waterwheel." Sandrine stood next to him, studying the contraption. The camshaft was made of an oak log well over a foot in diameter and it looked as if a crane had been needed to install it here. "The camshaft presses down the rear end of the helm; the iron head rises until it is released. Then it falls onto the anvil."

"You forge with that?" Léon asked.

"Absolutely. The hammer works flawlessly, requires little maintenance, and is environmentally friendly. Simply perfect. Otherwise, shaping the iron would be a real hassle. Tomorrow morning, I'll show the school class how it's done. We'd be delighted if you stayed and watched."

"We'd love to," Léon promised.

"The waterwheel not only powers the hammer. When the hammer is not needed, we use water power to produce the electricity we need for the mill. It's even enough to supply the manor," Lilou explained. "Our goal is to be self-sufficient."

"That's great," Sandrine replied, knowing how important Lilou's independence was to her in every facet of her life. "It works like the tidal power plant on the Rance," she added, drawing a parallel.

"Yes, that's why this type of mill is also called a tidal mill. There were several of these in Brittany. About a dozen are still preserved. The tide pushes the water up the Rance and drives the waterwheel. The basin fills with river water, which slowly drains away at low tide and flows over the wheel again. This way, we produce electricity almost all day. More reliable than a wind turbine and much more aesthetically pleasing. The mill has been standing here for centuries and will continue to do so if properly maintained," Alain explained enthusiastically.

Léon walked over to a massive workbench against the wall at the head of the room, where some axes, a morning star on a chain and several knives lay.

"Your latest creations?" he inquired.

Alain picked up one and handed it to Sandrine. The axe was slightly longer than her forearm, with patterns burned into the wooden handle that she didn't recognise. The widening blade shimmered softly in the light of the ceiling lamps. She ran a finger along the sharp edge. It was definitely not a weapon meant to hang decoratively on a wall only.

"Celtic?" she asked.

"Yes. It corresponds to discoveries in the Celtic graves found in Brittany. I've stuck as closely as possible to historical techniques," Alain explained, taking a second axe and almost caressing the blade. "I'm quite satisfied with the result." He was clearly proud of his intricate work, and rightfully so.

"Who are they for?" Léon inquired.

"I forged half a dozen. Two are going to regional museums, and the rest to collectors. One is even going overseas," Alain said, swinging the axe effortlessly from his wrist and laughing. His eyes sparkled with joy. It seemed he wasn't just capable of crafting weapons but wielding them as well.

"They look really impressive," Sandrine remarked, placing the axe back on the workbench.

"Beauty is only a minor aspect of their value," Alain replied, looking at Lilou.

"Isn't it time to tend to the food?" Lilou reminded him, as if she could read his thoughts.

"They don't need me at the grill. I'd just get in the way," Alain said, winking conspiratorially at Léon. "We should check how well balanced these axes really are," he added playfully.

Lilou sighed softly. "Do as you please. I need to tend to my teenagers before they get bored and into mischief," she said with resignation.

"Then come along," Alain said to Sandrine and Léon, handing each of them their own axe and heading towards the door.

"What's he up to?" Sandrine whispered to Léon.

"We're sort of the quality control managers," he replied, chuckling softly. Léon waved the axe through the air and followed his friend.

"He's finally found someone to join in his little games," Lilou remarked. Sandrine had never seen the usually stern woman smile so gently before. *She must truly love Alain.*

"Where are you?" Léon called out to her. "You're missing all the fun."

She followed the two men to the back of the workshop, where they stopped in front of a wall made of wooden planks. Sandrine estimated it to be about three metres high and roughly the same width. Deep grooves covered the boards. At eye level, someone had painted a white circle on the wooden wall, about the size of a human head.

"The axes weren't meant for chopping down trees or splitting wood; they were forged for war," explained Alain as he ran his hand gingerly over the blade. "Let's see if my work paid off."

He stepped back a few metres, balanced the axe in his hand, focused on the target and hurled the weapon which struck the centre of the circle and quivered as it stuck.

"Direct hit," exclaimed Léon. "Now it's your turn, Sandrine."

"Stand here. Left foot slightly forward, keep your eye on the target. Generate momentum from your hips," instructed Alain.

The grip felt smooth and solid in her hand. The weapon was lighter than she had expected. Slowly, Sandrine turned her right shoulder back until she felt the tension in her muscles, then she flung the axe at the wall. It crashed into the wood with a loud thud.

"A true talent," cheered Alain.

"I'm at least an arm's length away from the target. In a battle, my opponent would laugh at me, and I'd be as good as dead."

"At least it's stuck in the wood, which not everyone manages on their first throw. A little practice, and no one would dare laugh at you," reassured Alain.

"Thanks for your encouragement," she replied.

She waited until Léon had also thrown. He missed the target as well, but only by a hand's width.

"Nice aim," she said, going on her tiptoes to kiss him. Her stomach rumbled loudly, and Léon looked at her with an amused expression.

"Keep practicing as long as you enjoy it," Sandrine said, "but I desperately need something to eat now."

The men exchanged looks and grinned.

"I'll be right there," said Léon, not sounding particularly convincing. She left them behind and strolled across the meadow to the grill.

"You've come at the right time." Lilou waved her over, a long carving knife in her right hand. "Grab some sides while I carve the beef brisket." In front of her lay several massive pieces of meat with a blackened crust, likely from the barrel-like smoker. The woman glanced at a grill thermometer she pulled out of the roast and nodded in satisfaction.

"Looks delicious."

"This thing has been cooking and resting for twelve hours. I'm curious to see what it looks like inside. Plates are over there."

Sandrine took her time to survey the colourful buffet set up on a long wooden table. Most of the guests had contributed something. She recognised the bowl of seafood salad brought by Léon, which seemed to be quite popular as only small remnants remained. Alongside the salads were various baguettes and a tray of oven-roasted potatoes with dips. They looked good. She grabbed a plate and placed a fist-sized potato on it, which she cracked open with a fork and added a piece of butter. Small bowls of chives and spring onions were available, which she generously sprinkled on top. A platter of baked scallops on a bed of spinach smiled at her, and she took two. With her free hand, she broke off the tip of a baguette and tucked it into her pocket. That should do for now.

Lilou had sliced the beef brisket into thin slices and placed one on Sandrine's plate.

"Give it a try, if you don't like it there's plenty more on the grill," Lilou offered.

"It certainly smells delicious." The meat was light pink, and a fine juice ran out.

"The crust is just coarse sea salt and crushed pepper. We keep it pretty simple," explained Lilou as she began to serve the other guests. Sandrine strolled with her plate to the Rance and sat down on a rock by the riverbank. She could stay here for a while. She looked back at the smithy and saw Léon chatting with Alain and some people she didn't know. He noticed her and waved. She was glad she had come here with him.

"Madame Perrot?" someone addressed her, and she turned around. The sister of Adel Azarou stood before her. The usually chic young woman was wearing jeans, a plain T-shirt and sturdy shoes. She had forgone jewellery and makeup today.

"Hello, Jamila, nice to see you again," Sandrine greeted the girl. "Adel told me you would be here."

"I'm in Madame Lanvers's history class."

Sandrine looked at her in surprise; she'd never heard anyone address Lilou by her last name. But then, she was Jamila's teacher.

"I hope you're not here on official business," the girl joked. "Or is there a criminal you want to arrest?"

"Not today. That's Adel's job," Sandrine replied.

"Sorry about how I look," she said, wiping some black marks off her trousers. "I have to take care of the charcoal."

"Are you in charge of the grill, then?"

"No, not at all." She lowered her voice and stepped closer to her. "I'm a vegetarian, and there's enough food on the grill to feed a pack of wolves. Not my thing." She shook her head slightly in disgust, and a strand of her long, wavy hair fell into her face.

"So what's the charcoal for?"

"For the furnace." Jamila pointed to a small round structure, just over a metre high, that strongly resembled a termite mound to Sandrine.

"What's that?"

"A blast furnace. We built it last weekend. Luckily, the weather was mostly warm and dry, and during the short rain showers, we stretched a tarpaulin over it. By now, the clay has dried and hardened so we can try it out later. I'm quite excited."

"It will definitely be exciting." Sandrine hadn't expected the girl to be enthusiastic about historical iron-making, but she had clearly underestimated her. Something that spoke to Lilou's quality as a teacher.

"During the past few weeks, we've been collecting bog iron ore, which will go into the furnace today. I'm in charge of mixing it with the charcoal. It does mess up your clothes, but it's more pleasant than operating the bellows for hours to keep the temperature up."

"A wise choice."

"Who are you here with?" Jamila asked, smiling. She seemed to hope to find out something about Sandrine's private life.

"I know your teacher from sports. Also, a friend is accompanying me." She looked toward the mill and spotted Léon near the blast furnace, which Alexandre de Tréchet also seemed interested in. At least he was examining it closely while a man who could have been his son in age and appearance was talking to him. He seemed to pay little attention to him, and the stranger abruptly turned around and marched off in a huff. It hadn't seemed like a friendly chat.

"The holidays are starting soon," Jamila began, bringing Sandrine back from her thoughts. "Maybe there could be an opportunity..." She hesitated as if her courage had left her.

"What opportunity?"

"You're the only cop I know, and a pretty cool one at that," she said nervously.

"What about your brother?"

"No way!" she vehemently stated. "He's as uncool as they come and treats me like a child."

Sandrine waited until Jamila gathered her courage and came out with her request.

"I need a work placement, and I thought about applying to the police."

"Why not? Talk to Adel; he's popular at the station and can surely get you a spot."

Jamila sighed deeply. "He's the problem."

"I see," said Sandrine. "He's concerned about you, which is understandable. Our clientele is not exactly good company for a young girl."

"Wouldn't it be advantageous if more women worked in the police force? It could significantly improve their reputation."

"You're right about that. I'll see what I can do." Sandrine would talk to Inès Boni. If anyone knew whether interns were being hired, it was the office manager. "But only if your parents agree."

"I don't see a problem with that," said Jamila confidently.

Sandrine only shared the young woman's enthusiasm to a limited extent. Adel would voice his objections. Convincing him to agree to her internship wouldn't be easy, especially since she could understand many of his concerns quite well. Her own family was also highly dissatisfied with her career choice, albeit for different reasons.

"Should I talk to your brother?" she offered.

"That would be great. He always worries too much. I'm not a little kid. All I want is to get a taste of the work, and he already imagines me in the middle of a shootout with gangsters," she said.

Sandrine laughed. "He knows you won't be given a gun."

"Sure. But he acts as if the job is incredibly dangerous."

"That's not unreasonable."

"In France, more people die from doing household chores than policemen on duty. But he has no objections to me helping around the house."

"Good point," Sandrine murmured.

"Can I count on your support?"

"I'll put in a good word for you, but I can't promise anything."

"That's enough. He really values your opinion." Jamila glanced to the smelting furnace. Lilou stood among some students, waving her over. "I have to go. It's time to fill up the furnace."

"Have fun."

Sandrine watched Jamila go. The girl seemed to know exactly what she wanted. She would talk to Adel, find some harmless activity at the police station. Maybe with Marie Abondio in the forensics lab or with Inès Boni in administration.

It was highly unlikely that anyone would be shooting wildly there.

* * *

Sandrine sat with Léon in front of the blue dome tent he had set up. The tent salesman hadn't exaggerated; to her surprise, it had popped up on its own and looked somewhat sturdy, albeit quite small. She was sceptical whether she could stretch her legs without touching the tent fabric. Two used plates and glasses lay in the grass, which they would wash later. The sleeping mats and bags were already rolled out inside, and she had checked the ground several times for stones that could ruin her sleep.

"You even thought of two pillows," she said.

"Nothing stands in the way of a comfortable night," he replied, placing a battery-operated camping lantern next to her in the grass. "Instead of candles. I hope it's romantic enough."

Sandrine opened a bottle of cider and filled two cups she had brought from home. She handed one to Léon. "To our first night in a tent. Maybe we'll become enthusiastic campers."

She lay down in the grass and looked towards the mill. The meadow sloped gently towards the riverbank. The water of the Rance had receded, and the mill wheel turned evenly and silently in the draining pond. She saw Jamila standing next to Lilou at the smelting furnace, which had been burning for almost two hours now. A boy pressed on the bellows, air flowed into the lower part of the furnace, and sparks flew out like startled fireflies from the open mouth. She almost believed she could hear the hissing of the embers. It wouldn't be long before they broke open the wall to get to the pig iron.

"She's really great with the kids. They all look so enthusiastic. When I think about my history lessons..." Sandrine rolled her eyes and sighed.

"Lilou organises something like this every year with her oldest class. But it's the first time here at the mill."

"The two of them have put their heart and souls into the building."

"It's paid off. Alain is happy with his workshop, and Lilou loves living in nature and being as independent as possible from other people. They'll probably move into the mill house soon. After that, maybe a garden or a herd of goats. Who knows?"

The thought of watching Lilou milk a goat made Sandrine chuckle softly.

"Sorry, I'm being silly. It must be the cider."

"Or the pleasant company."

"No doubt." She kissed him on the cheek. "I'm enjoying being here with you."

"Same here." He put his arm around Sandrine and gently pulled her close. She rested her head on his shoulder and relished the peaceful evening. Camping might not be so bad after all.

* * *

Carefully, Sandrine peeled back the sleeping bag. Another thunderstorm had not occurred, which pleased her as she didn't trust the thin tent to be particularly waterproof. The summer night remained pleasantly warm, and she hadn't closed the sleeping bag zipper. She reached for her clothes and crawled out as quietly as she could into the open air. A cloud had moved in front of the moon. The mill and the tents of the few guests who had stayed, along with those of the school class, were only dimly visible at the other end of the meadow. The river lay behind them like a black ribbon. A light breeze brought fresh sea air from the nearby ocean, masking the smell of ash from the remnants of the smelting furnace. She slipped into her washed-out jogging bottoms and shook out her shoes before putting them on. She wasn't keen on stepping on beetles with her bare feet.

Too much cider, she thought. Although the mill was not inhabited, Alain had left it unlocked so his guests could use the toilet. *Well, here goes.*

No light pierced the darkness. After the exhausting day in the fresh air, everyone seemed to be fast asleep. Only a few of Lilou and Alain's friends were staying overnight on-site. Most had left late in the evening. Sandrine suspected some would reappear tomorrow for the scheduled brunch.

A bat zigzagged wildly across the sky, and Sandrine watched it for a while until it disappeared towards the château. The estate loomed dark against the forest like an abandoned haunted castle. Only a gentle light shone behind a window on the ground floor. *I guess I'm not the only one awake.*

The sound of a door hastily closing broke the silence. It came from the mill. Sandrine switched on the camping lantern and strained to see in the direction of the noise. *Probably just another visitor to the toilets.* A shadow darted away. The faint light of the lantern wasn't enough to discern more than a human silhouette that quickly vanished into the night. The policewoman in her wished she had her flashlight, but it was at home in a kitchen drawer.

Don't be childish, she scolded herself. She took the lantern and headed towards the mill. The workshop was locked. She gently rattled the door, but the latch seemed securely anchored. *I must have been mistaken.* Nevertheless, she turned back and looked across the open space up to the château. A shadow darted through the sky and disappeared into the forest. Probably an owl. Everything was peaceful tonight. Time to find the toilet and quickly get back into the sleeping bag.

She yawned deeply and entered the mill house.

The Man in the Mill

"Sandrine?" someone called outside the tent, fumbling with the zipper of the entrance.

"Yes," she said, sitting up and yawning extensively. She couldn't have slept for long, and her back ached. *Maybe I'm too old for a night on the ground.*

With a soft rasp, the flap opened and a woman peered in. Leon turned around and pulled the sleeping bag over his head, annoyed. The glow of a lamp illuminated her face.

"Genevieve? I didn't see you yesterday."

"We were working on the exhibition for a long time. When we finally finished, everyone was already in their tents sleeping."

"And now you want to fetch me for breakfast?" Sandrine looked outside. The edge of the sun was just scraping the horizon. "Isn't it a little too early for that?"

"You need to come to the mill. It's urgent."

"At this hour? Can't it wait?" The sleeping bag was warm and cosy, and she didn't feel like leaving it.

"No. We need a police officer."

"It's my weekend off," she grumbled. "If something was

stolen, call Adel. He's on duty and will be glad to find a reason to come here."

"He's already on his way and was very insistent on waking you up immediately. So come on, get out of the sleeping bag. This is an emergency."

"What happened? Did someone steal the leftovers from the buffet?"

"Alain's claimed that something terrible has happened. He sounded quite upset, which scares me, considering he's usually the epitome of calm."

"Stay here, I'll be back by breakfast time," she said to Leon, who sat up and shot Genevieve an annoyed look. She hoped she was right, but the concerned look on the young woman's face gave her an uneasy feeling. *I was really looking forward to this weekend.*

She pulled Sandrine by the arm and dragged her along. With one hand, Sandrine grabbed her jogging bottoms and shoes, putting them on as she walked.

Gazing sternly and arms crossed in front of his chest, Alain Nebot was guarding the door to the workshop, which stood open by a hand's breadth. He looked determined to protect the forge by any means necessary and not allow anyone to pass. Sandrine wondered why he didn't hold a battle-axe or any other weapon in his hands.

"I haven't touched anything," he greeted her. "Not a thing."

"What haven't you touched?"

He pushed the door further open with one hand, just enough for Sandrine to squeeze in.

"Stay outside!" he ordered Geneviève in an unusually stern tone.

"I'm not a little child," she retorted, stopping in front of the door.

Sandrine walked a few steps into the dark workshop. The

smell of cold bitter smoke hung heavily in the air. Faint light from the early morning sun shone through the windows, but it was enough to see why she was needed here.

Alain switched on the overhead light. Harsh light flooded the room, and Sandrine squinted for a moment.

"Damn it," she cursed softly.

A human body lay face down on the anvil. The head of a sledgehammer was stuck between his shoulder blades, preventing the corpse from sliding down. Blood smeared the metal and the sleeve of the jacket. The arms hung limp. At the fingertips, almost touching the ground, hung thick, red drops. The clay floor had absorbed the moisture and shimmered dull in the light of the ceiling lamps. The man couldn't have been dead for long. At most a few hours. Sandrine recognised immediately that it was Alexandre de Tréchet. He wore the same suit as yesterday, and his cane lay beside him on the floor. Searching for a pulse or any other sign of life seemed unnecessary. No one could possibly survive such injuries.

Sandrine stood in the middle of the room. She had come here to celebrate with friends, not to investigate a crime scene. Overshoes and disposable gloves were in her car in Cancale. She decided not to approach the body any further. The risk of contaminating the crime scene or trampling evidence was too great. She would hardly gain any deeper insights before the forensic technicians and the medical examiner had completed their work.

"Who found him?"

"I did," said Alain, stepping beside her, briefly glancing at the body then turning his gaze away. She noticed how pale he looked.

"Last night we brought in the bloom so we could work on it today." He pointed to a dark lump lying in a metal tub.

"The what?"

"The pig iron that Lilou's class smelted in the blast furnace. It needs to be heated again to remove the impurities before it can be used. Otherwise, you can't do anything with it. That's what I use the sledgehammer for. Lilou's students were pretty excited."

"I'm afraid they'll have to wait a while until the forensics team is done here and we can release the workshop again."

"I'm aware," he said, taking a step towards the corpse but Sandrine held his arm. "It's Alexandre, even though he's hard to recognise. The sledgehammer is made for forging iron. Human bones can't possibly withstand the force behind it."

"That's clearly visible," she agreed.

"He was a good man. Who would do such a thing?" Alain sounded upset and confused. He must have had a great deal of affinity for the man.

"That's what I wanted to ask you, actually," Sandrine replied.

"Me?" he asked, astonished. "I certainly didn't touch him."

"I don't assume so either, but you knew the man. Did he have any enemies or was he threatened?"

"Enemies?" he repeated thoughtfully. "There have been some family quarrels lately, but you don't kill someone over that."

"Let's go outside and wait for the police."

"Good idea, the sight is turning my stomach." He turned around and walked slowly to the door.

Alain led her to the long table where the buffet had been set up yesterday. Bags filled with croissants and a stack of baguettes were now ready for breakfast, which would hardly take place as planned. They sat down at the end of the table next to Geneviève. The sight of the corpse had ruined Sandrine's appetite.

Lilou came with some bowls of coffee and hot milk, which

she placed on the table before sitting down with them. She remained silent, but in her eyes Sandrine recognised that the man's death had also disturbed her. Most people needed a while to grasp such a violent act.

"Tell us how you found him," she urged Alain.

"There's not much to tell. I got up early, about half an hour ago around five, to start preparing. The forge needs to be fired up so we can finish the school project today. The plan was to forge a knife from the iron according to an old Celtic pattern."

"A weapon?" Sandrine asked.

"The class discussed and voted on it," said Lilou. "They're supposed to not only learn something but also have fun. The dagger would have ended up in one of the display cases at school."

"At any rate, I went into the workshop and found Alexandre," he continued.

"It's good that you didn't touch anything," Sandrine remarked.

"At first, I was frozen at the sight. I'm not used to corpses." Alain's hands trembled as he poured milk into the bowl and took a sip of café au lait.

"And then?"

"It didn't take an expert to see that he was dead. Just to be safe, I grabbed a hammer to defend myself, but there was no sign of the perpetrator."

"That was wise."

"I watch crime dramas on TV. Once you leave traces, you're always somehow a suspect."

"Well, it's not quite as dramatic as that." In any case, his traces were inevitably on every object in the forge.

"I was here to deliver the baguettes for breakfast," Geneviève said, "and to help with the preparations. I ran into Alain, and he asked me to notify the police and fetch you. I knew Adel was on call, so I phoned him directly."

"My phone is somewhere in the tent or in the forge," explained Alain. "Those things are just nuisances."

"When he needs one, he spends hours looking for it." Lilou leaned over to her boyfriend and kissed him. Sandrine had never seen the woman so tender. She constantly surprised her.

"Was the door locked when you arrived?"

"Yes. I hide the key on the beam in the evenings. You saw it today. But it's no big deal to break into the forge. The lock is more of a toy than an effective deterrent."

Sandrine nodded. Last night she had also found the door locked. Whoever was responsible for Alexandre de Tréchet's death either knew where Alain hid the key or possessed a similar tool to unlock the door and lock it behind them again. The idea that it could be anything other than murder was absurd.

"What could he have wanted here in the middle of the night?" she murmured, more to herself than to the others.

"Nothing," said Alain. "He was hardly ever in the forge. The man suffered from asthma, and the smoke from the charcoal caused breathing problems for him. Besides, he retired to the château relatively early last night."

"Which room was he staying in?" Sandrine asked.

"He lived on the ground floor, in the east wing."

She nodded. She had seen the faint light there. Perhaps from a reading or bedside lamp.

"You also live in the manoir, right?" she asked.

"No. Alexandre provided us with a small apartment in the farmhouse. It's just a short walk behind the château. But last night, we slept in a tent with Lilou's students." Alain lifted his coffee cup and looked thoughtfully over the rim at Sandrine as he took a sip

Sandrine watched him silently until he continued.

"He often said how lucky he had been in his life and that he wanted to give something back to society. At the beginning of last year, he came to us with the idea of turning the farmhouse into a sort of cultural centre. He was thinking of exhibitions by local artists, maybe even a small museum about the history of Brittany."

"A lavish undertaking," she commented.

"We are currently preparing some rooms for an exhibition on medieval Breton literature," Geneviève chimed in. "He was a great support." She fell silent and shook her head slightly, as if she were just realising that she would never speak to him again. Medieval literature. Of course, she would be involved in such a project. Geneviève had completed her PhD on the tragic love story between the theologian and philosopher Abelard and Héloïse from the 12th century.

"Did he have a family?"

"Oh yes." Lilou grimaced, as if the thought of them was enough to make her uncomfortable. "His son Xavier was here yesterday. He didn't seem particularly thrilled about his father's plans."

It must have been the man she had seen with Alexandre de Tréchet. They had obviously argued.

"The entire family arrived at the estate throughout the day," Geneviève said. "None of them seemed happy to find us at the farmhouse."

She looked at Alain, who nodded in agreement.

"Alexandre invited them. The clan gathers at the château once a year."

"A family celebration?"

"More like a board meeting." Alain chuckled bitterly. "A pack of starving wolves has more family spirit than the de Tréchets."

"The château is the family seat, but none of them except Alexandre lives here," said Lilou. "The two sons, a daughter with her husband, and the manager of the family foundation were invited. At least that's what Alexandre told me."

"There's a foundation?" Sandrine inquired.

"Régis Marceau manages it. Unlike the family, he was here yesterday and visited the mill. He was also present during the purchase negotiations. If you can call them negotiations," said Alain. "It was basically given to us, with the condition that we restore it."

"It's likely gained significantly in value by now," speculated Sandrine.

"We've put a lot of work and money into it," said Lilou.

"And it's now a real gem." Sandrine glanced over at the building, illuminated by the first rays of sunlight.

"That's true. But only for us. There's no demand for a tidal mill with a forge using a replica of a medieval trip hammer instead of modern equipment." Alain hesitated briefly as he mentioned the trip hammer. The murder must have significantly dampened his enthusiasm for the device.

"As you can see, we don't gain any advantage from Alexandre's death. The mill already belongs to us," said Lilou.

"I didn't suspect otherwise."

"I know, but I wanted to spare you from asking. It's part of your job to explore the deceased's surroundings for possible motives."

"True."

Geneviève gestured towards the tent. Léon had woken up and stuck his head out. He stretched and ran his hands through his dishevelled hair. Unfortunately, the weekend wouldn't go as they had both hoped. From now on, she was no longer just a guest, but an investigator with a murder to solve.

The sound of a car engine approached. It was still hidden by the trees, but it could only be Adel. Shortly afterward, a white-blue Renault Duster from the police emerged at the edge of the forest. He must have left directly after the call. Geneviève wanted to greet him, but Sandrine signalled for her to stay seated.

"I'd like to speak with him first."

"Understood," said the young woman. "I guess I'm somewhat of a witness, even though I didn't see the crime. That's certainly better than being a suspect."

"Bonjour," Sandrine greeted her colleague and friend after walking over to him.

"What happened? Geneviève was quite vague and only mentioned a dead body."

"Ugly story," said Sandrine. "I hope you haven't had a hearty breakfast yet."

"That bad?" Adel looked over at his girlfriend. "Did she find the body?"

"Don't worry, she didn't see the victim. Alain Nebot, Lilou Lanvers' partner, found the body this morning in his workshop. No one has entered the forge since then, he made sure of that." She looked at the tents of the student group. "And they're still oblivious."

"That's good. Let's make sure they don't find out any more than necessary." The relief was evident in his voice. "Jamila is quite sensitive. A dead body would upset her quite a bit."

Sandrine refrained from commenting. Adel seemed to have a completely opposite image of the girl than she did. Probably most men saw their little sisters through different eyes than the rest of the world. To Sandrine, Jamila seemed more like a young woman firmly grounded in reality who knew exactly what she wanted.

They walked to the forge, and Sandrine opened the heavy

wooden door. Adel handed her disposable gloves and shoe covers.

"The forensic team should be arriving soon. Jean-Claude is also on duty. Doctor Hervé has been notified."

"Another person I need to apologise to for ruining their weekend."

"Why? You didn't kill the man."

They entered the forge, and Adel stopped at the entrance. A brief glance at the body was enough for him before he began examining the crime scene and committing it to memory. They didn't know which detail would be important during the investigation.

"The victim's name is Alexandre de Tréchet. He owns the château on the edge of the forest, an ancient estate with extensive land in the surrounding area. I spoke with him briefly yesterday. He seemed in good spirits; I didn't notice any fear or nervousness that someone wanted to harm him."

"Was he killed here?"

"I assume so." Sandrine pointed to the damp spot next to the anvil. "If the body had been transported here, there would be less blood. I suspect the fatal blow hit him here in the forge. The man fell forward, and the assailant finished him off with the sledgehammer. But Doctor Hervé will be able to tell us more once he examines the body."

"This looks like the motive was very personal."

"That would be my first suspicion, too."

"And then this huge thing." Adel pointed to the head of the sledgehammer. "A strange murder weapon."

Sandrine approached the victim and crouched beside the anvil.

"I assume the murder weapon was much smaller and more manageable. The sledgehammer was only the final act of the crime, adding the necessary dramatic effect." She pointed to a wound on the back of the head that had bled heavily. "Probably the first blow. I would assume it was enough to kill the man."

"It looks like a staging," Adel concluded. "The victim was supposed to be found this morning. But why?"

"That's what I assume," she agreed. "The de Tréchet family meets once a year. Currently, they're all at the mansion. His death and the family gathering don't seem like a coincidence to me; there must be a connection."

"Wouldn't it be more appropriate to kill him at the château?" Adel asked.

"Perhaps the mill has special significance, or suspicion is meant to be directed at the owners. I hope we'll learn more when we question the de Tréchets. The question is, what was he doing here in the middle of the night? Alain claims the victim suffered from asthma and avoided entering the forge because of the smoke."

"He could have been lured here under false pretences or accompanied someone into the workshop," Adel suggested.

Adel stepped further away from the body. The forensic team would arrive soon, and he wanted to be careful not to contaminate the crime scene.

"Both point to someone he knew and probably trusted."

"Another indication that leads to the family and his personal environment."

A car pulled up in front of the forge. Shortly after, they heard the voice of Jean-Claude Mazet, the head of forensics. Adel looked at the watch on his wrist and nodded approvingly.

"Looks like they hurried even on a Saturday morning. Jean-Claude has his team well organised."

"Then the forensic team will take over the crime scene, and we'll go to the château before the de Tréchets have a chance to conspire among themselves. I'm curious to hear what they have to say." She was glad to escape the sight of the victim.

They stepped out of the forge, and Sandrine took a deep breath. After the smell of smoke, metal and blood, the fresh air coming from the nearby sea felt liberating. Thermos cups were placed on the hood of the van. At this hour, the forensic team, who had likely been dragged out of bed by Jean-Claude, had probably had no more than a cup of coffee for breakfast. He and two men put on blue disposable overalls, while a fourth one took some plastic boxes from the cargo bed and placed them on the ground.

"Hello, Sandrine," greeted the head of forensics. "Can't your clients ever die during normal working hours?"

He zipped up around the noticeable bulge of his stomach and winked at her. He had an unshakable sense of humour, which he undoubtedly needed to keep the disturbing aspects of the job at bay. Sandrine had come to appreciate the meticulous work of the man and his team during her time in Saint-Malo. She relied on his insights and sought him out often when the available evidence seemed contradictory.

"I'd prefer if they didn't die at all," she replied.

"The two of us probably won't live to see the day."

Alain Nebot and another man approached them.

"When you're done with the investigation, come over," he offered the forensics team, pointing to the table where Geneviève and Léon sat. "There's a hearty breakfast waiting. We cancelled the guests who had signed up for this morning. It would be inappropriate to hold a celebration after what's happened to Alexandre."

"And the students?" Adel asked glancing towards the tents, likely hoping to spot his sister.

"We'll bring breakfast over, and they can eat in the tents. The school principal and the bus company have been informed. They'll be picked up in an hour. Lilou is with them and explaining what happened. We'll keep them out of sight of the forge. They don't need to see a body being removed. I assume most of them saw Alexandre yesterday, maybe even spoke with him." His last words came out in fragments. It was visibly difficult for him to refer to Alexandre de Tréchet as a body.

"I can hardly believe it. How terrible," stammered the man accompanying Alain. He wore a thick wool jacket and a checkered tweed cap, as if expecting a cold snap on this early July morning. The victim had worn an almost identical cap yesterday. Otherwise, they bore little resemblance. The man's figure suggested he was not averse to a good meal. His cheeks were round and rosy.

"And you are?" Sandrine asked.

The man's hand flew towards her almost eagerly.

"Régis Marceau. Lawyer. I manage the de Tréchet family foundation. Everyone is shocked by this incomprehensible and cruel act."

"Who informed the family?"

"I'm an early riser and noticed Alain standing in front of the forge. Naturally, I wondered why he looked as if he were guarding the door and asked."

"I'm sorry if I shouldn't have said anything, but I was quite distraught," Alain apologised. "After all, you don't usually find a friend who..." He couldn't finish the sentence.

"It's okay." The element of surprise had been lost, but she tried not to show her annoyance.

"Do you have any idea why Monsieur de Tréchet went to the forge in the middle of the night?" she asked the lawyer.

"Not in the slightest. Unlike me, Alexandre was a night owl. He often spent whole nights with a book in an armchair. Anyway, I saw him at the window of his library when I returned from my evening walk. That must have been around 7 p.m. Then I looked through some documents and went to bed early. Normally, the annual de Tréchet gatherings are quite tiring and go on for a long time." His shoulders slumped at the thought of the family members, and he sighed softly.

"Let's go over to the estate," she suggested. "We can continue talking on the way. There's no time to waste."

"I'm sure everyone is already expecting the police."

The forensics team entered the forge, and Alain returned to Geneviève and Léon. Sandrine would have liked to exchange a few words with Léon, but that would have to wait. Right now, she was acting as a police officer who needed to question the victim's family as quickly as possible.

"Did you speak with Monsieur de Tréchet yesterday?" she asked the lawyer as they walked.

"We had three people at the château yesterday who go by the name Monsieur de Tréchet." The man chuckled in a way that suggested he didn't like all of them. "I saw Alexandre around 5 p.m. We both had a snack at the mill. The rest of the family dined at the château, as usual."

"Did you notice anything unusual about him? Did Monsieur de Tréchet seem different to you? Perhaps he had something on his mind, or he was afraid of someone?"

"No, not at all. He seemed happier than he had been in recent times. After his wife died almost ten years ago, the mansion became quite quiet. The two sons haven't lived there for a long time. Xavier lives in Rennes, and Fabius in Saint-Malo. Marie, his only daughter, moved to Paris with her husband, but she and her father had a rather complicated relationship."

"When did the children arrive?"

"Marie has been at the château for a week already, and the two sons arrived yesterday afternoon."

"This meeting takes place once a year?"

"The majority of the de Tréchet's assets are managed by a

foundation, which covers the living expenses of the family members with part of the profits."

"Which can be considerable, I assume."

"The children only sit on the foundation's board nominally; Alexandre had the say. They were all given the best educations money can buy, as well as a financial cushion beyond that. None of them are struggling financially, but it cannot be said that he showered his family with money, at least not in comparison to his considerable wealth."

"The mansion and the surrounding land also belong to the foundation," Sandrine guessed.

"You are mistaken. The château and the lands are Alexandre's personal property. The estate traditionally passes to the eldest son."

"So, now there are three heirs who can look forward to significantly higher allowances."

"If you want to put it that way, I can't disagree," said the lawyer.

"Is one of the children in financial trouble?"

"You'll have to ask the three of them yourselves. Only..." He hesitated to continue.

"Yes?"

"Marie is quite naive when it comes to financial matters, and it's obvious that her husband is excellent at spending money but terrible at making it."

"That doesn't sound like a love marriage."

"I won't offer an opinion on that," Régis Marceau replied diplomatically.

"And what exactly is your role?"

"I am the executive director of the foundation. The assets are strong and very conservatively invested. My job is to ensure that everything runs smoothly. It's purely an administrative job."

"So, you're the one who transfers the monthly allowances to the children?"

"Alexandre determined who receives what share. I just implement his decisions. However, not for much longer. It's time for retirement."

"Will anything change for you with his death?" She scrutinised him attentively, but the man's expression remained composed. He either didn't understand her question as a suspicion or was skilful at ignoring it.

"As you correctly assumed, I will have to issue significantly higher cheques in the foreseeable future. Furthermore..." Monsieur Marceau shrugged. He seemed to see this aspect of his employer's death fatalistically. Or he believed that his time at the foundation was coming to an end. The children would possibly appoint a different managing director.

A man in jeans, mid-high hiking boots and a red-black chequered shirt opened the entrance door to the château for them. Clearly taken aback to see them, he openly stared at Sandrine.

"Bonjour, Marcel," the lawyer greeted the man in his early twenties.

"Is it true what they're saying? Monsieur de Tréchet is really dead?" His voice trembled, and he didn't take his eyes off Sandrine.

"I'm sorry," she said.

"Who could do such a vile thing?" he stammered.

"That's what we're going to find out."

"I wish I could help you, but I haven't seen Monsieur de Tréchet since yesterday afternoon."

"And what is your role here?"

"Marcel Dumont," he introduced himself. "I'm sort of a caretaker here, responsible for everything that keeps the place running, from chopping wood for the fireplace to repairing the antique heating." He smiled at them.

"We'll definitely come to you, but for now, we'd like to speak with the family."

"They're all in the dining room and ... can hardly believe what's happened."

The man had paused briefly, clearly swallowing what he actually wanted to say and replacing it with a fib that would make the family appear in a better light.

Monsieur Marceau led the way, with Adel and Sandrine following him into the dining room, located in the rear part of the manor.

At a round table covered with a white cloth sat two men. One was in the process of slicing a Kouign-amann, the popular Breton butter cake, while the other was sipping his coffee. The age difference must have been at least ten years, but the resemblance left no doubt that they were brothers. The younger one with the cake could only be Fabius. He wore casual but expensive leisure clothing. The other seemed to prefer dark business suits even in his down time. A woman, roughly Sandrine's age, sat in a chair by the window, her legs crossed over the armrest, flipping through a magazine. She had imagined children shocked by the death of their father behaving quite differently. Both men raised their heads and looked towards them. The woman wasn't bothered by their entry.

"Is it true?" asked the older one, eagerly staring at the lawyer.

"I am Capitaine de Police Sandrine Perrot, and this is Brigadier Chief de Police Adel Azarou. Unfortunately, we must inform you that the news is true. Monsieur de Tréchet passed away last night."

"What happened to him?" asked the older one in a sharp tone. He seemed accustomed to giving orders.

"We are still investigating, but we can rule out natural death or an accident."

"You're suggesting someone murdered my father?" The woman in the chair set the magazine down on a side table and sat up straight. "That doesn't make sense; no one wanted to harm him. He was a man without enemies." The look she shot her older brother indicated a contrary opinion.

"Someone must have harboured deep resentment against your father," Sandrine replied, still picturing the face of the victim in her mind, "and it is the police's task to find out who that is."

"Only one person comes to mind: our farmer, Bertrand Barais," interjected a tall man who had just entered, blond, dressed in sporty attire as if he were about to embark on a sailing trip. "He showed up here yesterday and had a heated argument with Alexandre." He traversed the dining room without introducing himself, kissed the woman on the forehead, and took a seat on a sofa.

"And you are?" Sandrine asked.

"Auguste Brunel," he answered, as if she should have already known him.

"My husband," the daughter clarified.

"We live in Paris," he added, as if this were of special interest.

"A beautiful city," Sandrine remarked dryly.

"Oh. You're familiar with Paris? A few days' vacation?" Arrogance dripped from his voice, addressing a provincial woman as if she were beneath him.

Sandrine smirked. Most Bretons called her a Parisienne, as she had grown up there and joined the police force. Being mistaken for a Breton was a pleasant change.

"What happened?" She returned to his accusations against the farmer.

"Nothing out of the ordinary," Xavier de Tréchet, the elder of the two brothers, reassured. "Barais was upset because we had to terminate the lease for the land he currently farms."

"What exactly prompted your father to take this step? Were there any prior disputes?"

"We have more profitable plans for the land."

"*You* have other plans," the younger brother interjected. Fabius, as far as Sandrine could recall. "No decision has been made yet."

"It was just a formality. I spoke to Father, and he fully supported my project."

"I find that hard to believe," Fabius de Tréchet murmured, casting a sceptical glance at his older brother.

"What plans are these?" Sandrine inquired.

"I fail to see how that concerns the police," he retorted sharply. The man seemed intent on making it clear who was in charge at the château. He was in for a rude awakening. *Best to get it over with immediately.*

"Your father died a violent death, and his tenant has just been accused of having been in a dispute with him. Therefore, the reason for terminating the contract does concern us."

Xavier de Tréchet leaned back in his chair and crossed his hands defensively over his chest. Judging by the furrowed brow, he was contemplating whether to engage in confrontation. Yet, he was wise enough to opt against it.

"We intend to open a golf club here. With the château as the clubhouse and some moorings for boats on the Rance."

"How inventive," Auguste Brunel smirked.

"None of that concerns you in the slightest. You're not a member of the board," Xavier bluntly put him in his place. His brother-in-law obviously had to endure some of his resentment towards Sandrine.

"But it concerns me very much what happens to my wife's inheritance," the man shot back.

"So she can continue supporting you?"

"That's outrageous." Auguste Brunel rose up and took a step toward his brother-in-law, who stood up and faced him. His wife jumped up and approached him.

"Don't let him provoke you. Surely, he didn't mean it that way," she finally said in a soft voice, turning to Xavier. "Right?"

The man hesitated, then shook his head. "I may have gone a bit too far. I'm sorry, Marie."

In all likelihood, nobody in the room believed his remark was not serious. Sandrine couldn't help but notice that he apologised to his sister, not to his brother-in-law, who had endured the insult.

"You see. It was just a misunderstanding." She took her husband's arm, gently led him to the sofa, and sat down beside him. He shot her an irritated look, shook her hand off, and pulled out a golden lighter from his pocket.

"Father doesn't want smoking in the house," Fabius de Tréchet reminded him.

"He can hardly..."

The hostile glance Xavier shot him silenced him. Reluctantly, he pocketed the lighter again.

"We need to know where all of you were last night." Adel took out his notepad. Returning to the facts seemed like a decent way to defuse the emotional tension, but he was mistaken.

"Why? Are we suspects?" Xavier snapped at him loudly.

"Just routine," Sandrine reassured him. "No one is accusing anyone in this room. But we need to know where each of you was at the time of the incident."

Seeing the disdainful grin on Auguste Brunel's face, it was clear he viewed the matter in a different light. He seemed to believe his relatives were capable of murder. His wife had retreated into her thoughts again, and Fabius began eating his cake calmly. Either they were well-acquainted with Xavier's choleric nature or had decided to ignore his behaviour.

"As I said, I returned from my evening walk yesterday at 7 p.m., did some work to prepare for today's meeting, and went to bed around 9 p.m. When I entered the estate, I saw Alexandre sitting in his reading chair by the window, reading. However, we did not speak again." Régis Marceau repeated his statement to break the ice. "Nothing unusual caught my attention during the night until I met Alain Nebot outside the smithy this morning."

"Then we have another suspect. Him and his girlfriend," Xavier interjected. "The two who swindled Father out of the mill."

"That's not entirely accurate," Régis corrected him. "There was hardly anything left of the building other than a dilapidated ruin that the next storm would likely have swept into the Rance. Alexandre was glad to have found someone to restore the eyesore."

"I came from Saint-Malo in the afternoon and had dinner with the rest of the family," Fabius recounted. "Madame Sérian was kind enough to prepare her delicious beef bourguignon. I tried to ignore the loud spectacle at the mill and went to bed early. Xavier woke me up this morning with the news of my father's death. It's still hardly believable." He shook his head to express his shock.

"I sat here in the dining room for a while and went through some files. Not everyone has the luxury of taking a weekend off. Business doesn't run itself." Xavier de Tréchet couldn't resist a dig at his relatives. "I went to bed around eleven, and Auguste's sports car woke me up at midnight."

"I was out with some friends in Saint-Malo," his brother-in-law explained.

"Probably at the casino. Throwing my sister's money out the window," Xavier snapped at him.

"Says the sourpuss in the family who stashes his bills under the mattress."

"And you, Madame Brunel?" Sandrine stepped further into the room, positioning herself between the two quarrelling parties.

"Me?" she asked, surprised, as if she hadn't noticed anything happening around her. Perhaps she found it remarkable to find herself among the suspects.

"Yes, you, Madame."

"In the afternoon, the caretaker drove me to Saint-Malo for shopping. Father's library offers nothing appealing, so I brought back some magazines from the city and went to bed early."

"My wife was already fast asleep when I arrived," Auguste Brunel confirmed. "Neither of us left the room until my brother-in-law woke us all with the news of Alexandre's death."

"Thank you," Adel said, closing his notebook.

Xavier stood up and leaned on the table, which wobbled slightly. Coffee sloshed from the brim of his over-filled cup, leaving a brown stain spreading on the white tablecloth.

"Even though it's downright ludicrous to be accused of murdering one's own father, you now have solid alibis. We would ask you to leave us alone," he said, turning his head to his siblings. "We have much to discuss. Father wouldn't want us to neglect foundation matters."

"We will," Sandrine acquiesced to his request. "One more question: is there a will?"

Xavier opened his mouth to make a heated retort, but the lawyer intervened.

"Of course. Alexandre recently updated it. A notary working for the foundation drafted it, with me and his secretary as witnesses. He appointed me executor of the estate. The document is kept at the notary's office, but there's a copy in the foundation's safe, as Alexandre wished it to be read to the heirs here at the château in case of his death. I'll do that on Sunday."

"Tomorrow?" Sandrine expected a remark from Xavier, but it was Auguste, the son-in-law, who spoke up. "It's only a short drive to Saint-Malo. We could get it done today."

"Tomorrow," the lawyer replied curtly. "Some of us are mourning Alexandre, and we need to give them some time before the harsh realities of business consume us again." He held Xavier and Fabius in his gaze until they nodded reluctantly. Marie had already returned to flipping through one of the magazines she had taken from the table. The testament seemed to interest her no more than the arguments of those present.

"I would like to have a look at his last will," Sandrine said.

"Understandable," Régis Marceau replied. "It could be useful for the investigation. I'll discuss it calmly with the family. If there are no objections, you're welcome to join."

"Then we'll just take a quick look around Monsieur de Tréchet's apartment," Sandrine concluded.

"I have a key; it would be best if I accompanied you," offered Marceau.

The lawyer unlocked the oak door leading from the entrance hall to Alexandre de Tréchet's living quarters.

"The upper floors are uninhabited and, as far as I know, locked. Apart from the family and the staff, no one should have been here at the time of the incident."

"And those preparing the exhibition in the courtyard?"

"Several guest rooms have been prepared for them. There's no reason for them to visit the château."

"We'll take a look there as well."

"After you." He stepped aside, allowing Sandrine and Adel to enter first.

"We'll manage from here on our own. We'll keep the key in case the forensics team needs to examine the rooms."

"Of course." He didn't seem particularly affected by their rejection, handing Adel, who was closer, the door key, and pulling out a business card from the pocket of his jacket.

"If you need me again, give me a call. I'll be spending the night at my apartment in Saint-Malo. There's much to organise before we can read the will tomorrow."

"We'll certainly do that."

Régis Marceau left them alone, and Sandrine entered the apartment. The antique floorboards creaked loudly under her feet. No intruder could enter here unnoticed without waking half the house. The shelves made of dark wood were filled with books and mementos. She surveyed the collection: mostly French classics. Nothing modern. What caught Sandrine's eye was the absence of pictures. Not a single family photo stood on the shelf, not even on the desk or the mantelpiece. Alexandre de Tréchet didn't seem to have been a particularly family-oriented person.

"He didn't seem to care too much for them," she muttered.

"I can understand that," Adel replied, knowing what she meant.

By the window stood two reading chairs with matching foot-stools and a small table on which several books lay, with book-marks protruding from their pages. They were biographies and history books. On top was a picture book about tide mills in France. Some photos of the mill were tucked between the pages. The man had been deeply engaged in the work of Alain and Lilou. It seemed he was proud of the gem they had created from the ruins. It wouldn't surprise them if he had preferred the company of those two over that of his own children.

Adel opened a door leading to the bedroom and stepped inside. Sandrine was more interested in the man's study. On the desk were letters concerning the foundation's work, but also a brochure of the golf course. Xavier must have brought it, the question was when? Did Alexandre already know about his son's plans when Bertrand Barais arrived here angrily, or had the farmer confronted him with something new? Alain, at least, claimed that the deceased had never mentioned the topic to him.

One of the drawers was ajar, and on the floor under the desk lay a splinter of wood. She put on gloves and bent down to examine it closely. Someone had forced the drawer open. The break in the wood looked fresh. It was probably done just last night. The perpetrator must have been searching for something important enough to kill for.

Carefully, she pulled open the drawer. It was empty. The burglar had taken its entire contents. Either he wanted to go through the findings at leisure, or he was in a hurry and had grabbed everything to make a quick getaway. There would be nothing left to find here.

Sandrine stood up, returned to the living room and briefed Adel on her discovery. They would have to have Jean-Claude and his team search the apartment.

Together, they left the château and walked over to the mill.

Alain and Léon were lugging camping tables into the small student tent area; Lilou and Geneviève followed with trays and large shoulder bags containing breakfast ingredients. Jamila stood in front of one of the tents, rolling up a sleeping mat. Her curly hair cascaded down her back, gently swaying in the wind. She glanced over and waved to Adel.

"I spoke with her yesterday," said Sandrine. "She's nice and seems quite clever, just like her older brother."

"She won't see it that way," he replied, waving back at Jamila. "I'm not exactly her favourite person."

"I wouldn't be so sure. She seems more interested in you and your life than you think. Anyway, she finds police work pretty exciting."

"Only until I catch one of her friends doing something stupid and have to lock them up."

"Maybe you should tell her more about what your daily life is like."

"Better not. I'm glad she has as little to do with the people we encounter daily as possible."

"What are the people we deal with daily like?" Sandrine asked curiously.

"Drug dealers, robbers, and murderers. People I wouldn't want any of my family near."

"Criminals are everywhere, and most of them don't look like it. We just spoke with a part of Brittany's elite. It's not unlikely that one of them has committed murder."

"You think those types are capable of murder?" He shook his head lightly. "I wouldn't suspect more than tax evasion from them."

"When the stakes are high enough, anyone is capable of anything," she replied. The likelihood of him allowing his little sister to intern at the police station was low. The man wanted to keep her in a protective bubble. *She'll probably run away at best. I'd better get support from Inès. He'd rather see Jamila under her wing than with me.*

"There's Dr Hervé's car," she said, changing the subject.

They approached the open gate of the forge. The photographer was taking crime scene photos.

The doctor knelt beside the body, putting a thermometer back into his old-fashioned leather bag. He looked up at them as they approached.

"Bonjour," Sandrine greeted him. "Not a pleasant weekend for us."

"Better than his, I'd say."

"What can you tell us about the body?" Adel asked.

"Not much at the moment. I'll be able to tell you more after the autopsy."

"I'll tell you the time of death, and in return, you give me your initial assessment," she offered.

"Now I'm curious," the doctor said, looking at her expectantly.

"The man was killed around 2 o'clock this morning."

Doctor Hervé took a half-step forward, leaning slightly on his toes to meet Sandrine's eyes directly.

"And how do you know that?"

"Experience." Of course, she had glanced at the clock when leaving the tent and observed someone at the smithy, but she wouldn't reveal that to him, at least not now.

"I'm impressed. That's pretty accurate."

"Now it's your turn. How was he killed? By the drop hammer or a blow to the head?"

"Probably the latter." He retrieved a pen from his breast pocket and held the tip close to the back of the man's head, exactly where she and Adel had noticed. "Here, he was struck with force by a hard object. The bone splintered, and the wound bled heavily." He pointed to the ground, about a metre from the anvil. "According to the blood splatters, it happened there. But the forensic team will be able to answer that in more detail."

"Did he survive the blow?"

"Based on my experience, I wouldn't assume so. If he did, then only for a very short time. Someone then placed him on the anvil and released the hammer's holder. The spine was pierced, and rib fragments were driven into the lungs. I can say more once the autopsy is completed."

"The assailant wanted to ensure that Monsieur de Tréchet didn't survive the attack?" Adel asked.

"I wouldn't assume that. Look at the wound on the back of his head; even a layman would recognise that he had no chance of surviving something like that."

"Why then the staging on the anvil?" Sandrine murmured.

"That's happily your job, not mine. Crawling into the minds of these people is not for me."

"What kind of weapon could it have been?" Adel asked.

The doctor chuckled throatily and spun around once.

"Just look around here. It's like being in a well-stocked armoury. Hammers in various sizes, heavy pliers, and back there, medieval axes hanging on the wall. Somewhere, I also saw a sword and a medieval spiked club called a morning star lying around. Jean-Claude's team will use a ton of Luminol to examine every possible murder weapon."

"If it even comes from here." Sandrine glanced at the axes hanging on the wall, which she had handled earlier in the afternoon. The doctor was right. There was a plethora of deadly weapons here. But she couldn't rule out that the perpetrator might have brought their own. The act didn't seem impulsive. She was convinced that the murder of Alexandre de Tréchet was meticulously planned.

"Then I'll let you continue your work in peace," she said, turning away and heading for the door. Adel remained behind, chatting with a forensic technician.

Sandrine noticed Alain sitting alone at the table.

"May I?" she asked and he nodded, inviting her to sit with him.

"I thought it would get easier, but I can't get the sight out of my head," he said, massaging his temples with his fingertips. Small scars covered his hand. She suspected they were from glowing sparks while forging.

"Memories fade with time, even if they never completely disappear," she said. She considered herself quite professional in

dealing with the dead, but occasionally they surfaced unexpectedly in her dreams. Especially those whose killers she hadn't
found.

"Not comforting."

"I could lie to you, Alain," she said cautiously. Yesterday, it
had felt appropriate to address the man informally, but now
Alain was a witness in a murder case, which significantly altered
their relationship. Yet, she hesitated to return to a formal "Monsieur Nebot".

"I spoke with the family."

"A pack of wolves has more compassion than this bunch.
They only show up when it comes to protecting their financial
interests." He pushed a clean cup toward her and poured coffee.
He lifted the small milk jug and turned it over the grass. A
single white drop fell to the ground. "Unfortunately, the milk's
out, as is the sugar. I can go back inside and get more."

"No need, I'll take it black. But I'll have a croissant." He
pushed the basket in her direction, and she picked up one.

"Alexandre was quite ill last winter. None of the family
bothered to check on him. Madame Sérian and both of us took
care of him. Régis Marceau came by occasionally. The two have
known each other forever; that's probably why he got the position as managing director of the foundation. In any case,
Alexandre's death hit him hard, even though he's trying not to
show it."

"The family claimed one of the tenants was here yesterday
and had an argument with Alexandre."

Alain pursed his lips and nodded thoughtfully.

"When you say 'the family,' do you mean Xavier, or am I
mistaken?"

"You're not."

"He has big plans. His current fantasy is building a golf
course on the de Tréchets' land. He claimed to Alexandre that

he'd found the necessary investors. They were still discussing it yesterday."

"A golf course near Saint-Malo and Dinard seems like a profitable venture," Sandrine offered.

"I have no idea. Hitting a stick against a small ball and chasing after it isn't exactly a pastime that appeals to me." Alain shrugged.

"And the tenant was here?"

"Bertrand Barais was quite upset after Xavier threatened to terminate the lease. He came over to talk to Alexandre. He slightly scratched the sports car of the son-in-law with his tractor. The lad started screaming immediately."

"And Monsieur de Tréchet?" she pressed.

"I saw them standing by the riverbank, having a conversation. Then Xavier joined them. He and Bertrand started shouting at each other, after which he drove off angrily, leaving Alexandre and Xavier behind. I can't tell you what the two of them discussed afterwards. I was busy here, and it wasn't any of my business. But none of the three looked particularly happy yesterday."

"Perhaps it does concern you after all."

"Should I learn to play golf?" Alain looked at her questioningly and slightly amused.

"Xavier is planning to convert the château into a clubhouse. Presumably, he needs the farmhouse for the remaining facilities."

Alain fell silent and lowered his head. Slowly, he stirred his coffee cup. Sandrine gave him the time he needed to think.

"His father would never have allowed that," he said finally. "Alexandre had other plans for the farmhouse. We talked about expanding the area for exhibitions and workshops for local artists just last night. You should ask Geneviève; the two of them discussed the current project at length. I got the impression they were on the same wavelength."

"I will."

"I feel sorry for her," he said softly. "After his death, the eldest son will inherit the château and the land, as in previous generations. Xavier can do whatever he wants with it."

"Then the golf course will come."

"And they'll try to push us out of the mill," he said, looking over his shoulder at the building. "Perfect for a golf shop."

"But it belongs to you and Lilou."

"That's true, but they'll make our lives as difficult as possible. The access to the mill goes through the family's land." He looked up and met her gaze. "At least that helps me to be taken off the suspect list. Lilou and I gained nothing from Alexandre's death, quite the opposite, as I now realise."

"You were not among the suspects," Sandrine assured him.

It was Xavier de Tréchet who currently topped the list. He benefited the most from his father's death.

Léon joined them. He refrained from kissing her. She was on duty and being watched by her colleagues. It mattered less to her, and she leaned in to him, kissing his cheek.

"I've stowed the stuff in the car. I still need to fold up the tent," he said.

Alain chuckled. "I saw."

"It was really easy to set up, but..."

"You couldn't get it back together?" she asked.

"There must be a trick that I haven't figured out yet. But I'll manage."

"At least the cargo space of your SUV is big enough in case it doesn't work out."

"Should I wait until you're done?" he deflected.

"The celebration is cancelled. There's no reason for you to hang around here. I'll ride to the station later with Adel. Either he'll take me home after work, or I'll take one of the duty cars. See you tonight," she promised.

"Alright." His tone was sceptical, which she could well understand. Whenever she had a case, she always ended up getting home very late.

She waved to Adel and his sister, who were strolling over the meadow toward them.

"Could you help Léon?" Alain asked the girl. "He can't fold his tent anymore, and I saw you have a similar one."

Jamila nodded. "No problem, I can do that in a snap. You just need to know the trick of how it works."

Léon said his goodbyes, and the two of them walked across the meadow. All the other guests had already left, leaving only the small blue dome tent standing alone on the grass.

"The forensics team is finished, and Dr Hervé is ready to leave," Adel informed her.

A hearse was parked in front of the forge. Two men in dark suits carried out a stretcher, which they pushed onto the bed of the vehicle. Alain's gaze seemed glued to them until they got in. They avoided the extended dirt road, instead driving across the meadow to the château and taking the paved road from there to the main street.

"What are you going to do with him?" Alain asked.

"He's going to the coroner's office, and Dr Hervé will determine the cause of death and the exact time," Adel replied.

"I still have the sight in my mind vividly. There can hardly be any doubt about the cause of death," Alain remarked.

"I'm not expecting any surprises either. Other than that, we need to know if he had alcohol or drugs in his system. If he entered the mill voluntarily and with a clear mind."

"When can I reopen the forge? There are plenty of orders waiting to be completed soon."

"The forensics team has finished their work. You'll need to

check if the perpetrator took anything or if anything else stands out. Every little detail could be important."

"No problem. I know the forge like the back of my hand. If the perpetrator touched or moved anything, I won't miss it." Alain stood up and approached Jean-Claude Mazet, who was loading plastic boxes of evidence into the van.

Sandrine would stop by the forensics department at the police station later. Perhaps they had something for her.

"The sandwiches are good," Adel remarked, taking a filled baguette from a basket. "Turkey with salad and pickles. Your friend with the red hair did an excellent job catering to the forensic team."

"I feel genuinely sorry for them. They probably have enough food leftover for the next few weeks," Sandrine commented.

"The school class had a hearty breakfast, and everyone received a small lunch pack for the road," Adel added.

She watched as Adel's sister lifted the tent, held it at two corners, and folded it down with a swift motion. Léon held the bag open, and she stowed it inside.

"Jamila is quite skilled," Sandrine observed.

"She is. And clever too. I hope she decides to go to university. She has the opportunity," Adel remarked.

"She'll definitely choose something that brings her joy," Sandrine replied vaguely. She kept the topic of the internship at the police station to herself. This wasn't the right time to bring it up.

"Can I catch a ride with you?" she asked him.

"Of course. Do you want to come to the police station with me, or should I drop you off in Cancale so you can get your car?" Adel inquired.

"I'd prefer to go home first. But before that, I'd like to talk to Geneviève and the farmer who had a dispute with the de Tréchets," she replied.

"With Geneviève?" Adel sounded surprised.

"She might be able to confirm something Alain mentioned. Don't worry, she's not among the suspects," Sandrine assured him.

"As if she could ever harm anyone," he said quickly. There was a slight indignation in his tone. The idea that she could be involved in anything illegal seemed absurd to him. The brigadier seemed very much in love with the young woman; Sandrine was happy for them.

"What does her grandmother think of your relationship, or haven't you had the courage to inform her yet?" Sandrine remembered the resolute woman who lived opposite a murder victim and had reluctantly allowed them to conduct an interrogation in her apartment.

"She still doesn't think much of women and foreigners in the police force," he replied.

"I can imagine. People don't change so easily at that age," she remarked.

"She celebrated her ninetieth birthday recently. To my surprise, I was invited," he revealed.

"You're getting closer," she said, grinning broadly.

"I think so too. She knows that Geneviève and I plan to move in together, and she offered us an apartment in her rental property. With a view of the beach and at a bargain price," he shared.

"You make a lovely couple. I wish you all the best," she replied.

"Thank you." Adel glanced over at Léon, who was carrying the tent bag to the car.

"He seems nice too."

Before she could reply, Jamila joined them and sat down beside Sandrine.

"The bus is about to arrive and pick us up," she informed them.

"I'm sorry about your party," Sandrine expressed.

"Madame Lanvers promised to reschedule it," Jamila replied.

"She'll definitely follow through. I know her well enough." Sandrine nodded reassuringly.

"Is it true that both of you regularly step into the ring to beat each other up?" Jamila asked.

"Jamila!" Adel reprimanded her.

"Sorry. For a competitive boxing match," she corrected herself.

"We're in the same martial arts club, and occasionally I spar with her. But she's much better than me," Sandrine explained.

"I don't believe that," the girl contested. "Maybe I should try martial arts too. It could come in handy for a girl."

"You'd better focus on getting through your schooling properly. That's enough to keep you busy," her brother advised, to which she theatrically rolled her eyes in response.

"I remembered something that might be relevant. I woke up in the night when someone walked past my tent. At first, I thought the guys were playing a prank on us, but the footsteps faded away, and nothing happened," Jamila shared.

"Did you check who passed by?" Adel inquired.

"No. If I had known what had happened, I would have secretly followed them," she replied.

"Then I'm glad you didn't know," her brother said. "Whoever attacked Monsieur de Tréchet wouldn't hesitate to attack an unwelcome witness." He avoided speaking of murder.

"At any rate, he came from the mill, crossed our camp and disappeared toward the château. It must have been shortly after two," Jamila added.

"That helps. It's good that you were so attentive," Sandrine said. It aligned with her own observation. The time of the crime was clear, and it didn't surprise her that she had to look for the perpetrator in the mansion. Everyone who might benefit from Alexandre de Tréchet's death currently resided there.

* * *

Adel turned onto a well-maintained dirt road leading to Bertrand Barais's farm, the farmer who cultivated the de Tréchets' land.

"Is that him?" The brigadier pulled up next to a tractor, its rear wheels towering over the Dacia Duster. The man behind the wheel glanced down at them, not particularly pleased by their arrival.

"Monsieur Barais?" Sandrine inquired after stepping out of the car.

"And who are you?" Friendliness didn't seem to be one of the man's prominent qualities.

"Captaine Perrot." She held up her police badge.

The farmer turned off the engine, donned a brown corduroy hat and climbed down from the tractor.

"So, did that bastard really file a complaint against me?" He pulled up his trousers, tucked into green, mud-splattered rubber boots and spat on the ground. He clearly didn't hold Auguste Brunel in high regard. Likely not the police either, if he suspected they'd send a Captain of Police over for a scratch on a car.

"I have no record of any complaint."

"If the son-in-law didn't file a complaint against me, then why are you wasting my time?"

"You had an argument with Alexandre de Tréchet yesterday?"

"One could say that. Less with the old man, more with the son. But what does this have to do with the police?"

Adel had exited the car and circled around it, careful not to step in any puddles. Bertrand Barais eyed the brigadier's expensive leather shoes and smirked disdainfully.

"Alexandre de Tréchet died last night."

"He's dead?" His jaw dropped, and he stared at them in astonishment. The man didn't seem like a particularly skilled actor, and Sandrine believed he genuinely hadn't known. Bertrand Barais took a step back and leaned against one of the tractor's huge wheels.

"What happened to him?"

"Were you angry with him because he intended to terminate the lease agreement?"

"I was furious. I've been farming the de Tréchet's land for over twenty years. There's never been an issue, and the rent has always been paid on time. And now, some slimy businessman comes along and wants to take it all away from me. Wouldn't you be angry?"

"Angry enough to kill Monsieur de Tréchet?" Sandrine interjected quickly, trying to provoke an impulsive response from him.

"The old man? No. He's okay. If anyone, I would have run over his son if he ever wandered onto my land again." He tapped the deep treads of the rear wheels with the flat of his hand. "That leaves marks."

Just like the sledgehammer in Alain's forge, she thought to herself, but refrained from making the comment.

"In any case, you visited them yesterday."

"Of course. That nonsense about a golf course had to be stopped before the crazy idea took hold."

"Did you reach an agreement with the de Tréchets?"

"The old man seemed unaware of his son's plans, or at least that's how it appeared to me, and he wasn't thrilled either. He intended to discuss it with the family over the weekend and make a decision."

"Not the most reassuring response," Sandrine replied.

"We've known each other since his kids were still in diapers. He wouldn't just take my land away like that. Additionally, he's got a new project underway, turning the farmhouse into some kind of museum; he definitely won't let Xavier mess that up. Fatherly love only goes so far."

"At least he planned to discuss the matter with the family."

"I assume he didn't want to embarrass his son in front of me."

She could understand the man's impression. The museum seemed important to him.

"Where were you last night?"

"Me?"

"Yes."

"Well, right here on the farm, in my bed to be precise. Why would I harm the old man? I'm not that stupid. If the son takes over, I'll lose the land." He took off his cap and scratched his head. "Which apparently won't take much longer."

He's probably right about that. Sandrine didn't completely remove him from the list of suspects, but he slipped down quite a bit.

"That's all I wanted to know, actually. We won't bother you any longer."

"I don't know if this helps, but the son-in-law raced past the farm last night around midnight. Towards the mansion."

"Did you see him?"

"Don't need to. The roar of his racing car scares my geese and they make quite a racket. That bastard does it on purpose."

"Thank you. Every clue is helpful."

She had only just met Auguste Brunel, but she could easily imagine him seeking childish revenge for the scratch on his car.

She got into the patrol car. The brigadier had already placed a rubber mat in the footwell in front of the passenger seat for her to put her dirty shoes on.

* * *

Adel dropped her off at her house in Cancale. She preferred to have her own car at hand, not wanting to depend on others.

Rosalie Simonas, her friend and tenant of the main house, opened a window and leaned out.

"You're back early. Was the party boring?"

"Boring wouldn't be quite accurate; more like it abruptly ended."

"Tell me!"

"The host was murdered, which pretty much killed the festive mood," she said curtly, with a touch of sarcasm she didn't particularly appreciate in herself.

"Come in, you must tell me all about it."

Rosalie was her best friend and an extremely successful author of detective novels featuring Commissaire Hugo Delacroix. She loved nothing more than discussing criminal cases with Sandrine and incorporating some details into her books. Plus, Rosalie was an excellent cook and often supplied Sandrine, whose fridge was usually empty, with delicious home-made dishes.

Rosalie was at the stove, and Sandrine sat down at the kitchen table. In a baking dish lay four blanched heads of chicory, each wrapped in a large slice of cooked ham.

"I don't want to disturb you while you're cooking," Sandrine said.

"You'll only be a bother if you try to help me. As long as you sit at the table and tell me about your investigations, everything's fine." It wasn't a secret between them that Rosalie didn't think much of Sandrine's culinary skills, which she was usually right about.

Even Léon thinks I'm a terrible cook.

The heated butter in the pot crackled softly, and Rosalie sprinkled flour into it, stirring vigorously with a wooden spoon.

"Do you know the de Tréchets?" Sandrine asked. Her friend was well connected in Brittany.

"Of course. The family owns a château and lands on the Rance. That's where you were for the celebration, right?" She glanced briefly over her shoulder while continuing to stir in the pot, ensuring the flour browned but didn't burn, ruining the sauce. Sandrine handed her friend the glass carafe of warm milk.

"Thanks." Rosalie slowly poured the milk into the pot, continuing to stir.

"Alexandre de Tréchet, the family patriarch, was murdered last night."

"My God, the poor man. He didn't deserve that."

"Actually, hardly anyone deserves to be bludgeoned to death."

"I hope the sight wasn't too horrific," Rosalie said in her caring manner, though her – thankfully fictional – murder cases were always particularly bizarre and blood-soaked.

"What can you tell me about the family?"

For a while, she stirred the milk in silence, as if rummaging through her memories, then she sat down at the table with Sandrine.

"This needs to simmer and thicken," Rosalie said.

"What are you planning to make with it?"

"Chicory wrapped in ham with gratin. You're invited, of course." She pulled a bowl, a cheese grater, and a block of Gruyère towards her and began grating the cheese vigorously. She probably doubled the amount the recipe called for.

"I have to work," Sandrine reluctantly declined.

"Then come for dinner," Rosalie brushed off the objection. "It's Saturday, and you won't be out late, I'm sure."

"Alright. Thank you." It would be a while before she could hope for any insights from the forensics team. The police station was lightly staffed on weekends, and investigations would certainly run at a slow pace.

"Most people would describe the family as wealthy. As far as I know, Alexandre de Tréchet kept a tight rein on the fortune, to keep the children from squandering it."

"He didn't really seem like he led an extravagant lifestyle. Except for the château on the Rance. The ongoing costs must be immense," Sandrine commented.

"The oldest son, to my knowledge, lives in Rennes and is trying his hand at project development or construction, I can't say for sure. However, it seems he's not very successful at it. Fabius, the younger one, I know vaguely. He lives in Saint-Malo in a family-owned house." She absentmindedly stroked her cheek. "I'd be surprised if he actually held down a job."

"So, he's living off the foundation's allowances. Then he must have a keen interest in loosening the reins on the family fortune. Definitely a motive. We urgently need to review his finances. The daughter, whose name escapes me, moved to Paris with her husband."

"Marie," Rosalie interjected.

"Yes. Not exactly the outgoing type, from what I hear."

Sandrine remembered that during the questioning, the woman had paid more attention to her magazines than to the conversation, unlike her husband. He probably saw an opportunity to profit from Alexandre de Tréchet's death if he played his cards right. *A genuinely pleasant family,* she thought sarcastically.

"Rumour has it that the father wasn't particularly thrilled

about the match. The son-in-law is said to be quite a spendthrift, blowing money and unable to keep away from gambling."

"Judging by the car he drives, that might be accurate."

Rosalie stood up and stirred the grated Gruyère into the sauce, which bubbled gently in the pot.

"A Mornay sauce simply needs a strong cheese and some time to thicken. Then it goes over the chicory, and everything goes into the oven." She looked at the four heads of chicory in the dish. "That should be enough for us. I also have an excellent cider."

"Sounds delicious, but I need to shower and put on something respectable for the precinct."

"I'll expect you for dinner at eight."

"Looking forward to it," she said, heading back to her little cottage.

* * *

An hour later, she entered the open-plan office. It was deserted, and Sandrine made a phone call before starting her search. In the meeting room, she found Adel. To her surprise, Inès Boni, the office manager, was also present.

"What are you doing at the office on a weekend? Don't you have better things to do?"

"We have a murder case to solve, of course I'm here. I'll log these overtime hours and take time off when things are slow here."

"Alright, any help is welcome."

They pushed several pinboards together and pulled their chairs up.

"We don't have much yet," Sandrine said, taking a photo and pinning it to one of the boards. "Alexandre de Tréchet, the victim: wealthy and head of the family foundation. He was bludgeoned to death last night around two at Alain Nebot's mill."

"With the infamous blunt object?" Inès asked. "Or do we already have a murder weapon?"

"We're not there yet. The killer had free rein in the forge," answered Sandrine.

"Jean-Claude has examined the possible weapons but hasn't found any blood traces yet. However, Alain Nebot claims that two axes and a morning star spiked club he made are missing," Adel read from his notepad.

"An axe would match the wound, but we should wait for the forensic results. Was it found on the property?" asked Sandrine.

"A search team is combing the area and the surrounding forest. Nothing has been found yet. Maybe our killer is keeping it as a souvenir, or it's lying at the bottom of the Rance." Adel didn't sound overly optimistic that the weapon would be found.

"I'd prefer that to the alternative of him needing it for another victim," Sandrine said thoughtfully. But this was exactly the premonition that nagged at her. Taking items from the crime scene was a big risk if they were later found by the police. Maybe the murderer planned to use them again.

"A rather unusual weapon," Inès commented. "Should we assume a male perpetrator?"

Sandrine remembered the axe-throwing behind the forge. She hadn't hit her target, but delivering a surprising blow to the back of an unsuspecting person's head hardly posed a challenge, even for an untrained person.

"I wouldn't rule out a woman, although I don't have a female suspect in mind at the moment. The daughter has a motive, like all family members, but I can't imagine she'd choose such a violent method."

She paused for a moment before continuing. "Lilou Lanvers can certainly handle an axe, but she lacks the motive for the crime. There's nothing for the two mill owners to gain from Alexandre de Tréchet's death. On the contrary, the heir to the house hinted at contesting the sale of the building." Still, she wrote down the names of Marie, Lilou, and Alain on different slips of paper and pinned them to the wall. She trained with Lilou, and Alain was likeable to her; perhaps she saw the two in too friendly a light.

"Can we gather more information about the sale of the mill and the financial situation of the two?" asked Sandrine. She didn't want to be accused of favouring anyone in the investigation. Prosecutor Judge de Chezac would be looking for a reason to accuse her of incompetence or worse.

"Will do. However, I doubt we'll make much progress over the weekend," replied Inès.

"That's fine. The family's lawyer can surely provide us with some information. But now, back to the victim. Have we found his phone?"

"It hasn't been discovered yet. The forensics team searched the smithy and the living quarters. The tracking yielded nothing. It's probably turned off. If I were the perpetrator and it contained incriminating evidence, I would have sunk it in the Rance by now."

"Too bad. Perhaps he had contact with his killer in the evening, and they lured him to the mill in some way. We urgently need the victim's phone data, as well as that of the rest of the family and Régis Marceau."

"That will be difficult." Inès's enthusiasm was dampened. "As long as there is no reasonable suspicion, the prosecutor is unlikely to give his consent, especially when it comes to Monsieur Marceau, who is the deceased's lawyer. The communication between lawyer and client is protected to a high degree."

Antoine de Chezac had a strong dislike for Sandrine and

torpedoed all requests that weren't airtight. She was convinced that the de Tréchets wouldn't willingly hand over their phones.

"Let's hope it turns up soon."

"Otherwise, we still have Bertrand Barais, who had a confrontation with the de Tréchets in the morning. Whether the victim wanted to maintain the lease agreement, as he claimed, we don't know. Xavier de Tréchet denied it, though," said Adel, writing the name of the farmer on a card and handing it to her. "The man seemed hot-headed enough to resort to violence."

"But murder?" Sandrine doubted.

"They argued, and things got out of hand. The man grabbed the nearest object and struck. I could see him acting in the heat of the moment."

"Unlikely, but possible." She pinned the card next to those of Alain and Lilou. "I find the siblings who stand to benefit from their father's death more interesting."

"Who will have control of the foundation's board in the future?" asked Adel.

"We should ask the family's lawyer about that; after all, he is the managing director of the foundation. I would assume that the children sit on the foundation board on an equal footing," Sandrine said.

"And can set their own monthly allowances," he finished her thoughts. "Being able to determine my own salary would suit me well." Adel grinned at the idea.

"If it's true that their father controlled the purse strings, then the three of them are definitely winners. We need to know about their respective finances." She directed the last sentence at Inès, who nodded in agreement. If there was something to find, she would uncover it.

"Don't forget the son-in-law," Adel said. "Xavier claimed that he spends his wife's money faster than it comes in."

Sandrine pinned more index cards to the wall.

"Xavier will also inherit the mansion and the associated lands. A substantial fortune." She tapped the end of a pen on the card with his name.

"Nothing would stand in the way of the golf course project," Adel added.

"At the moment, he's quite high on the list of suspects," Sandrine replied. "Love for his father would hardly have stopped him from solving his problems with a single blow. Moreover, he has no alibi. No one can confirm that he was in his room at the time of the crime. Just like Fabius and the lawyer. Only Marie and Auguste provide each other with an alibi."

"What would Régis Marceau have gained from the victim's death?" Inès interjected.

"At first glance, nothing. The children might try to get rid of him, then he would lose a lucrative position. On the other hand, he mentioned that he plans to retire soon." Sandrine wrote his name on another card. "We need to find out more about him."

"I'm on it." Inès noted her tasks on a pad.

There was a knock on the door, and Jean-Claude Mazet, the head of forensic science, peeked in.

"Is this a bad time?"

"Not at all," she waved him in. "We're hoping for some news that will move us forward. Right now, we're still pretty much in the dark," Sandrine added.

"Unfortunately, I don't have much to offer," he said, taking a seat in the chair she pushed towards him. "We can rule out a robbery-murder. Money, credit cards, a hefty gold ring and the walking stick with the solid silver handle are untouched."

"Still no trace of the victim's phone?"

He shook his head. Although she had expected it, she felt

disappointed. His call log and possible text messages would have helped her.

"But we found this in the apartment." He placed a transparent folder containing an envelope on the table. A quick glance was enough for her to see that it was empty.

"The victim's fingerprints are on it. He opened the letter and kept it in the desk. Whoever broke into the drawer and emptied it must have dropped it. At any rate, it was under a chest of drawers."

"I'd prefer the contents over the envelope."

"I can understand that, but one may lead to the other," he replied, turning the transparent folder over and tapping the sender's address label with his index finger.

"Do we know who it is?"

"Now it gets interesting," Jean-Claude Mazet looked at her and smiled knowingly. "We know the man pretty well: Patrick Pradel. A private detective from Dinan. A rather shady character, cunning and unscrupulous."

"Interesting," murmured Sandrine, taking a seat. This information added a new twist to the case. What could have troubled Alexandre de Tréchet so much that he hired a private investigator? And why one with a bad reputation? With his wealth, he could easily afford a reputable detective agency.

"We have an address; let's go there," Adel suggested. "This man could hold the key to the case."

"I know him personally; he used to be in the gendarmerie. His methods were..." The forensic scientist shook his head disgruntledly. "Anyway, he overstepped the mark. To avoid being dismissed, he resigned and opened a detective agency."

"That doesn't sound like someone Alexandre de Tréchet would do business with." Adel had the same thought she did.

Something about it bothered Sandrine. What could de

Tréchet have wanted from the shady Patrick Pradel? The man would be able to tell them. He surely had a copy of the letter.

"I tried to reach him. Only got the answering machine at the office, and his phone is switched off," said Jean-Claude.

"Not everyone has to work on weekends."

"Pradel has neither family nor friends. No one can stand him for long it seems. The job is his entire existence."

"Maybe he's out on a job, snooping on adulterers. We'll keep trying; he should be reachable for clients by Monday at the latest," decided Sandrine.

"Or he'll get in touch with us as soon as he hears about his client's death," Adel hoped.

"Only if he sees no chance of extorting money from someone," said Jean-Claude, clearly rather pessimistic about the man.

"Blackmail?" Sandrine asked.

"Definitely a possibility. He wouldn't shy away from it if it was worth it."

"As long as we don't know the contents of the letter, it's anyone's guess who would be willing to pay for the information," said Adel.

"Or if it was even related to Alexandre de Tréchet's death." She pinned a card for the detective next to the witnesses. "We don't have much choice but to keep calling him until he picks up."

"I talked to Doctor Hervé," the forensic scientist continued. "The time of death matches when the figure was seen fleeing the crime scene. Around two in the morning. The victim didn't survive the first blow. Everything else was staged. No idea for whom. For the police, the family, or the mill owner." He glanced briefly at his notepad, probably to make sure he didn't forget anything. "Definitely a right-hander," he read aloud. "More details will follow during the week."

"That doesn't help us. I observed the family at breakfast and didn't notice any left-handers."

"The perpetrator must belong to the inner circle of the de Tréchets or his acquaintances. Otherwise, the man would never have met someone in the smithy at night, surely," Adel interjected.

"Maybe he needed a discreet place for the meeting? His visitor could have been discovered by sheer coincidence in the château," Sandrine remarked.

"What are the next steps?" Inès asked.

"Each of us has their tasks." Sandrine looked at the clock. It was already late afternoon. "Let's call it a day and meet here again tomorrow morning. Hopefully, we'll have found something by then to move us forward."

They said their goodbyes and left the conference room. Only Sandrine remained seated for a while, gazing at the pinboards adorned with maps and names, yet no connection emerged that brought her closer to solving the case. Likely, the investigation would keep her restless in the coming days, haunting her even in her sleep. She decided to call it a day as well. At home, a delicious meal and pleasant company awaited her.

* * *

On her way home Sandrine received a text message from Sébastian Hermé, the prosecutor from Rennes, asking her to meet him in person in Cancale at the harbour. She was curious to see what information he had for her, and now she sat on a bench at the end of the promenade, waiting. The sea had receded, leaving the flat boats of the fishermen resting on the muddy bottom revealed by the ebb tide. Seagulls flew closely overhead, not on the hunt for fish or crabs, but seeking inattentive tourists from whom they could snatch a baguette. A fine mist hung lazily over the bay, turning the Normandy coastline into a grey strip on the horizon. Mont-Saint-Michel, visible from here on clear days, remained hidden today. It was late afternoon, and oppressive heat gripped the place tightly. She had taken off her light jacket, draping it over the bench. The dark T-shirt reached down to her hips, concealing the Glock 17 snug in its holster. She didn't often carry her police weapon, but she was on the trail of a murderer, and it was uncertain if she would make it to the station tomorrow before work. Better safe than sorry.

"I'm pleased to see you again so soon." Sébastian Hermé, the prosecutor from Rennes with whom she had collaborated on her last case, joined her. The subtle scent of his deodorant wafted towards her, and the mischievous smile she liked about him gave her a pleasant sense of appreciation, something she couldn't imagine feeling about de Chezac, his colleague in Saint-Malo.

"I feel the same, though a phone call would have sufficed. It's quite a journey from Rennes to the Emerald Coast."

"That's true. But it's the weekend, the weather is splendid, and I couldn't pass up the opportunity for a seaside excursion."

"And what does your partner think about it?" Sandrine had never met him, but Sébastian Hermé mentioned him regularly. He seemed happy in his relationship. She, on the other hand, tried to keep Léon out of anything related to her job as much as possible.

"We've booked a room and a table for tonight at La Mère Champlain. He preferred to stroll along the promenade, enjoy a glass of wine, and people-watch. Police work doesn't particularly interest him."

"Who can blame him? We deal with the unpleasant side of life a lot."

"You were called about Xavier de Tréchet." He circled back to the reason for their meeting. "Let's take a few steps. I've been stuck in traffic for an hour; some movement will help loosen my stiff back."

The oyster market was just a few metres from the bench, and they strolled between the blue-and-white-striped market stalls. Sébastian Hermé looked with great interest at the offerings and exchanged expertise with a seller about the quality of the oysters. Sandrine glanced at the expansive oyster park revealed by the receding sea. Tractors pulled heavily loaded trailers across the beach and up the flat concrete ramp onto the street lined with restaurants advertising multi-tiered seafood platters. However, most of the harvest went directly to wholesalers and would land in Parisian restaurants in a few hours.

The prosecutor took half a dozen oysters and brought the tray to one of the high tables in front of the red-beige painted Camion à Vins, a 1950s Citroën van converted into a wine bar that regularly stood at the oyster market. Sandrine fetched two glasses of white wine.

The seller had already opened the shells with the short oyster knife and placed them on the tray. The oysters lay in mother-of-pearl and glistened moistly. You couldn't get them fresher than here at the market.

"May I offer you one?" He took a shell in his hand and held it out to her.

"Thank you, but I'm expected for dinner."

"From your boyfriend?"

"No. Léon is already at work."

"I heard the charges against him were dropped. Congratulations."

"I wish they had never been made."

"You can't choose that, unfortunately, but the situation could have turned ugly for him. He should be grateful to have a friend like you, a policewoman."

He wouldn't have been in that situation if not for me, she thought, but didn't say it aloud. In the presence of a prosecutor, it was better to refrain from such conjectures.

"Did you find out anything about Xavier de Tréchet?"

"I've encountered the man several times, though never professionally. He has a completely clean slate, not even a parking ticket. It's hard for me to see him as someone who could cold-bloodedly bash his father's skull in."

Hermé applied the knife and detached the first oyster from the shell.

"The man owns several properties in Rennes and dabbles in property development," he said, squeezing half a lemon until several drops fell onto the oyster, then he held the shell to his lower lip, raised it, and slurped up the oyster.

"Delicious. Just that alone was worth the trip."

"Is he facing financial difficulties?"

"The de Tréchet's fortune is considerable."

"But it's tied up in a foundation, and none of the children can access it."

"That makes things more complicated. Rumour has it he's lost several major tenants in one of his office buildings and is desperately seeking replacements. A financial boost would certainly come in handy. An inheritance would suit him well."

"Xavier de Tréchet plans to build a golf course on his family's land. On the other side of the Rance, a few kilometres from Saint-Malo."

"A perfect location. Since he already owns the land, a significant portion of the costs is eliminated. He would have to be very clumsy to mess up this project." He set the shell aside and looked at Sandrine curiously. "I suppose not everyone is an enthusiastic supporter of a golf course."

"You could say that. The tenants are losing their livelihoods, and the rest of the family views his plans sceptically. His father didn't seem to support the project."

"That problem is now off the table, which probably makes him one of the main suspects."

Sandrine nodded thoughtfully. "He currently has the strongest motive, at least until I learn more about the other siblings and their surroundings. Who knows what else we might come across."

"These old families bear the weight of their past sins intensely," Hermé said softly, as if he had another family in mind besides the de Tréchets.

It would be easy to focus on Xavier de Tréchet, but she resolved to dig deeper.

They chatted for a while, drank the wine, and Sandrine bid him farewell. Rosalie was waiting with the meal.

Sandrine found a set table. Rosalie kissed her on the cheek and pushed her into one of the chairs at the kitchen table, probably to prevent her from interfering with the preparations.

"How's your case progressing?" she asked, opening the stove. The scent of melted cheese wafted into the kitchen. With thick oven mitts, she lifted a glass baking dish and placed it on the table.

"There's no shortage of suspects, just a tangible lead that leads me to the culprit."

"It'll come together. Piece by piece, the picture will come together."

"You and Adel are always so damn optimistic."

"You should adopt that attitude, too. Hugo always assumes he'll solve his cases."

Commissaire Hugo de Lacroix, the hero of Rosalie's crime series, was a second Sherlock Holmes, only with more love for the female gender, something that never lacked in her books. Surely one of the main reasons for the popularity of her series.

"If I assume I'll catch the culprit, I'll become arrogant and careless. A fictional hero can afford that, but I can't."

"Hugo is only as good as his author, and you're cleverer than I am."

"Thanks for the compliment. I wish I felt particularly clever right now. Instead, I'm stuck in a dead end. The culprit left barely any traces, and basically everyone at the château had access to the crime scene."

With a knife, Rosalie cut through the gratin and lifted a chicory wrapped in ham onto Sandrine's plate. The sauce Mornay oozed out under the cheese crust. The smell of Gruyère filled her nose, and her stomach rumbled quietly in anticipation. She tore off a piece of baguette and dipped it in the sauce.

"Delicious." *Even if it means I'll have to put in one or two extra sessions at the gym.*

"And how do you plan to proceed?"

"How I always do: narrow down the list of potential suspects until hopefully only one remains. Right now, there are about half a dozen suspects on the list, but that will change over time. Now I have to weed out those whom the victim would never meet in the middle of the night in a secluded place. That significantly reduces the number of potential suspects."

"Do you think the killer's from the family?"

"Or from the inner circle of friends." She couldn't ignore that Alexandre de Tréchet would likely have agreed to Alain Nebot's request for a conversation. The forge wasn't an unusual meeting point, except for the time, which didn't fit the habits of the two men. Or they shared a secret she hadn't uncovered yet.

Rosalie opened a bottle of cider and handed Sandrine a glass.

"Thank you, but I can't do this too often, otherwise my pants won't fit anymore."

"You can handle it."

"Besides our friendship, is there another reason for the invitation?"

"I've always said you're clever." Rosalie raised her glass and toasted her.

"Spill the beans."

"Doesn't a certain Marcel Dumont work for the family?"

"Do you know him?"

"Before you moved to Brittany, he occasionally worked for me, maintaining the garden."

"He works as a sort of caretaker on the estate, so to speak, a jack-of-all-trades."

"Marcel is a nice guy, with a regrettable weakness for the wrong company."

"Do you think he's capable of murder?"

"Never in a million years." Her reaction was spontaneous, and Sandrine believed her. "If it were about a few things going missing in the house, he'd be my first suspect, but he's never been violent."

"So far, I don't see a tangible motive for him. He had nothing to gain from his employer's death. His work couldn't have been particularly laborious, and he'll likely lose his job due to Alexandre de Tréchet's death."

"The poor guy," said Rosalie, looking out the window into the garden. Sandrine suspected she was considering which hedge to trim or which bed to dig up to find him some paid work. He really seemed to matter to her.

"Nothing is decided yet. Maybe something will come up at the estate for him."

"I'd be happy for him."

Sandrine cut through the chicory and speared a piece of ham. They avoided talking about the investigation for the rest of the meal.

The Last Will

The forest thinned out, revealing the view of the Rance River gently flowing through the valley. Shortly after, Sandrine and Adel reached the port of Dinan. Joggers did their morning rounds, passing by the boats moored alongside the quay. There were no lights on in the restaurants, and the tables and chairs on the narrow terraces along the street were still firmly tied together.

"We're early."

"Good for parking," Adel replied, pulling into one of the free spaces. "In a while, it'll be swarming with tourists." He was right; it was Sunday just before the holiday season, and Dinan, with its picturesque old town, was one of the most popular destinations in Brittany.

Inès had managed to reach Patrick Pradel yesterday and arrange a meeting in his office. On the phone, he refused to reveal anything about Alexandre de Tréchet's request. The man was either extremely suspicious or wanted to first gauge what the police knew about him and his relationship with the victim. Sandrine leaned towards the latter. The murder had made headlines in the newspapers, which was hardly surprising, given that the de Tréchets were among the well-known families in Brittany.

"We still have half an hour. Let's grab a bite to eat," she suggested. Her preference for sleeping in until the very last minute on a Sunday morning and his habit of always allowing enough buffer time in the schedule to arrive on time had left them with no time to eat at home. "I don't want to sit with this man while my stomach keeps growling."

"There seems to be a shop open up ahead," Adel pointed to a typical Breton stone house with 'Boulangerie and Pâtisserie' written on it.

"Looks perfect."

They entered the bakery and chose a breakfast from the counter, which they took outside. Several wooden tables with benches were set up on a small terrace, offering a view over the river. The shop was located at the lower end of Rue du Petit Fort, a narrow alley leading from the old port up to the city centre. Shops of various artisans lined the steep path, which was part of Dinan's tourist attractions. From here, it was only a few minutes' walk to Patrick Pradel's office.

"Did Inès find out anything else about this detective?" she asked Adel.

"Not more than Jean-Claude told us. The man has a bad reputation. Rumour has it he occasionally took bribes and turned a blind eye to what was happening in his district. He left the police force before my time, so I don't know him personally. He inherited the house in Dinan, which is why he moved here."

Sandrine took a piece of the toasted baguette and spread some salted butter on it before adding a dollop of strawberry jam. The place felt exceedingly peaceful to her. Not exactly an ideal working area for a private detective.

"I'm betting on cheating husbands," said Adel, who had

guessed her thoughts. "There won't be much else for him to do around here."

"That would be my guess too. But what could a widower like Alexandre de Tréchet want from him?"

"We'll find out." Adel broke off a piece of his Kouign-amann and dipped the tip into his latte before taking a bite. A sparrow landed on the table, pecked up some crumbs from Sandrine's baguette, and quickly fluttered away. Probably the boldest thieves around here. But compared to the seagulls in Saint-Malo, just harmless amateurs.

"Régis Marceau got in touch. He's going to read the will to the family at 11 a.m."

"You want to listen in?" Adel guessed.

"Of course. The question on my mind is who knew about the contents of the victim's last will and who is in for a surprise."

"As far as I understand, there won't be any surprises. The fortune is tied up in the foundation, which the heirs can't touch, and the château always goes to the eldest son. What's left?"

"I'll be there," Sandrine decided. "It could be crucial to find out who benefited from Alexandre de Tréchet's death, aside from his children."

"Go ahead," said Adel. "Meanwhile, I can question more witnesses. I'm thinking of that caretaker."

"Marcel Dumont?"

"According to our database, he's no saint. He has a prior conviction for burglary. One year on probation, which hasn't expired yet. Maybe de Tréchet caught him red-handed in the mill stealing, and the guy didn't want to end up in prison."

"There must be plenty worth stealing in the château. Why would he target the mill?"

"To divert suspicion. Everyone associates him with the estate, but no one with the mill. Suspicion wouldn't automatically fall on him. Plus, Alain Nebot seems to keep some valuable pieces in his workshop, and his security measures are pathetic," said Adel.

"That's true. Marcel Dumont is so inconspicuous that I've hardly considered him in my thoughts, which might be a mistake," she said thoughtfully. "I just wonder why Alexandre de Tréchet would surprise him in the mill in the middle of the night. The man had no reason to be there."

"We're at the beginning of the investigation. Much remains in the dark, so let's hope that will change soon," Adel, often the more optimistic of the two of them, said. "But for now, we have to go. Our private detective is waiting for us."

Patrick Pradel opened the door to his office, located above a pottery workshop. Sandrine's first thought was that he probably earned more from the rent than from his work as a detective.

"Have a seat." The rather slender man gestured to two padded chairs in front of his desk. He wore a white shirt with stains under the arms, suggesting it hadn't been washed today, and a black leather tie.

"How can I assist the police? After all, I used to be in your club," he said in a tone of comradeship that sounded oily, as if he wanted to pull Adel and her down to his level. Sandrine sat down and pushed her chair slightly back. Cracks ran across the orange faux leather armrests. On the desk lay some files with coffee stains on a wavy desk pad, as well as a half-empty bottle of discount cognac. With every passing moment she spent in the run-down office, it was increasingly unclear what had led someone like Alexandre de Tréchet to hire such a dubious detective.

"You worked for Monsieur de Tréchet?"

"We were in contact." He admitted to knowing the man but kept a backdoor open. He'd probably only admit what they could prove.

"You're aware he's dead?"

"Of course. I read the papers." He glanced at a sofa made of the same faux leather, which stood against the wall. A newspaper and a plate with a bitten baguette were on the worn cushion.

"What tasks were you supposed to carry out for him?" she began.

"The poor man," Pradel diverted, as if trying to buy time to think. "Is it true he was murdered?"

"That's correct."

The man poured himself a glass of cognac and downed it in one gulp.

"Back to my question: what tasks did he entrust you with?"

"How do you know I worked for your deceased?" He certainly didn't intend to make it easy for them.

"We understand you wrote a letter to Monsieur de Tréchet."

"I assume you've read the report. Then you're fully informed. I really can't say more," he said firmly.

Sandrine clenched her jaw for a moment. She hated having to admit to this guy that they hadn't found the letter, but she had no choice.

"The report you're referring to wasn't among his documents." She omitted that the murderer had stolen it.

"Why did you come to me then?" Distrust weighed heavily in his voice, and Sandrine wondered what the man had to hide.

"We found the envelope you sent in his study. Your address was on the back."

"Ah, I see," he said slowly. "I suppose the rest was taken by his murderer." His shoulders relaxed, and a slight smile appeared on his face. The man seemed relieved, and Sandrine's curiosity about what he knew skyrocketed.

"So, what were you supposed to do for Monsieur de Tréchet?"

"What I'm good at. I investigate doubts about marital fidelity and almost always find something. People simply aren't made for monogamy. It's a law of nature."

"He wasn't married," Adel interjected.

"It wasn't about him."

"Then?"

Patrick Pradel refilled his glass, this time only halfway.

"He seemed blessed with a son-in-law who wasn't exactly one of the model specimens of our species."

"Did he suspect him of infidelity?" Sandrine asked.

"He was convinced of it. I suspect he was looking for reasons to convince his daughter to finally leave the wannabe playboy and file for divorce. From what I hear, the girl isn't exactly the brightest lamp on the street."

Sandrine remembered how absent the young woman seemed during the family interrogation. Most of her attention had been devoted to gossip magazines. She couldn't say if she was happy in her marriage, and her father's death didn't seem to have affected her much. But ultimately, she and her husband provided each other with an alibi for the time period during which Alexandre de Tréchet had been murdered.

"Could you confirm his suspicion?"

"The infidelity? Unfortunately not. But the rest, yes. The couple arrived a week ago, and every evening he hits the casinos and clubs in the area. He's not very lucky, neither at the gambling table nor with the ladies. He hits on anything that crosses his path, but his success rate remains consistently at zero. That's quite an accomplishment," he said, injecting a dose of spite into his voice.

"You've been tailing him for a week?" Adel asked.

"Every time he leaves the estate. Every evening."

"Even on Friday?"

"Of course." He leaned back, crossing his thin arms over his chest and looking at them arrogantly. He possessed information they wanted, and judging by his gaze, he was considering what he could get out of it for himself. Either from them or from someone else who might have an interest in it. It hadn't taken long for them to believe the stories about his alleged corruption.

"We're listening," Sandrine said.

"Would I then have something coming my way from you?" He tried his luck.

"Sure," she replied. "We would kindly mention it to his executor if he hesitated to settle your bill."

"His executor," he said, drawing out the words. "That would be that lawyer from Saint-Malo? A certain Marceau, isn't it?"

"Stop playing games. Where was Auguste Brunel on Friday?"

"Alright. He drove from the estate to Saint-Malo. He spent the evening at the casino and lost quite a bit. After that, he stormed off in a rage. Straight back to the estate. He arrived there around midnight. The man was already drunk, and I assumed he wouldn't leave the estate again, so I called off the surveillance and headed back to Dinan."

She nodded. It matched Auguste Brunel's statement. Around midnight, he had gone into the bedroom and, according to his wife, hadn't gotten up again.

"Thank you. That helps us. We'd need a copy of the report."

"Of course. Unfortunately, the file is on my secretary's computer, and I can't access it today. She handles all the computer stuff and paperwork; I don't understand any of that. I'll print a copy on Monday and send it to you."

"A colleague will come by to pick it up," Sandrine said. She wanted to make sure to get the report as soon as possible, even if it only confirmed existing statements and didn't bring any new insights.

They bid the man farewell and set off. It was almost half an hour to the Château de Tréchet, and they definitely didn't want to miss the reading of the will.

* * *

Adel parked in front of the estate. He wanted to speak with some witnesses again while Sandrine went to the will reading. The former stables and servants' quarters formed a self-contained rectangle with a large elongated courtyard. The entrance led through an archway high enough to allow a modern tractor with a loaded trailer to pass through. But the de Tréchets had given up working their land decades ago. It was more profitable and less labour-intensive to lease it to local farmers who put a lot of work into tilling the fields. Surely Bertrand Barais wasn't the only tenant who was angry with Xavier de Tréchet.

Marcel Dumont, the caretaker, appeared under the archway. He paused briefly, as if considering how best to avoid them, then quickly marched on.

"Monsieur Dumont," Sandrine called. "We would like to speak with you."

The young man didn't stop, and she called out to him again. Finally he stopped, turned around and looked at them with exaggerated curiosity. Then he pulled out two headphones from his ears.

"Sorry, I didn't hear you."

His left eye was swollen and bloodshot. He probably couldn't see much with it.

"Who gave you the black eye?" she asked.

"I tripped and fell like a clumsy oaf."

He was clearly lying, but at least he didn't come up with the worn-out story of walking into an open door.

"It looks more like a solid punch to me." She approached and examined the face of the young man, who took a step back from her. "And I know about these things."

"Who would want to pick a fight with me?" He raised his hands to emphasise his cluelessness.

"That's what we'd like to know as well."

"You're barking up the wrong tree. I haven't had any quarrels with anyone," he insisted.

"As you wish." If he wanted to keep it a secret, she had to accept that. At least for the moment. Sooner or later, she would come back to it.

"You've had time to think things over. Anything else come to mind that could help us?" Sandrine asked.

"Like I said, it was a tough day at work. I hit the sack early and slept soundly. Madame Sérian, the housekeeper, told me about the murder during breakfast. She was pretty shaken up," Dumont recounted.

"Now that Monsieur de Tréchet is no longer alive, what will happen to her?" Sandrine inquired.

"No idea," he replied curtly, aware that he faced the same fate as the housekeeper. "It depends on what the heirs plan to do with the château. But things probably won't get any better for us," he added, crossing his arms defensively and giving Sandrine a dismissive look. She realised she wouldn't get anything more out of the man.

"If you happen to remember anything unusual, don't hesitate to give us a call," she said, handing him a business card, which he glanced at briefly before pocketing it indifferently.

"Now I have to go; my work won't get done by itself," he said, turning around and marching briskly toward the château, which loomed behind a row of trees.

"Someone gave him a good punch," Adel remarked.

"I'd like to know who gave him that black eye. When

tensions rise to the point of physical altercations, there are usually some useful clues to be found," Sandrine speculated.

"I'll ask Geneviève; perhaps she overheard something about the argument," Adel said.

"Do that. In the meantime, I'll head to the château and listen to Alexandre de Tréchet's last will," Sandrine replied.

She found the family gathered in the salon. To her surprise, Alain and Lilou were also seated on one of the antique brocade-covered sofas. She could imagine how uncomfortable Lilou felt here. Most likely, was wondering how long the fragile-looking legs of the sofa would hold up their weight. The woman she often trained with at the gym shot her a questioning glance, which Sandrine responded to with a brief nod. She was here on official business and needed to avoid any suspicion of bias towards her acquaintances.

Régis Marceau took a seat behind a table usually reserved for card games and laid out several sheets of paper. The Brunel couple sat on another sofa, a decorative cushion between them and as far apart as the furniture allowed. Auguste kept his eyes fixed on the lawyer every second, while his wife gazed absently out of the window. Xavier had chosen the widest armchair in the centre of the room, where he perched himself like a king on his throne. He seemed to relish his role as the new head of the family. Despite his black suit and the mournful expression he wore, he reminded Sandrine more of a child eager to unwrap his Christmas presents. She briefly thought about his investors for the golf club and whether he had already informed them about the impending inheritance.

His younger brother was occupied with staring at his phone and occasionally typing something. Madame Sérian and Marcel, the caretaker, sat farther away in the salon, both looking uncomfortable. They must have both been included in the will, otherwise why would they have been invited to the reading?

Sandrine took one of the padded chairs and sat at the end of the room, where she could observe the faces of those present. Their reactions would be revealing, even though she hardly expected any surprises in the will. As she understood from the lawyer, the foundation would go to the children, and the château to the eldest son.

Régis Marceau straightened in his chair and let his gaze sweep across the room until he had the attention of everyone present, except for Alexandre's daughter, who still stared out the window. He cleared his throat, and she slowly turned her head to him, only to look out the window again afterward. The contents of the will seemed to hold no interest for her, unlike her husband. What didn't escape Sandrine's notice were the furtive glances Marcel cast her way and the abrasion on the knuckles of Auguste Brunel's right hand. So that's where the black eye came from. The question was whether the young care-taker's interest in Marie de Tréchet was one-sided or recipro-cated by her. She would have to talk to the woman, even though she didn't yet see any connection between a possible affair and her father's death.

"Now that all individuals mentioned in the document are present, I will begin reading the will. Alexandre entrusted me with the execution of his last wishes, as you all know," Régis Marceau announced.

He took the first sheet and began to read. The document was rather concise. As expected, the seats on the board of the foundation were divided equally among the three children. He left a substantial sum to the housekeeper. He probably knew his heirs well enough to know that their time as employees would end with his passing. Marcel Dumont also received a severance package, although significantly smaller. Nonetheless, Auguste Brunel shot a disdainful glance across the room. He seemed unwilling to grant the man a single penny.

"'Traditionally, the Château de Tréchet would be passed down to my eldest son, Xavier'," the lawyer continued.

A smile crept onto Xavier's face, which he quickly suppressed. However, the rest of the family noticed.

"'The de Tréchet family is deeply rooted in the history of Brittany, and fortune has always smiled upon us,'" the lawyer continued reading. "'It is time for us to give something back, so I bequeath the estate to Alain Nebot, with the condition that he – according to our joint plans – develop it into a cultural centre'."

"Damn it, what is this?" Xavier exclaimed, jumping to his feet. He must have already detailed plans for where the golf shop would be set up within the estate.

"'The income from leasing the land will be used exclusively for the development and maintenance of the cultural centre'," Régis Marceau finished.

The blood drained from Xavier de Tréchet's cheeks. His knees buckled, and he sank back into the chair. His plans for a golf course were definitively dashed.

For the first time, Sandrine noticed genuine interest in the situation and a hint of a smile on Marie's face. The young woman seemed to dislike her brother and relish his defeat.

"You knew about this," Xavier stammered, staring at Alain. "You not only swindled the mill from him but also the farmhouse and our land." His voice grew louder with each word until he was shouting at the man.

Alain raised his hands defensively and looked to the lawyer for help. "We legally purchased the mill. I had no idea he had intended a role for me in his plans for the farmhouse."

"You can't tell me that," Xavier snapped at him before turning to Monsieur Marceau. "My father must have been out of his mind when he wrote this will. I shall contest it."

"That will not lead to a different outcome," the lawyer replied, keeping his voice deliberately calm. "I was present in the room when his notary drafted the document for him, and he signed it in the presence of several witnesses. He was of sound mind; there is no doubt about it."

The muscles in Xavier's jaw protruded as he clenched his teeth, and his fingers gripped the sofa's armrest. Sandrine feared he might tear the leather. Suddenly, he stood up and turned to her.

"He knew about the will. Father agreed with my plans, and that guy got scared he would lose his illegitimate inheritance. That's why he killed him before he could change his will."

"That's nonsense," Alain exclaimed, visibly upset. "I had no idea what was in the will. Besides, I would never harm anyone."

"What do you intend to do?" Xavier snapped at Sandrine.

"Carry out my job. I will continue to investigate until the perpetrator is apprehended," she replied calmly.

"You haven't accomplished much yet," Xavier snarled.

"Calm down. The police will find out what happened," Fabius de Tréchet stood up and placed a hand on his brother's upper arm, which he roughly brushed aside.

"They're all in cahoots," he snarled in Sandrine's direction and stormed out of the room.

Fabius turned to her. "I apologise for what he said."

"It's okay. You've tragically lost your father, and he was confronted today with his last will, which contained something he did not expect. That can easily throw one off balance," she replied.

"Thank you for your understanding. I'll go check on him before he does anything rash," Fabius said before leaving the salon.

A heavy silence fell over the room. Marie seemed detached again, avoiding the glances Marcel threw her way. Judging by the furrows on Auguste's forehead, he was keenly aware of these looks.

Alain and Lilou looked at each other and stood up. "We better go. The family would probably prefer to be alone," he said.

He looked to Sandrine, as if he needed her permission to leave the château, and she nodded to him. The testament had propelled the two of them up the list of suspects. Even though they were friends, she couldn't ignore that. Especially since she could easily imagine Xavier de Tréchet calling her superiors and complaining about her. Commissaire Matisse knew her well enough to have her back, but for prosecutor de Chezac, it would be a triumph to discredit her and remove her from the investigation.

The caretaker and the housekeeper joined Alain and Lilou and left the salon.

"And I thought this would be a boring event," Auguste said, crossing his arms and stretching out his legs. It seemed he had enjoyed his brother-in-law's performance. What happened to the estate didn't seem to interest him. Important to him was his wife's voting rights on the board of trustees. If the brothers disagreed, Marie would be the deciding vote. Sandrine suspected he saw Fabius in a similar situation as himself, dependent on the family's money, which would now flow more generously than under Alexandre de Tréchet's regime. Certainly a motive, but was his greed strong enough for him to gather the courage to kill his father-in-law? Perhaps. Did he meet with the shady guy in the middle of the night in the forge and turn his back on him? That's not how she perceived the victim.

Marie de Tréchet stood up and silently left the room. Auguste looked at her with irritation, then followed his wife. Sandrine was left alone with Régis Marceau. The lawyer approached her and took a seat on a chair next to her. Something seemed to weigh on him that he wanted to get off his chest.

"I hope not all your meetings with the family are as turbulent as this one," she said.

"My hopes are rather low. The family members' interests are not exactly aligned," he replied.

"Will you remain as the director?"

"I assume so, at least for some time. Even if Alexandre's children can't stand me, they understand that I've been managing the foundation for almost thirty years. Finding a successor who can navigate the often complicated company structures will be a difficult task. Even if they want to dismiss me, they're unlikely to agree on someone else, as they distrust each other too much. Each will assume the other wanted to elevate a confidante to the position to gain more influence. I don't have to worry about my job," he explained.

"I'm unsure if I should congratulate you," she remarked.

"Just a few more years, then I'll retire," he added.

"Alexandre de Tréchet hired a private detective. What can you tell me about that?"

"How do you know about that?" he asked quickly.

"We found an envelope from the detective agency under a cabinet. The man must have submitted a report, but it's unfortunately missing. The perpetrator broke open the drawer and stole everything inside," she explained.

"Alexandre mentioned something about it casually, but he didn't want to elaborate. I suspect the assignment didn't lead to any success, otherwise he would have told me. Do you know what it was about?" he inquired.

"Without having the report in hand, it's hard to say," she replied, not intending to give the lawyer too detailed a glimpse into the investigation. "Do you have any idea if there are other hiding places in the house, perhaps a safe?"

"The de Tréchets are extremely proud of their long history

in Brittany and plaster their family crest on every envelope and napkin. I believe Alexandre recently had cuff-links made with the crest. The whole moral talk about how much luck the family had and that he should now give something back to Brittany is absolutely hypocritical. The root of the de Tréchets' prosperity lies in smuggling and the exploitation of the people who depended on them. Even when they started presenting themselves as law-abiding Bretons, they still had some hiding places and secret storage rooms built into the château. If Alexandre wanted to hide something, he had plenty of options here. I'm afraid you won't find the report," he concluded.

"Likely it has nothing to do with the murder," she said. After all, the private detective had admitted to not discovering anything incriminating about Auguste Brunel. At least not what his client had hoped for.

"Now I must go, my colleague is probably already waiting for me." She bid farewell to the lawyer.

She suspected Adel was in the farmstead. He hadn't been able to question Alain and Lilou, as they were present at the reading of the will. He was probably using the time to meet with Geneviève. It was Sunday, and she felt he deserved a break from work. She couldn't see the farmstead from the château, even though it was only a short walk away, as it was behind a narrow grove. She passed through the archway and stopped in the courtyard.

"I'm here," Adel called out from one of the buildings, where he stood with Geneviève. The wide door with two wings indicated it was a former stable, but there was hardly any evidence of it now. Grey limestone slabs covered the floor. The walls were plastered with clay, tinted with a warm orange tone. The roof beams were exposed and looked as if they had been recently renovated. Large-format pictures and display boards hung on the walls. Movable display panels were distributed throughout the room, and at the back, three camp beds were set up, with sleeping bags and bags on them. This was where Geneviève and her helpers had slept on the night Alexandre was murdered. No wonder she hadn't noticed anything. The farmstead was too far away from the mill.

"So, this is the exhibition you talked about?" she asked the woman.

"Well, it will soon be an exhibition. Currently, there's not much to see," Geneviève replied.

"A beautiful renovation," she remarked. She herself lived in a renovated sheepfold, albeit much smaller than this one. Therefore, she could well appreciate the effort and, above all, the costs needed to lovingly restore this building.

"This is just a part of the estate. Now that Alexandre is dead, I don't know if his project will continue," Geneviève said.

"Did he talk to you about what he intended to do with the farmstead?" Sandrine wanted to hear from Geneviève what the victim had told her without her knowing about the content of the will.

"Of course. He was passionate about the project. He often called it his museum," she said, signalling Sandrine to follow her, and stepped out into the paved courtyard. "He wanted to set up seminar rooms in the old servants' quarters and studios for local artists in the stables across. But that's probably history now. Where an artist would have painted, a golf shop will soon move in or those little carts will be parked," Geneviève lamented.

"Talk to Alain; he can inform you about the status of the planning," Sandrine instructed Adel. She didn't want to reveal more. It was up to him and Lilou to figure out how things would proceed here. If they proceeded at all. She didn't take Xavier's threat to contest the will lightly. He wouldn't easily accept defeat.

"But now I have to take Adel with me. After all, we have a case to solve," she continued.

"I hope you catch the monster who murdered Alexandre. The poor old man," Geneviève remarked.

"We'll do everything in our power," Adel assured her.

They said their goodbyes to Geneviève and left the farmstead.

On the way, Sandrine briefed the brigadier on the content of the will and the family's reactions.

"Geneviève will be pleased. She has put a lot of work into the exhibition. But I also understand why you didn't tell her," Adel commented.

"I didn't want to pre-empt Alain or Lilou," she replied.

"This will kill Xavier de Tréchet's grand project," Adel observed.

"I watched him closely. Either he's an Oscar-worthy actor, or he genuinely didn't know the contents of the will," she said.

"If he's our culprit, he killed his father without it benefiting him. He must have assumed he would inherit the entire package – the château with the farmstead and the land," Adel speculated.

"That would be tragic. However, he now has access to the foundation. Compared to the family's wealth, the income from a golf course is negligible. People have killed for much less," she remarked.

"The same goes for Fabius and Marie," Adel agreed.

"Don't forget about Auguste. If Patrick Pradel didn't deceive us, Monsieur de Tréchet didn't think much of him and would have liked to see a divorce. But I still don't get it. Everyone seemed to know what a scoundrel the guy was. Why did he need proof from a detective?" she pondered.

"Geneviève mentioned to me that she had seen Auguste and

Marie arguing on the evening of the murder. She suspects it was about her outing with Marcel," Sandrine shared.

"She claimed he only drove her for shopping," Adel noted.

"People lie, it's been known to happen," Sandrine replied dryly. "Marie seemed to have spent a lot of time with the young caretaker, which didn't sit well with her husband," she continued.

"But wouldn't he have been better off killing Marcel Dumont instead of his father-in-law? The two aren't easily confused, even in the dark."

"The picture isn't clear yet, but it will come together eventually," Adel concluded.

"You really are the more optimistic one between us," Sandrine remarked.

"True. So, what's our next move?" he asked.

"I'll sit by the river and dip my feet in the water while you talk to Alain and Lilou. Perhaps something they considered insignificant yesterday might now be relevant, especially after Xavier accused them of killing his father. We need to carefully verify their statements," Sandrine suggested.

"Shouldn't you talk to them? After all, you're friends," Adel countered.

"Exactly for that reason, you'll do it for me. Our approach must be strictly textbook," she insisted.

"Are you thinking about de Chezac?" he asked knowingly.

"The prosecutor is just looking for a way to make trouble for me. If there's any hint of bias, he'll take the case away from me. Not even Commissaire Matisse can protect me from that," Sandrine explained.

"Understood," he acknowledged.

"You know where to find me," she said, heading towards the Rance.

A sandy strip stretched along the river, a few metres wide.

She took off her shoes and socks, rolled up her trouser legs, and waded into the water a few steps. Occasionally, sailboats passed by slowly, but most were moored to buoys and rocked gently in the breeze coming from the sea. The sails cast harsh shadows on the river's surface, and the water in the Rance was surprisingly warm even for a summer day. She wished she could take a few strokes for a swim, but she didn't have the time.

Sandrine turned her back to the river and looked over to the mill, where Adel stood with Alain at the entrance to the forge. Occasionally, they glanced over at her, and she wondered if her suspicion regarding their innocence, both his and Lilou's, was correct. The farmstead and the accompanying land represented a considerable fortune, which they could now use at their discretion as a labour of love. Her gut feeling reaffirmed her trust in Alain, that he hadn't known the contents of the will, but she couldn't rely solely on her instincts. It was her duty to find a murderer, not to exonerate her friends.

Adel said his goodbyes, and Sandrine walked towards him, shoes in hand.

"To the police station?" he asked.

"We can't do much right now. Let's call it a day," she suggested.

"Agreed."

They got into his Peugeot and drove back to Saint-Malo.

Sandrine sat on a bench, watching Léon spar with a partner in the ring. Her T-shirt clung damply to her, and her muscles burned with exertion. In the past hour, she had worked out her tension on the punching bag. The gloves lay beside her. She reached for her towel, wiping the sweat from her face. She wanted to watch Léon train for a while longer before taking a thorough shower. She hadn't wanted to refuse his suggestion of grabbing a bite to eat. A pleasant evening together could perhaps salvage some of the otherwise ruined weekend. At the police station, she and Adel had taken care of the absolutely necessary paperwork, updated the bulletin boards, and organised a patrol of the gendarmerie to pick up the detective's report tomorrow morning. She didn't want to give the slimy detective more time to delay until he found someone to sell his information to profitably. So far, his name hadn't appeared in the press, but that wouldn't last long. A journalist like Deborah Binet wouldn't hesitate to shell out a few bucks for insider information.

"Léon is in good shape," Lilou remarked.

Sandrine turned around. Lilou Lanvers stood behind her. It was noisy in the studio, and she hadn't heard the woman approach.

"I understand why you sent your colleague to question us," Lilou continued.

"I want to avoid being perceived as biased, especially since we know each other," Sandrine replied.

"I witnessed Xavier's outburst. He will do everything in his power to contest the will, even if he has to aim in your direction," Lilou observed.

"I questioned Régis Marceau. According to him, Alexandre de Tréchet's last will seems to be airtight. At least, that's his assessment," Sandrine shared.

"We didn't know his intentions, honestly. Of course, he often talked about what he planned to do with the farmstead, but he assumed he would have enough time to see his work completed himself. The fact that he intended to transfer the responsibility to Alain and me if something happened to him was a considerable surprise to us," Lilou explained.

"I could see that," Sandrine replied.

"Are we now suspects?" Lilou asked, concern evident in her otherwise confident voice, which caught Sandrine's attention.

"I believe you when you say you didn't know about the will, but that can't be proven and the accusation is hanging over your heads. You and Alain are beneficiaries and therefore have a motive," Sandrine clarified.

"You assume..."

"I don't. While you're considered suspects, you're not accused. Furthermore, you're in good company; the entire de Tréchet family is on the list. Each of them benefits from Alexandre's death," Sandrine explained.

"Some have stronger motives than we do," Lilou noted.

"And those individuals will do everything in their power to divert suspicion from themselves. That's where the two of you come in handy," Sandrine agreed.

"If Xavier manages to pin the murder on us, we wouldn't be entitled to the inheritance anymore, and the farmstead with the land would fall to him," Lilou added.

"That's how I would proceed in his place," Sandrine concurred.

"Alain and I have an alibi for the night Alexandre was killed. We were camping with the school class," she said, exhaling deeply and looking at Sandrine thoughtfully. "Probably not a particularly good one, is it?"

"Either of you could have slipped away to meet him in the forge," Sandrine replied.

"Then I guess you're not available as a sparring partner anymore," Lilou remarked.

"Only until I catch the culprit," Sandrine replied.

"Hurry up, I need a partner who isn't easily intimidated in the ring by Friday," Lilou added.

"I'll do my best."

As Lilou stood up, Sandrine grabbed her arm.

"If you ever wanted to kill someone, it wouldn't be from behind. I can't imagine that," she said.

"That would be cowardly," Lilou agreed. "'Thank you," she said softly before turning away and heading to the punching bags. Sandrine couldn't help but feel sorry for Lilou; surely she had her own frustrations and tensions that needed to be released.

Dinan

Sandrine stood in the kitchen, brewing a coffee. There wasn't much more than that in the tiny room. *After all, I had to work on the weekend, how could I have gone shopping?* she reasoned, although it was more of a constant state. Léon had quickly learned to bring everything he needed to cook when he visited and stayed overnight. After training yesterday, they had eaten a little something at the Crêperie Corps de Garde in Saint-Malo before he headed to the Équinoxe. Her galette saucisse bretonne had tasted excellent, and the view from their table of the beach and the offshore islands was unbeatable.

She glanced at the kitchen clock. It was seven. He couldn't have been home in bed for long. The weekend was his main working time; in return, he allowed himself the luxury of taking Monday to Wednesday off. The weather forecast predicted a pleasant week with slightly declining temperatures, ideal for finally embarking on the long-planned tour along the coast.

Her phone rang. It was the number from the police station.

"Sandrine Perrot," she answered.

"Inès."

"What's so urgent that it can't wait until I'm in the office?"

"A dead body was found in Dinan."

"Pradel?" It was her first guess. Otherwise, she didn't know anyone there, and the gendarmerie wouldn't have called the Saint-Malo police district about another corpse.

"Exactly. Your business card was found next to the body, so they called here."

"Where's Adel?"

"Already on his way," she replied.

"Tell him I'll need about forty-five minutes."

Her plan to take the Citroën had just fallen through; it would take too long. She put on her motorcycle boots and grabbed her helmet and jacket. As she left, she ate the rest of a dry baguette from the day before.

* * *

Sandrine pulled up on her motorcycle outside the bakery where she'd had breakfast with Adel. The entrance to Rue du Petit Fort, which led up the hill, was restricted to residents only. She decided that murder investigations were a valid reason and drove slowly over the rough cobblestones up the narrow alley. In sight of the old city gate, the Porte du Jerzual, a police car was parked outside the pottery shop located on the ground floor of Pradel's house. Adel was talking to a major from the gendarmerie and waved to her.

"I didn't expect you this early," he said in a slightly reproachful tone. She knew her colleague thought she had been driving too fast.

She handed him the helmet, dismounted and set the motorcycle on the kick stand.

"Albert." The policeman extended his hand to her.

"Capitaine Perrot." She shook the man's hand. "What's happened?"

"The owners of the shop opened up this morning and found bloodstains on the crockery."

"It came through the floor from Pradel's office?" she asked, surprised.

"It's a very old house, and the ceiling is basically just a floorboard," the policeman explained. "We gained access to the apartment and found him dead. Someone bludgeoned him."

"Has his secretary been notified?" she asked. There was a high probability that the perpetrator was after the detective's report, just like the break-in at Alexandre de Tréchet's apartment. She urgently needed to get a copy.

"Secretary?" The major looked at her in surprise. "I've known Patrick Pradel for several years, but he's never had a secretary. I'd be surprised if the detective agency could support him alone. Without renting to the pottery shop, he'd barely make ends meet."

"Then he lied to us yesterday."

"He was never particularly truthful." The man chuckled bitterly. He probably had a closer relationship with the deceased than he wanted to admit.

"You knew him well?"

"Well is an exaggeration, but it's a small town, so we all know each other. He used to be a policeman himself and never quite let go. As a private detective, he still felt somewhat like a cop, and he liked to hang out in the cafés we policemen often frequent."

"Did he mention his last assignment?"

"Not to me."

"Can you take us up?" she asked.

"The doctor has already been here. Two forensic experts are still upstairs. They'll allow you to take a look at the crime scene," said the major.

Adel handed her some gloves, shoe covers and a disposable coverall.

"We'll be careful and not touch anything."

At the end of the steep staircase leading to Patrick Pradel's office and apartment, another policeman was waiting who opened the door for them. In the hallway and the office, several aluminium stepping plates were placed so that Sandrine could walk over them without leaving any traces on the floor. The gendarmerie was well-equipped and seemed to be working professionally. One technician was taking fingerprints while another was snapping photos of the crime scene.

The detective was lying on the floor. She lifted the blanket covering the body. There was a deep wound on the back of his head, which had bled profusely. Sandrine recognised Patrick Pradel instantly. The man hadn't even changed his stained shirt since their visit. His mouth was open, and his hands lay flat on the floorboards. The blow reminded her of the wound on Alexandre de Tréchet, only this one was rounder and deeper. The man must have been dead before hitting the ground. The murderer obviously killed swiftly and always from behind.

"It happened last night, between nine and eleven," said the policeman. "We'll get the exact time after the autopsy."

Sandrine looked at the pool of blood and was no longer surprised that it had seeped through the cracks in the old floorboards.

"Are there any witnesses?"

"Not yet. The shop was already closed at that time, and there were hardly any tourists on the street."

"The perpetrator chose a convenient time."

"A resident witnessed someone throwing an object into the river. Divers are already searching for it. Unfortunately, we couldn't get a description of the person. It was dark, and our witness wasn't wearing his glasses."

"That would have been too much luck," murmured Sandrine.

Pradel was lying in front of a cabinet. The door of a built-in safe was open.

"What was in it?"

"Nothing. It's completely emptied," said Major Albert.

Like the drawer in Alexandre de Tréchet's apartment. The perpetrator took everything, perhaps to conceal what he was actually looking for.

"We're treating it as a robbery-homicide," said the major. Sandrine turned around and looked at him questioningly.

"We found some banknotes under the victim. He must have dropped them when he received the blow and fell on them. The perpetrator seemed to hesitate to turn him over to search for money. He grabbed what was lying around and disappeared."

"Your theory makes sense in many ways, but I have my doubts. The crime bears too much resemblance to the murder of Alexandre de Tréchet, which I'm currently investigating," Sandrine explained.

"I read about that in the newspaper. Do you believe Pradel's death is related to your investigation?" Major Albert inquired.

"I have no doubt about it. It would be too much of a coincidence for the man who worked for de Tréchet to be murdered, and the report he'd prepared to be stolen both at the château and here in his office," Sandrine replied firmly.

"And the banknotes?" the major pressed on. "It appears to be a robbery."

"As you mentioned earlier, the detective agency wasn't exactly a cash cow. Who would expect to find a fortune here and break in?" Sandrine countered.

"What else could the perpetrator be looking for? This report?" the major asked.

"I assume Monsieur Pradel intended to sell something or

blackmail someone. Unfortunately, he crossed paths with the wrong person. When he had the money in his hands, his vigilance decreased. We see the consequences," Sandrine reasoned.

She turned around and walked back over the stepping plates. There wasn't much more for her to do at the moment.

"Would you be so kind as to send us a copy of your report? And fingerprints if you find any that don't belong to Pradel," she requested.

"I'll do that gladly," Major Albert agreed.

"Thank you very much." It wasn't common for collaboration to go as smoothly as it did with Major Albert.

Sandrine and Adel descended the alley to the harbour, where a police van was parked. Several uniformed officers were standing on the quay and two divers were entering the water. The search for the murder weapon had begun.

"Should we wait?" Adel asked.

"I'm curious to see if they find anything. The coffee at the bakery was nice, and I haven't had breakfast yet," Sandrine replied.

"Sounds good," Adel said, leading the way.

The elderly woman behind the counter smiled at them. "Back again? It must have been good."

"You noticed that?" Sandrine said, surprised. The bakery was definitely busy, especially on weekends.

"Strangers rarely come back. Especially not two days in a row. Usually, tourists just visit the old town, walk up and down the alley to the harbour, take a break here, and then continue on. But our little town would be suitable for a longer stay. What's your next destination?" the woman asked.

"We're not tourists; we're here on business," Sandrine replied.

"Police?" the woman guessed, looking at Sandrine suspiciously. Policewomen with leather jackets and motorcycle boots were surely a rare sight here.

"How did you guess?"

"You're here because of Patrick Pradel, I assume," the woman said.

"You know about it?"

"Everyone knows about it now, from the harbour to the Porte du Jerzual. The police cars in front of his house are hard to miss. Plus, the owners of the pottery and their seller had breakfast here. The three of them were quite shaken," the woman said, tilting her head slightly and looking up at the ceiling. "Just the thought of blood dripping onto my pastries..." she shuddered.

"Did you know Monsieur Pradel?" Sandrine inquired.

"Of course. He was one of the regulars who come in every morning for their baguette. Although he wasn't exactly an early bird," the woman replied.

"Did you see him yesterday?"

"I don't spy on people, but he was standing on the quay, right in front of my window, talking on the phone. I couldn't miss that. It must have been a pleasant conversation, at any rate."

"How do you figure?"

"He came into the shop with a wide grin and grabbed a strawberry tart and a Kouign-amann to go with his baguette. That's not something he usually does," the woman explained.

"Did he say anything?"

"No, just placed his order. The shop was quite busy, too."

"Thank you, that's helpful," Sandrine said.

"I'm happy to help the police. Unless, of course, they're handing out tickets to my customers who park their cars in front of the café or drive up the alley to the centre of Dinan," she said, winking at Sandrine. The historical alley was one of the most visited places in Britanny and closed for cars. Not everyone in the neighbourhood was happy about this.

"Does that happen often?"

"Many tourists drive up the alley to pick up their purchases. Especially the heavy ones, like those from the pottery. It is not allowed and the municipal police are quite diligent. But you're safe in that regard."

"Unless there's an official reason, I have to abide by the regulations like everyone else," Sandrine replied.

"Then be careful, those tickets are expensive," the woman warned, sounding like she spoke from experience.

Sandrine placed two cups of coffee and pain au chocolat on a tray and took it outside. Adel was sitting at one of the tables, watching the policemen. They could only see the bubbles from the divers' oxygen tanks when they moved away from the quay and searched closer to the centre of the river.

"We'll take the time to enjoy our coffee. If they haven't found anything by then, we'll move on. The family members are still at the château and are expected to stay until the end of the week. I'm curious to see if any of them will admit to knowing Patrick Pradel," Sandrine said.

"You've already talked to the lawyer about the detective, the others will deny it," Adel remarked.

"I assume the same, but it's part of our job to ask that question," Sandrine replied.

Major Albert was standing on the quay, waving to them. "That was quicker than expected," she commented, downing her coffee and tossing the cup into the trash can next to the entrance.

"The divers found something, but whether it's related to the murder is hard to say," the major reported. In front of him lay a peculiar-looking object. A flail, consisting of a chain attached to a wooden handle with a spiked ball at the end.

"A morning star," Adel remarked, kneeling down to inspect

the medieval weapon more closely. "One like this is on the list of stolen items from Alain Nebot's forge."

"With this discovery, it's clear that both murders are connected," Sandrine said to Major Albert. "I'd wager it's the same perpetrator."

"Who would use such an unwieldy weapon? And where would one find such a thing?" the officer asked.

"Our victim was bludgeoned in a forge where such historical weapons are crafted. The perpetrator took some of them. We'd like to photograph this one and show it to the blacksmith. I'm fairly certain he'll identify it as his morning star," Sandrine explained.

"The guy must have had a backpack or bag with him to conceal the weapon," Adel speculated. "After handing over the money to Pradel, he took advantage of the detective's distraction to get rid of him."

"Do you believe he was an extortionist?" The officer furrowed his brow, looking at Sandrine.

"Would that surprise you?" she asked the man.

"I don't consider Pradel to be criminal, but if an opportunity arose to make a lot of money with little effort, he probably wouldn't have said no," the officer admitted.

"In this case, he was too greedy and misjudged his victim," Sandrine remarked.

"Since it's most likely the same perpetrator, will you be taking over the investigation?" the major inquired.

"It would make sense, but that will be for the prosecutor in Saint-Malo to decide," Sandrine replied.

"I'll certainly keep you updated," he assured her.

"Thank you. We'll do the same," Sandrine replied, bidding him farewell and heading back to Adel's car.

"What's your plan?" he asked.

"I'm going to Château de Tréchet to speak with the family and Alain," she replied.

"Should I come with you?"

"I'd prefer it if you inform Commissioner Matisse about the progress of the investigation and keep an eye on the forensic team. Maybe they've found something. I'll come to the police station later," she explained.

The news of the detective's death had not only reached the friendly bakery vendor but also the press, who were crowding around the entrance to Pradel's apartment and the van of the forensic technicians. A police officer was doing his best to keep them at a distance. Most journalists ignored Sandrine, but one woman stood near her motorcycle: Deborah Binet, the journalist whose calls she had ignored over the weekend. She was smarter than the others and had caught her here.

"Madame Binet, what a pleasant surprise," Sandrine greeted.

"Meeting a crime reporter at a crime scene shouldn't really be a surprise," Deborah countered.

"I was just being polite."

"Polite would have been returning my calls," Deborah retorted.

"On the weekend? Isn't that a bit much to ask?" Sandrine quipped.

"The violent death of Alexandre de Tréchet has shaken Saint-Malo. What can you tell me about it?" Deborah pressed.

"No more than what was in your article. I assume there will be a press conference soon."

"This afternoon, to be precise, but I'm sure you can answer a few questions now," Deborah said.

The woman was better informed than Sandrine. De Chezac hadn't wasted much time before gathering the press around him.

"The prosecutor will surely answer all questions in detail," Sandrine deflected.

"You're not coming to the press conference?"

"One has to work, after all." Besides, Sandrine knew that the reporter hadn't been invited and she didn't want to rub it in the woman's face.

"If you're here, there must be a connection between the two deaths, or should I say murders?" Deborah prodded.

"Maybe I'm just a tourist wanting to see Dinan. As you know, I haven't been in Brittany for very long, and there's so much to explore here. It's a charming city, and the pastries at the café at the end of the alley are excellent," Sandrine replied.

"A tourist chatting with the head investigator of the gendarmerie in Dinan? Not very imaginative," Deborah scoffed.

"There's nothing wrong with having a chat when meeting colleagues," Sandrine maintained.

"Patrick Pradel was also a colleague."

"An ex-police officer, and that was quite a while ago. I'm sure you're familiar with his background," Sandrine retorted.

"But he had been working as a private detective. What kind of hornet's nest did this man stumble into?"

"To be honest, I can't say yet."

Deborah Binet tilted her head slightly and scrutinised her, then nodded thoughtfully.

"That's the first thing you've said I believe. So, the cases are connected."

"I won't provide you with internal investigation results, but I'm sure you can put two and two together." She knew that Sandrine was involved in the investigation at Château de Tréchet and had encountered her at the crime scene in Dinan. Even someone less clever than her would draw the right conclusions.

"Information for information," the journalist offered.

"Shoot."

"The daughter has been seen in Saint-Malo several times in

the past few days, always accompanied by a man who wasn't her husband."

"We're aware of that," Sandrine fibbed. "What's suspicious about being driven into town and bringing an employee along to carry the groceries?"

"Rumour has it the handsome young man does more than just carry her bags." A smug smile crossed her face.

"Who's spreading these rumours?"

"People who work in bars, restaurants, or hotels and take an interest in their fellow humans."

"Who?" Sandrine pressed.

"What happened up there in the apartment? Was it murder or an accident?" Without information, she wouldn't reveal her source.

"The man didn't die of natural causes, that's all I can say for now. I'm on-site because I questioned Patrick Pradel yesterday about another matter. Whether there's a connection between our conversation and his death, I can neither confirm nor deny." She had bent the truth a bit, but not too much. She doubted her questioning had spooked the murderer. It was more likely the alleged extortion that led to his death. Patrick Pradel would have died even if she hadn't tracked him down.

"Marie Brunel has eaten at Le Sillon several times with her companion, and the two seemed quite intimate. Nothing that would please her husband if he found out."

"Thank you."

"Do you think Auguste Brunel is behind the murder?"

"Wouldn't he have killed his wife or her alleged lover instead of his father-in-law and an unrelated private detective?" Sandrine didn't want to disclose the connection between Pradel and de Tréchet.

The journalist looked at Sandrine, clearly considering where to start her research.

"There's more to this," she said. "And I'll find out what it is."

"Do that. And don't forget to keep me informed." Sandrine zipped up her jacket and put on her helmet and gloves. The engine started, and she rode down the steep alley to the harbour. Deborah Binet was anything but stupid and had a keen instinct for a good story. If she had Auguste Brunel in her sights, it was worth finding out more about the man.

Under the brilliantly blue sky with a few scattered clouds, Sandrine decided to take the slightly longer route following the course of the Rance. She turned left at the end of the alley and leisurely passed the boats in the Dinan harbour. Along the way, small forests alternated with expansive fields and meadows. She enjoyed the peaceful ride and felt herself beginning to feel at home in Brittany. Nothing drew her back to the loud and bustling city of Paris.

Half an hour later, she turned onto the dirt road leading to the mill. The potholes posed no problem for the BMW, yet she was glad it hadn't rained in the past few days otherwise the road would have been too muddy. Above all, she couldn't show up for questioning at the château with dirty trousers.

Sandrine pulled up in front of the mill. At this hour, Lilou should be in school. Her class would surely be eager to learn more about what had happened during the night, leading to the cancellation of the trip. She didn't envy the woman her job.

Sounds of hammering emanated from the workshop as she approached the slightly ajar door. Smoke and heat hit her as she entered. The glowing charcoal in the forge and the sun shining on the roof drove temperatures inside the smithy up. Alain stood at the anvil, working on a long piece of iron held firmly with tongs. The fire cast a red glow on his face, sweat streaming down. She paused at the door, observing him for a while as he worked intently. He looked content, setting the hammer aside and placing the workpiece back into the glowing coals to heat it once more. Only then did he turn to her.

"Hello, Sandrine. Any news?" he asked.

"Some, which I'd like to discuss with you."

"Let's go outside." He grabbed a water bottle from the shelf and headed for the door. "It's too hot in here. I should work at night during the summer, when the sun has set. It's so secluded here that the noise wouldn't bother anyone."

They sat on two chairs in front of the mill. The tide was receding, and the mill wheel turned tirelessly in the running water.

"Thanks for releasing the forge again. I was afraid it would remain sealed for a while," he said.

"The forensics team is efficient and has collected everything. There was no reason to keep your workplace closed," she replied.

"You look like you've got bad news," Alain observed.

"You could say that. There's been another death."

"Someone I know?" he inquired.

"A certain Patrick Pradel from Dinan."

Alain seemed to ponder for a moment, then shook his head. "I've never heard that name. Does it have something to do with Alexandre's murder?"

"The man was a private detective and worked for him."

"He never mentioned a detective to me. Why would he need one? Or was he snooping around Lilou and me?"

"As far as I know, the man had nothing to do with you."

"Good, at least one murder where no motive can be pinned on me," he said, turning to Sandrine who sat silently beside him. "Or am I missing something?"

She powered on her phone and loaded the picture of the murder weapon.

"Damn," was his only comment.

"Am I correct in assuming that this is the morning star stolen from the forge?" she asked.

Alain took the phone and examined the picture. He zoomed in with two fingers to see the details.

"The pattern on the wooden handle is dirty, but I'm convinced it's mine."

"It was found last night in the Rance."

"I'm no detective, but doesn't that mean it's the same culprit?" Alain asked.

"That's what we're currently assuming. Someone used the forge to carry out their murders," Sandrine replied.

"If people around here are being attacked with historical iron weapons, everyone will immediately think of my work," Alain lamented.

"A morning star is quite an unwieldy weapon. Either the perpetrator didn't have suitable ones, which is unlikely, or they intended to divert suspicion," Sandrine remarked.

"And to pin it on me," Alain added, finishing Sandrine's thoughts as he stood up. Without explanation, he returned to the forge. She suspected he wanted to retrieve the blade he was working on and waited for his return. To her surprise, he brought back a similar-looking morning star and handed it to her. An iron chain with several links hung from a sphere the size of a tennis ball, from which protruded half a dozen spikes. Unlike the murder weapon, the wooden handle was tightly wrapped with a leather strap. Sandrine stood up and took the weapon in her hand. Carefully, she moved the handle and let the ball swing back and forth.

"It's lighter than I expected," she remarked. Initially, the choice of weapon had led her to exclude a female perpetrator, but now, holding the morning star, she doubted it.

"But still has a devastating effect," Alain said. "Absolutely deadly if you know where to strike."

The perpetrator had only needed one blow to the back of the head to rid himself of Patrick Pradel.

"Can you handle it?"

"Of course. I thoroughly test the weapons that leave my workshop, just like the axes we've thrown together."

"How difficult is it for an untrained person to aim with it?" Sandrine inquired.

"Not difficult at all. It's not a weapon that requires particularly sophisticated technique, like throwing axes. But I can show you."

Alain went into the house, shortly after returning with a watermelon about the size of a human head and placed it on one of the posts driven into the ground next to the forge.

"This is about the height of a person," he said, aligning the melon until it lay securely on the palm-sized surface. Sandrine stood next to him, letting the morning star hang from her outstretched arm. The iron ball swayed gently, and the spikes brushed the grass.

"This should be the correct distance." He indicated a spot about twice the length of an arm away from the post. "Swing the ball, take a half step forward, and strike. It's easiest to strike straight from above or from the side. Due to the chain, handling a morning star is similar to that of a flail, which is why it was popular among farmers. An unchivalrous weapon. But in the right hands, it's extremely efficient."

Sandrine focused on the target and swung the ball lightly. The weight pulled on her arm, but it was easier than she had feared. She swung the weapon in an arc, and as the ball reached its highest point, she stepped forward and struck. The shell burst upon impact, and the red flesh of the watermelon sprayed through the air. One of the spikes remained stuck in the post.

"Perhaps the most difficult part of the fight would be pulling the morning star back out of the skull," Alain said, cautiously grasping the ball with both hands and pulling it out of the wood of the post. Sandrine let go of the handle, and he placed the weapon in the grass.

"Lilou probably had plans for that melon, but I think it was helpful to see how easy it is to handle," he said, looking at the remains scattered on the ground.

"That was it. Thank you very much."

"I've never been suspected of harming another person. And now I'm considered a possible suspect in two murders?" Alain sighed, looking at her questioningly.

"It depends. Where were you last night between nine and eleven?" she asked.

"I was here, working late."

"Are there any witnesses?"

"Lilou was at boxing practice in Saint-Malo and didn't come home until late. Maybe someone passing by the mill heard me. One of the family or the staff."

"I'll look into it," she said, injecting optimism into her voice. It was unlikely that one of the de Tréchets would provide him with an alibi.

"I hope you don't suspect me of killing Alexandre?"

"I don't, just as I don't suspect Lilou, but I have to treat both of you like any other involved party. You understand that, surely."

"Of course, I understand you're just doing your job, but I'm glad at least you don't consider us murderers. Some people do."

She knew who he was referring to: Xavier de Tréchet. Perhaps others in the family were struggling with the loss of the farmhouse as well.

"Being part of a murder investigation is always stressful. Few can resist the temptation to point fingers at others to deflect suspicion. It's hard not to take the accusations personally."

"That's true, but I'm doing my best."

"In that case, I'll leave you to continue your work in peace and head over to the château. There are still some questions I need to ask the family."

Outside the entrance to the château, Sandrine ran into Fabius de Tréchet.

"Bonjour, Madame Perrot," he greeted her, a bit too casually, as if her presence didn't bother him in the slightest.

"Bonjour, Monsieur de Tréchet. It's a pleasant coincidence to run into you here."

"You want to speak with me?"

"With all the members of the family."

"You'll find Xavier in the salon; he claims to have important work to do. Marie just returned from one of her extensive walks and I saw her heading into the dining room. She's probably making herself some tea. I haven't seen her unpleasant husband yet. He probably stayed up late again last night and is sleeping until noon."

"You don't seem to have much affection for Auguste Brunel."

"The man is a spendthrift who squanders her money and is rather lax with fidelity, from what I hear. Marie deserves better."

"You saw him last night?" Sandrine inquired. Auguste Brunel was one of the family members whose alibis she was particularly interested in.

"No, I didn't see him. He left the estate around eight. He drove off in his sports car, and I didn't hear when he returned. My room faces the river. Fortunately."

"And you were here at the château the entire evening yesterday?"

"Why do you ask?"

"A private detective was murdered in Dinan around that time."

"A private detective?" He looked at her in surprise. "And you suspect me? How did you come to that conclusion?"

"I'm not at the point of suspecting anyone yet. I just want to establish where everyone was at that time."

"What reason would I or any of my siblings have to kill a detective from Dinan? That seems absurd to me."

"That's a good question," she replied. "Your father hired him, and I would like to know why."

"Why would he do such a thing? And if he did, it has nothing to do with the family, rather with the foundation's business. You'd better ask Régis Marceau; he can give you information."

"I will definitely do that when I'm back in Saint-Malo."

"Anyway, Xavier isn't exactly fostering a cosy atmosphere right now. The whole estate ordeal is weighing on him. That's why I retired after dinner, read a few more pages, and went to bed around ten."

"Is there anyone who can confirm that?"

"Unfortunately not. When I went to my room, Auguste was leaving the estate, Xavier was in the salon, and I hadn't seen Marie since the afternoon. I warned my sister against taking those walks she enjoys so much. After all, there's a murderer on the loose around here." During the last sentence, he looked at her critically, as if she should have solved the case long ago.

"I don't assume the perpetrator is attacking people he randomly encounters while they're out for a walk."

"You suspect someone is targeting the family?" He stepped back half a step, looking at her alarmed. Until now, he hadn't seen himself as being in danger.

"At the very least, your father wasn't a random victim."

"But who could do such a thing? He was one of the few people who I would say without a doubt had no enemies."

"What do you do for a living?" Sandrine changed the subject.

"I enjoy having been born into a wealthy family and not being forced to pursue a profession."

"Then it must be advantageous for you to now have voting rights on the foundation board."

"Ah... that's what you're getting at," he said, nodding in understanding. "You're barking up the wrong tree. Being part of a wealthy family doesn't necessarily mean living extravagantly. With what the foundation has granted me so far, I'm getting along just fine. I don't own a sports car or a yacht, and I live rent-free in a house provided for me. My only weakness is excellent restaurants." He smiled dreamily and placed a hand on his protruding belly, which was hard to miss. "Perhaps I should consider a gym membership in the future."

"So, the reading of the will wasn't a disappointment for you?"

"Certainly not for me. As expected, the assets remain in the foundation; my siblings will probably vote to distribute more generous benefits to us. Xavier needs money to invest in his projects, and Marie's husband can squander any amount of income in no time. I had no hopes for the estate or the lands. No, for me, it was neither a surprise nor a disappointment."

"And the farmhouse?" Sandrine inquired.

Fabius de Tréchet sighed deeply. "Xavier clung to his illusion that Father would support him in his golf club project. I visited him more often than any of the siblings. It's just a short drive from Saint-Malo to the château, and Madame Sérian is an excellent cook. My father was enthusiastic about his vision of a cultural centre and museum at the farmhouse. He would never have considered giving up his dream for something as mundane as a golf course. I warned Xavier not to indulge in such illusions. However, the fact that it was anchored in the will surprised me. I wouldn't have expected him to contemplate his own death."

"Your brother didn't take your father's decision calmly."

"Xavier can be somewhat fiery at times, and the will tore him from his daydreams. Reality can be harsh when you collide with it unexpectedly."

"Fiery enough to argue with your father?"

"Definitely. They shouted at each other in the salon on the evening of his death. It wasn't uncommon; the two of them were too similar. However, they never went beyond verbal attacks, and I cannot imagine for the life of me that he would become physically violent towards anyone. Absolutely not." To emphasise his point, he shook his head. In Sandrine's experience, anyone could become violent if the stakes were high enough.

"Who else might hold a grudge against your father?"

"I'm at a loss."

"Your brother accuses Alain Nebot."

"He's mistaken there. I saw Alain's reaction at the will reading, and I don't believe he was aware of the clause. In that regard, my father was as closed as an oyster. The mere thought of relinquishing control over something that mattered to him would have driven him crazy."

"How was his relationship with his son-in-law?"

"Difficult. Most fathers are convinced their daughters deserve better, and in this case, I agree. What Marie sees in the guy is absolutely beyond me. Anyway, he and Auguste couldn't stand each other, and neither made any effort to conceal it."

"He's also among the beneficiaries of your father's death."

"In essence, it's Marie, not him. The foundation provides each of the children with a certain sum for a decent livelihood, and it's up to us to spend the amount, which I hardly ever do, or to settle for less. Whatever remains of the stipend, Régis Marceau manages for us." He rubbed his chin with one hand, appearing to ponder something. Eventually, he said, "There's a prenuptial agreement, but I have no idea what it contains. Father insisted on it back then."

"Do you get the impression that their marriage is in trouble?"

"Like I said, I wonder every day how Marie puts up with the guy."

"Perhaps she'll confide in me, woman to woman," Sandrine joked.

"Certain things are easier to reveal to strangers than to family," he agreed. "She would find it hard to admit that we might be right about her marriage."

"One last question: who accompanied your sister on her walks? Auguste?"

Fabius let out a short, barking laugh.

"Definitely not. What garlic is to vampires, fresh air is to Auguste. I asked Marcel, the caretaker, to accompany her. It seemed safer for now, even though she resisted for a while."

"I can imagine," said Sandrine, suppressing a smirk. He evidently didn't have much insight into his sister's life.

Sandrine found Marie in the dining room. The woman had turned her chair toward the window, legs propped up on a stool. An open fashion magazine lay on her lap, but she paid it no attention. Instead, she sipped from a delicate teacup and gazed out at the river.

"A wonderful view, isn't it?" Sandrine didn't wait for an invitation but pulled up another chair beside the window and sat down next to the woman, who wore a simple but stylish black dress.

"I enjoy sitting here, watching the river, observing how the tide reverses its flow. There's something magical about the water rising and flowing inland," she said, casting a fleeting smile at Sandrine. "Despite the tide, it should be the other way around."

"Things are often more complicated than they appear at first glance."

"Life itself is complicated," she said, without elaborating further. Sandrine suspected she was referring to her own life.

"You must miss the château when you're in Paris."

"That's true," Marie admitted, then quickly added, "but Paris has its own charms." She sounded as if she were lonely in the city and yearning to return to the banks of the Rance.

Outside, Marcel Dumont passed by the estate, casting a furtive glance their way.

"You like him," Sandrine said softly.

"He's a kind man."

"Who appreciates your company."

"He occasionally drives me to Saint-Malo when I want to be among people. That's all."

"Why doesn't your husband accompany you?"

Marie raised her cup, stirred the tea with her spoon for a moment, and took a small sip. The woman appeared much more present and lively to Sandrine than in their previous encounters. She ignored the question, and Sandrine had no intention of further probing her relationship with Marcel Dumont. First, she wanted to verify the information she had received from Deborah Binet on-site.

"When do you intend to return to Paris?"

"If it were up to Auguste, as soon as possible, but we'll stay at the château for a while longer. My father's death prevented the annual board meeting of the foundation from taking place; we'll have to make up for it. Some important decisions need to be made."

"Do you expect disagreements?"

"My father's decision used to suffice in the past. Now, with the three of us, our interests are not necessarily aligned. It could take a while before we leave." She didn't sound sad about it. Sandrine suspected the woman enjoyed staying in her child-hood home, returning once a year for the foundation's board meeting. "Auguste will stay here until everything is settled."

And until his interests are secured, Sandrine thought.

"Everyone in the family assures me that your father had no enemies who might have wanted to harm him. Do you agree? Or were there conflicts in the family?"

"Fabius is a peace-loving person who deliberately overlooks unpleasant things in others, and Xavier never gave up seeking his father's love. Since it was not forthcoming, he tried to earn respect or recognition from him as a businessman. Neither of them would do Father any harm."

"Was Xavier successful?"

"The more he tried and begged, the more contemptuously Father looked down upon him. He's like a hamster on a wheel. No matter how hard he struggles, he doesn't get anywhere."

"Was that why he was so enraged when he wasn't mentioned in the will?"

Marie leaned her head back against the high backrest. The dark hair made her skin appear even paler, and in the subdued light of the salon, she seemed almost fragile. But this woman was anything but, and certainly not the naive girl that many clearly saw her to be.

"The château and the lands were rightfully his. It's a silly and outdated rule, but it has been a tradition in the family for generations. To be honest, I suspect Xavier doesn't really care for golf, but with this project, he posed the ultimate question: did his father love him, or at least trust him enough to pass the inheritance on to him?" She straightened up and looked at Sandrine. "You've seen the answer."

"If he had learned about the contents of the will beforehand, how do you think he would have reacted?"

"His world would have completely shattered. But who can predict how a wounded animal will react? I wouldn't put it past him to lose his composure."

"And to kill his father?"

"Why not? Deeply hurt people are capable of anything."

"Did your father hurt you as well?"

Auguste Brunel entered the dining room before she could answer, if she had intended to at all.

"Hello, darling, did you have a pleasant day?" she greeted him with a smile. Not one that spoke of joy or even love, but a meaningless one that she wore like a mask to hide her true feelings. Sandrine cursed silently. His appearance dashed her hopes of learning anything insightful from Marie.

He positioned himself behind her chair, casting a gaze down at the two women. Both hands grasped Marie's shoulders, who diverted her attention to the fashion magazine, flipping a page.

"I also wanted to speak with you," Sandrine addressed the man.

"Why's that? I've already told you and your lackey everything. Marie confirmed my alibi. Shouldn't that be enough?"

"You had a disagreement with your father-in-law?"

"Who said that?" His fingers tightened on his wife's shoulders, as if warning her against making a comment. She leaned forward, placing the magazine on a low table, and his hands released her.

"A considerable number of people."

"That's not accurate. I admit, we had little interaction, but that's no surprise considering we live in Paris, and he hardly ever ventured out of the countryside."

Marie Brunel picked up the magazine again and resumed flipping through its pages. The liveliness and intelligence she had just exuded vanished behind a facade of apathy. Was it due to the presence of her husband, whom she could only tolerate at a particular level of indifference?

"Do you know a certain Patrick Pradel from Dinan?" she asked Brunel.

"Never heard of him. The name sounds awfully dull, just like the tiny town he comes from."

"He's a private detective."

"They have those here? Country life never ceases to amaze me." He theatrically raised his eyebrows and smiled smugly.

"Your father-in-law hired him to shadow you."

"Nonsense." The word practically flew out of his mouth.

"Nevertheless, he's been following you for the past few days."

"So what?" He shrugged, attempting to sound bored with moderate success. "I have no secrets he could uncover."

"He was murdered last night in his office in Dinan."

The nonchalance he had displayed evaporated, and he stared at her, dumbfounded.

"Murdered?"

"The report he was preparing for your father-in-law was stolen. We're fairly certain the perpetrator wanted to make that document and anyone who knew its contents disappear."

"I have nothing to do with that."

"Who else would have an interest in destroying his investigations?"

"How should I know? Maybe some guy he caught cheating. My surveillance surely wasn't his only job, at least I hope not for the man's financial sake."

"And the incriminated husband takes the report on you away as well?"

"He must have taken everything that was in the safe."

"Why do you know that the man had a safe?"

"He didn't?"

"He did, but how did you know?" she repeated the question in a harsher tone.

"I assume that in this line of work, one needs it to store confidential documents."

"So you're sticking to your story of not knowing the man and never having been in his office?"

"Of course. I have nothing to do with characters who make a living slandering and denouncing others."

"So we won't find any fingerprints of yours in his office?"

He hesitated, as if considering what to say.

"Since I've never been there, you won't find any traces of me."

She observed the hands resting on the armrest of the chair. The skin on the knuckles of his right hand was scraped.

"You got hurt?"

He immediately tucked his hand deep into his pocket.

"An accident. I slipped."

"Just like Marcel Dumont, except he fell on his eye. Château de Tréchet seems to be an accident-prone estate."

"I was careless, that's all."

"Can you tell me where you were last night between nine o'clock and midnight?"

"Out with friends. Dining at that hour and later at the casino. You'll find plenty of witnesses."

She would have liked to ask for his fingerprints, but he would surely refuse. She didn't have enough evidence against him for a warrant yet, so she refrained.

"That's all then. I'm invited for sailing and must take my leave." Without another word, he turned and marched to the door. His wife neither watched him leave nor bid him farewell. Sandrine imagined a happy marriage quite differently.

"When did your husband return home last night?"

"I can't say. It was late, and he didn't want to wake me. Out of consideration, he slept on a sofa in the salon."

"Does he do that often?"

"Occasionally. I'm an early riser, and Auguste is more of a night owl." She noticed Sandrine's sceptical look. "Everyone has their own time to themselves. We don't need to constantly be on top of each other," she said a bit too quickly. Likely, she used that phrase frequently. So far, Sandrine hadn't met anyone who thought of them as a harmonious couple, joyously spending time together. What could have led the woman to marry this man? With Auguste, she believed she was sure that the monthly allowances from the foundation had been decisive. But her? Maybe just the desire to break away from the family and lead an independent life far away.

"Then I'll be on my way. I'd like to speak with your brother before I head back."

"I'm afraid that will be difficult. Fabius is on foot, and you just missed Xavier. He wanted to go to Saint-Malo. He didn't tell me what he was up to, and I didn't bother to ask him." A polite way of saying she hardly cared about her brothers' lives.

"Thank you. That saves me the trouble of searching for him."

Marie turned away and looked out the window again. Sandrine's presence seemed to become irrelevant.

As she left, she encountered Madame Sérian, the housekeeper and cook. The older woman, who looked like she was nearing retirement, carried a folded blanket under her arm. She scrutinised Sandrine's leather pants and ankle-high sturdy shoes. Policewomen who rode motorcycles obviously seemed suspicious to her.

"You tidied up in the salon?" Sandrine speculated.

"It's my job to keep things tidy. For now, at least."

"Somebody slept in the salon?" Sandrine didn't want to miss the opportunity to verify Marie de Tréchet's statement.

"Monsieur Brunel came back late yesterday and decided to spend the remainder of the night there." Her disapproval of the man's lifestyle was hard to miss.

"Does that happen often?"

"Several times in the past week." She tapped on the blanket. "I put a new one in the salon every day. This one smells like cigarette smoke and will be hung up on the rack to air out. I wouldn't subject the rest of the family to that stink."

"I understand. You're very attentive."

"Monsieur de Tréchet was always satisfied with my work."

"What are your plans now?" Sandrine asked.

"That depends on what the new owner plans to do with the estate. If he decides to do without my services, I'll retire. At my age, what choice do I have? My daughter lives in Morlaix. Maybe I'll find an apartment nearby and spend time with my grandchildren."

"I'm sure they'll be happy to have their grandmother around. Did you know about the sum you were bequeathed in the will?"

"Monsieur de Tréchet mentioned it. Of course, I didn't know the amount... and I would have preferred to wait longer." She sighed heavily, tears welling up in her eyes. She must have genuinely liked her employer. Suddenly, she straightened up and stared at Sandrine.

"I'm not a suspect just because I inherited a small sum, am I? I could never have harmed Monsieur de Tréchet. Never."

"Of course not. Nobody is accusing you of being involved in his death," Sandrine assured the housekeeper.

"That comforts me. Otherwise, I wouldn't have been able to sleep a wink tonight."

"Perhaps you noticed something unusual on the night of his death?"

"I've already told your colleague about it. The children had arrived, so I cooked for them. There was a soup, then a beef bourguignon, as Monsieur Fabius de Tréchet likes it, a cheese platter, and a homemade chocolate mousse."

"That sounds like a lot of work."

"You bet. There are no ready-made products from the supermarket in my kitchen."

Sandrine nodded approvingly, but also with a twinge of

guilt. She hardly cooked herself and instead used a delivery service. Unless Léon visited her and prepared something, or Rosalie invited her for a meal.

"Anyway, I was thoroughly tired in the evening and went to bed after serving coffee and tea in the salon and scrubbing the kitchen."

"You didn't hear anything?"

"My room is on the side opposite of the mill. The house was full of people, and the wooden floors are ancient. The creaking when someone sneaks through the hallway at night is hellish. It would have definitely woken me up."

"I understand," Sandrine said, trying to hide her disappointment.

"I must get going then. Work won't get done by itself." The housekeeper nodded at her and left her standing.

There was nothing left for her to do here at the moment, and it was time to drive to the police station in Saint-Malo. Perhaps Adel or the forensic team had found something that would help her progress. She was still poking around in the fog. A feeling she couldn't stand.

* * *

Sandrine was lucky and snagged one of the few parking spots in front of Brasserie du Sillon, a three-storey building made of brown stone masonry, right on the expansive beach. The entrance door, mullion windows, and signage were painted in the same inviting blue. She hadn't eaten here yet, but Adel praised the cuisine. She stowed her helmet and jacket in the side cases and entered the brasserie. She stopped at the entrance until a waiter noticed her and came over.

"I'm very sorry, but all tables are currently occupied."

"Perhaps another time," she said and looked around. She

couldn't spot a free table anywhere. Some Parisian restaurants preferred to give their tables to couples or groups during peak hours rather than to individuals. But that wasn't the case here.

"If you'd like a reservation, I can make one for you," the man offered.

"Perhaps you could assist me with some information," she said, pulling out her badge from her pocket.

"Oh."

"You know Madame Binet?"

"The journalist?" He nodded hesitantly. "She's one of our regulars."

"She hinted that this woman has eaten here several times during the past week." She held out her phone with a picture of Marie de Tréchet.

"Has the lady done anything wrong?"

"Not that I know of. It's just a routine question."

"That's good to hear. She seems to appreciate our cuisine very much, as she visited the restaurant three times last week." The man looked around. One of the guests waved, and he nodded to them. Sandrine wouldn't be able to question him for long.

"Did she come with anyone?"

"Yes. There was a young man with her."

"Are you sure?"

"Absolutely. The two of them seemed to enjoy each other's company. She was always impeccably dressed, but he..." The waiter shook his head.

She swiped the screen until a picture of Marcel Dumont appeared. "Was it this man?"

"But yes. That's him." The waiter looked at her curiously. "Did he get her into trouble?"

"Not that I'm aware of." At least, not into any trouble that concerned the police. That was something Marie would have to sort out with Marcel and her husband. She wouldn't make a very effective marriage counsellor.

"I'm sorry, but my guests are waiting," the waiter apologised.

"You've already been very helpful. Thank you for the information," she said and left the brasserie.

At the quay, Sandrine took off her boots and stuffed her socks inside. Carrying them in her hands, she walked barefoot across the beach. The sand felt warm, and a gentle breeze from the sea tousled her hair. The water was too high to reach Fort National on the offshore island without getting wet. Children splashed loudly through the puddles formed in the sand's indentations. Seagulls flew along the promenade in search of food they could snatch from the hands of careless tourists. She ducked as one hovered closely over her head. She continued walking until the waves' tendrils lapped coldly over her feet. She would have gone further if not for her leather trousers; she didn't want them to get wet. Salt stains were difficult to remove. She stood for a while, gazing out at the sea until she found her inner peace, and the irritation she always felt when a case wasn't progressing quickly enough dissipated. Sandrine wished she had more time for such moments. Perhaps then they would lose their appeal and become something ordinary. *It's alright the way it is.*

She thought for a while about Marie, whom she had initially misjudged. The bored and mentally absent daughter from a wealthy family seemed to be nothing more than a facade she used to conceal her emotions. During their last conversation, glimpses of the woman's true personality surfaced occasionally, one who observed and assessed her fellow humans accurately. The liveliness she had experienced had disappeared abruptly when her husband appeared. If she had ever seen a loveless marriage, it was this one. In contrast, the sympathy between Marie and Marcel seemed deeper than she had suspected. No one took someone out to eat multiple times in a week if they didn't mean something to them. Her husband seemed to have realised that as well. Marcel's bruise and Auguste's scraped knuckles left little doubt about it. But did the jealous behaviour of the two men have anything to do with Alexandre de Tréchet's death? She didn't have an answer to that yet. The private detective's report might provide a clue, but she would probably never get her hands on it. Marie's father had hired someone to shadow her husband. He could hardly have overlooked his daughter's unhappy marriage, even if she rarely visited. Was Patrick Pradel tasked with finding reasons to convince her to divorce? Then Auguste Brunel had a motive to get rid of his father-in-law and the detective. He wouldn't want to lose the income. She needed to talk to him urgently, convinced the man was hiding something. But now it was time to drive to the police station.

* * *

Sandrine found Adel at his desk.

"I hope you've made some progress, or else I'll have to spend the rest of the day typing reports," he greeted her.

She sat down at her desk and gave him an overview of what she had learned that morning.

"De Tréchet's daughter and Marcel are bothering me," she said. "Did they have an affair, or did she just need someone to talk to? Her husband strikes me as someone who likes to talk but hardly listens. Everyone I've met so far wonders what Marie sees in him."

"I might have an idea."

"Spill it."

"Alexandre de Tréchet gave the impression of being an affable and generous benefactor who poured his money into a museum. But that's just one side of him." Adel slid some papers over to her. "Compared to the family's fortune, the expenses for the farmhouse's renovation are small, but significantly more than what the foundation pays his children. The man kept them on a tight leash; if they needed money beyond that, they had to personally go to him and ask for it."

"Where did you get these numbers?"

"The foundation's manager printed them out for me."

"You think Marie wanted to escape her father's control and married the first man she came across?"

"And one who lives in Paris, far away from Château de Tréchet. After the marriage, her father could hardly keep her here, and she must have enjoyed her freedom."

"I doubt the joy lasted long. There's not much love and trust between them. Auguste slept on the sofa in the salon several times during the last week. She claims it was because he came home late and didn't want to disturb her."

"Does the guy look like he cares about how other people feel? Not to me."

"Not in the slightest," she agreed with Adel.

Inès walked over to them.

"Matisse is asking you to come to him. He and the prosecutor want an update on the investigation," she said.

"Tell him I'm in the conference room and have some time."

"It sounded like he'd rather speak to you in his office."

"Everything, including photos and evidence, is on the pinboards here. It's easier to keep track of things." Normally, the Commissaire always came to them when he wanted to be briefed on a case. It was probably because of the prosecutor. De Chezac intended to address issues not meant for the ears of the brigadier. Since Adel witnessed her conflicts with de Chezac firsthand, he could hear everything the man had to say.

"Should I bring in coffee and cookies?" Inès asked, more interested in defusing conflicts.

"Not necessary. Matisse is on a diet, we'll get coffee from the kitchen, and de Chezac won't get anything from me."

"It'll seem like he's not welcome," the office manager interjected.

"Then it serves its purpose perfectly." Sandrine got up. "You go ahead, I'll bring you a coffee," she said to Adel.

"Thanks. I'll call the forensic lab in the meantime. Maybe they've found a lead."

"Where do we stand?" Matisse broke the heavy silence in the room. De Chezac scrutinised her appraisingly, as if he didn't expect any particular progress.

Abruptly, Adel stood up, went to the monitor, and peeled off the film. Shortly after, a photo of the de Tréchet family, which she didn't recognise, appeared on the screen.

"An up-to-date picture taken on Friday when the siblings arrived at the château. Monsieur Marceau was kind enough to send it to me," Adel explained. With a laser pointer, he indicated Alexandre de Tréchet.

"The victim, his children, Xavier, Fabius, and Marie, the son-in-law Auguste, and Monsieur Marceau himself, the manager of the foundation. In the background stands Madame Sérian, the housekeeper."

"Do you believe any of them is behind the murder?" Commissaire Matisse asked sceptically, looking at Sandrine. The people in the photo clearly seemed too harmonious, in his opinion, for one of them to have bludgeoned someone with a Celtic battle axe just a few hours later.

"The children definitely have a motive. They're stepping up in the foundation's board now. Previously, they were more or less just silent observers; now it's up to them to make decisions. Especially regarding what allowances they will receive from the foundation's assets in the future. Their father is said to have been rather frugal in supporting his children, at least compared to the considerable family fortune."

"Would they kill their own father over it?" Jean Matisse seemed doubtful.

"I'm more likely to suspect Auguste Brunel of drastic action. He's burning through his wife's money at an alarming rate, which didn't make him particularly popular with Alexandre de Tréchet. So much so that the victim reportedly hired a private detective to keep an eye on his son-in-law."

"To find out what?" Matisse leaned forward curiously.

"Unfortunately, we can't say for sure. The detective's report was stolen from the victim's desk, and Patrick Pradel was killed before he could hand us a copy. Forensics found neither a computer nor files related to the case in his office." Sandrine doubted that the man ever intended to provide them with the report. He probably thought he had found a wealthier buyer.

"So it could have been anything, perhaps nothing to do with our case at all," de Chezac interjected in a slightly disdainful tone.

"It's possible, but many factors argue against it," Sandrine replied.

"Such as?"

"The perpetrator went to steal the report from Alexandre de Tréchet's apartment after the murder. Monsieur Pradel lied to us about his findings to stall us. I suspect he was looking for a more lucrative source of income rather than handing it over to the police."

"Speculation."

"Indications, not speculation. His safe was left open, and new banknotes that appeared to have recently come from an ATM were found under the body. Like Alexandre de Tréchet, he was struck from behind with a medieval weapon. The weapon comes from Alain Nebot's workshop and was stolen on the evening of the first crime. Additionally, the detective's report is missing in this case as well. These clues are enough for me to establish a connection between the crimes."

"Me too," Matisse supported her. "I took the liberty of speaking to the relevant investigators in Dinan. They agree and are leaving the lead to us."

"You should have consulted me on that," de Chezac interjected. Sandrine knew how much the man hated being bypassed.

"Even the press sees it as a fact." Adel pulled out a newspaper from his bag and pushed it across the table. De Chezac took it and scanned the headline. She forced back a smile that was welling up within her; it would only further infuriate the man, especially since he wasn't mentioned by name in the article by Deborah Binet. Another bitter pill for him to swallow. But he would correct that during the upcoming press conference and seize the spotlight. The de Tréchets were a well-known family, and the investigation was bringing a lot of attention to the responsible prosecutor. Something he craved. De Chezac carelessly let the newspaper fall onto the table and only shrugged slightly, as if the scribblings of journalists were of no concern to him.

"The de Tréchets are among the longstanding families of Brittany. The notion that the children might have treacherously slain their father sounds quite absurd to me." The prosecutor shook his head vigorously.

"It's about a considerable fortune. People have been killed for much less, and the alibis of the entire family are weak," Sandrine said.

"As long as you can't provide me with solid evidence, we treat them with kid gloves." It seemed very clear to him to what measure the de Tréchets could either boost his career or throw sand into the gears.

"Fingerprints were found in the private detective's office that we can't match. It would be helpful to be able to take the suspects' prints."

"What part of 'solid evidence' did you not understand?"

Sandrine spared herself further discussion. The man wouldn't budge an inch from his stance.

"Monsieur Marceau was also present at the château that night." Adel came to her aid to prevent the smouldering dispute from escalating.

"The lawyer and head of the foundation?"

"His alibi is equally weak, although it doesn't seem like he had anything to gain from his employer's death," Adel added.

"The children could dismiss him, then he'd lose a lucrative position," said Commissaire Matisse. Sandrine knew Marceau was not worried about losing his job, in fact he assumed he would keep it, as he didn't trust the siblings to agree on a new director.

"Who else benefited from the victim's will?" De Chezac was obviously seeking other suspects to shift the focus of the investigation away from the family.

"The housekeeper and the caretaker received a severance from the estate. Madame Sérian is quite elderly; she's unlikely to bludgeon anyone with an axe, and the amount Marcel Dumont received is too insignificant to murder for," said Sandrine. "To some extent, the two owners of the mill were also considered. Alain Nebot and Lilou Lanvers."

"What does 'to some extent' mean?" the prosecutor inquired. This direction of the investigation seemed much more agreeable to him.

"The victim bequeathed the farmhouse to Alain. However, with the condition to continue the vision of a cultural centre," explained Sandrine. "Xavier de Tréchet was particularly angry as he had other plans for the land."

"The murder happened in Alain Nebot's forge, with one of his own weapons, and he inherited a considerable fortune. You should investigate in this direction more extensively." De Chezac's voice gained sharpness. He seemed to sense an opportunity to circumvent the influential family and focus on two inconsequential individuals in the surroundings.

"Do the two have credible alibis?" Commissaire Matisse asked.

"Friday night, they were sleeping in a tent amidst the school class. For the time of Patrick Pradel's death, they claim to have been at home, which can't be corroborated by third parties."

"They could have slipped away. It was late, and teenagers can sleep till two after a strenuous day outdoors," Matisse mused. "Meeting with a family member in the forge seems unusual, but with the mill owner, it's a different story."

"They are on the list of suspects." Sandrine pointed to the pictures hanging on the pinboard. "Again, we lack solid evidence here, and I can't see a motive for the murder of the private detective, at least not at the moment."

"Increase the pressure," de Chezac demanded. "Eventually, they'll contradict themselves, and then we'll have them."

"As you wish." It was an empty phrase. She didn't believe the two were capable of committing murder. But a suspicion crossed her mind.

"Has a member of the family complained about our investigation?" she asked de Chezac.

"How did you come up with that?" he deflected.

"Xavier de Tréchet threatened to do so." At least, he seemed keen on shifting suspicion onto Alain and Lilou.

"I won't have my investigations meddled with, especially not by a potential suspect like Xavier de Tréchet. It's downright outrageous to insinuate that. Even by your standards." De Chezac didn't answer her question but acted offended, which proved that de Tréchet had complained about her and the investigation, probably had asked for her removal as lead investigator. He stood up and stepped in front of the pinboard. Either out of interest or to avoid her gaze. She suspected the latter.

"You know what to do," he said without looking at her.

Sandrine looked at Commissaire Matisse, who nodded hesitantly. He also seemed suspicious of de Chezac's eagerness to focus the investigation on the mill owners.

"We would like to discuss another topic with Capitaine Perrot," he addressed Adel.

"I have a lot of work on my desk that needs to be done." Adel quickly gathered his belongings and left the room. Sandrine picked up her cup and leaned back in her chair, which rocked slightly. She took a sip and silently observed her boss. It wasn't particularly difficult to guess what the two men wanted from her.

Commissaire Matisse crossed his arms over his chest, seemingly unwilling to broach the subject.

De Chezac sat back down. "What is your boyfriend up to?" He got straight to the point.

"Léon Martinau?"

"Who else, or do you have several?" he snapped at her impatiently.

"If you're so eager to know, you'd better ask him yourself," she shot back.

"We were hoping you could give us some insight," Matisse asked more conciliatory.

"We keep personal and professional matters separate, as I've said since the suspicions arose. I won't spy on my boyfriend."

"No one mentioned spying."

"I'm sure he and his lawyer will carefully consider how to restore his and his club's good reputation."

"He's represented by Madame Roche, isn't he?" Commissaire Matisse grimaced as if the lawyer's name caused him toothache.

"I don't like her much either," she admitted, "but she's exceptionally assertive." She couldn't praise the woman any further without feeling queasy. Lianne Roche was ruthless and used every means to win a case. Sandrine still wondered why she represented Léon, because she knew the lawyer would never forgive her for outsmarting her several times in the past. Probably, it gave her immense pleasure to outmanoeuvre the police and expose every dirty detail in public.

"Léon respects my work and will avoid putting me in an uncomfortable situation. That's why he keeps me completely out of this matter."

"But you're already neck-deep in it," de Chezac burst out.

"Absolutely not. Brigadier Poutin framed him with drugs and got caught. How could I have anything to do with that? In fact, I was at a hotel on Mont-Saint-Michel the night of the raid. With Léon Martinau."

Sandrine sought eye contact and silently warned de Chezac to be careful where he stepped. The ice he was treading on was extremely thin because she suspected him of being the mastermind behind the plot against Léon and her. Brigadier Poutin would never have committed such an offense without support from his superiors. It looked as though the policeman was being sacrificed. Poutin would be at least dismissed from the police force, probably charged with fabricating evidence. De Chezac must be sweating profusely at the prospect.

At that moment, the door opened and Marie Abondio peeked in.

"Am I interrupting?" She seemed to notice the tension in the room.

"No, we're done with the meeting." Sandrine looked at the two men. De Chezac appeared annoyed, while Commissaire Matisse seemed relieved to be able to end the conversation. The prosecutor must have pushed him to have it. He wouldn't have brought it up voluntarily. He was one of the few superiors who had always had her back.

"Then I'll get back to my work now." She stood up and walked with Marie to her workstation. Adel finished a phone call and looked up at them.

"What's new?" Sandrine had kept her curiosity in check in the presence of de Chezac. It was wiser to consider information before passing it on to him.

"The colleagues from Dinan sent us a bunch of fingerprints from the crime scene. We compared them with those in the system and got a match. A glass was touched by Auguste Brunel."

"The son-in-law," she said thoughtfully and sat down.

"Logical. The private detective was shadowing him. Perhaps he wanted to find out what he had discovered about him, and the conversation got out of hand," Adel speculated.

"Either he learned about the detective's existence through our questions and knocked on his door, or..."

"Or he already knew about it because he stole the report from his father-in-law's drawer after bashing his skull in," Adel finished her thoughts.

"What could Pradel have uncovered that was important enough to kill for? That Auguste Brunel gambled money away in the casinos was no secret. I wish we could find another copy of the report somewhere."

"If I were the murderer, I would have burned the documents long ago."

"That would be clever," Marie said. "Fortunately, few criminals are cunning enough to destroy all traces."

"I hope you're right because in this case, the fingerprints are our first real evidence that moves us forward."

"Nothing pleases us forensic technicians more than making you look good." She smiled in a self-assured manner, indicating that she was aware of her significance within the team.

"We love you too," said Sandrine. "Now Adel and I will pay another visit to the château."

* * *

Xavier de Tréchet met them outside the entrance of the estate.

"I was assured that you would finally do your job and scrutinise Alain and his girlfriend more closely. It's about time." The man had obviously spoken to the prosecutor and made no secret of it – unlike de Chezac, who had denied any interference. He wanted to demonstrate that he could speak to their superiors at any time and had significant influence.

"Rest assured, we are scrutinising everyone who could potentially be a perpetrator, without exception," Sandrine tried to appease him, but it bounced off. The wrinkles on his forehead deepened as he realised they wouldn't dance to his tune, no matter how good his connections were.

"It's completely absurd to assume that one of us could have killed my father."

"We're not accusing anyone. Not yet, anyway," she lied. At the moment, he had no right to know what steps she was planning against Auguste. Although she doubted Xavier saw him as a proper family member.

"Then you damn well better do your job." He gestured excitedly towards the river. "The guy wormed his way into my father's good graces and swindled the mill away from him. But that was just the beginning. He probably had his sights set on more from the start. He would have loved to get his hands on the château too."

"He claims he knew nothing about the will." It took her a great deal of self-control to remain calm, and an open argument would hardly advance the investigation.

"Then he's lying," he snapped at Sandrine harshly.

"Did you know its contents?"

"Of course not. Otherwise, I would have stopped this foolish plan to give away the family heritage."

"You and your father were close?"

"Absolutely."

"Then it seems unlikely to me that he would inform a stranger of the details of his last will, but not his eldest son and heir to the estate," she said gently, putting her suspicion that he was lying into the room.

Xavier de Tréchet paused in astonishment and took a deep breath. "As I said, I didn't know anything about his plans."

"It's just a consideration."

"They both fluttered around him every day, and he wasn't getting any younger. They brainwashed him, otherwise he would never have parted with the farmhouse."

"We'll keep that in mind during our investigation."

"You're friends with both of them. Is that why you're unwilling to investigate in this direction promptly?"

"As I said, we're investigating in all directions," she replied, emphasising the word 'all'.

"And what are you planning to do now?"

"We're going to talk to your brother-in-law."

"With Auguste?" he asked, surprised. "What does he have to do with Father's death?"

"Did you know that your father hired a private detective to shadow him while he was in Brittany?"

"No. That's news to me." He looked at her in astonishment, and she believed his ignorance. "Why would he do that? Everyone knows the guy drinks, gambles, and throws away Marie's money. Shadowing wouldn't reveal anything new."

"We're wondering the same thing."

"You'd better go find this detective; he'll be able to tell you." Xavier de Tréchet had recovered from his surprise and adopted his usual lofty tone.

"We'd like to, but he was killed. In a similar manner to your father."

"Another murder?" the man stammered, looking towards the mill as if expecting Alain to rush out and also bash his skull in with a battle axe. "You won't find him here, though. Auguste went to Saint-Malo. He had plans with some acquaintances."

"Do you know where this meeting is supposed to take place?" asked the brigadier.

"No idea. He babbled something about an oyster bar on the beach."

"I think I know which one he means." Adel nodded to her.

"Thank you very much. We'll find him."

"Does he have anything to do with the murder of this detective?"

"That remains to be seen." She glanced at her watch demonstratively. "We have to go now," she said, leaving the man standing and heading towards the entrance of the estate. Xavier de Tréchet stared after them in bewilderment.

Marcel Dumont left the château. The moment he noticed them, he changed direction to avoid a meeting.

"Monsieur Dumont!" Sandrine called out, loud enough for him not to be able to ignore her. The man took a few more steps, then stopped and turned slowly, almost reluctantly, towards her.

"You take care of what needs to be done," she told Adel and approached the caretaker.

"Capitaine Perrot. How can I help you?" He didn't sound particularly helpful, rather unsettled by her interest in him.

"Let's take a few steps together," she urged him.

"As you wish. I'm on my way to the estate."

"Then I'll accompany you on the way." A visit to the château wasn't urgent now that she knew Auguste Brunel wasn't to be found there.

"The path is muddy."

Ignoring his feeble attempt to shake her off, she continued as he swiftly headed towards the wooded area. Sandrine kept pace with the man.

"Do you like Madame Brunel?"

"She's the daughter of my employer."

"You spend a lot of time with her. Unusual for an employee. The château is a large and old estate, plus there's the farm, leaving little time. Yet you chauffeur Madame Brunel to Saint-Malo for shopping or keep her company on her walks, which are said to be quite extensive."

"She doesn't like being alone, and Monsieur de Tréchet asked me to drive her. He was... the boss."

"What does her husband think? Wouldn't it be his job to accompany her?"

"I can't say. How Monsieur Brunel views his marriage is his business." The sharpening tone belied his words. The relation-ship between the couple seemed far from indifferent to him.

"I find it hard to believe that he would approve of his wife spending so much time with a stranger."

"I've driven Marie Brunel and carried the groceries. That's all."

"The waiter from Brasserie Le Sillon had a different impres-sion. According to his account, you were very familiar with each other."

"She invited me once because she finds eating alone boring."

"Three times within a week. That hasn't gone unnoticed. Especially not by Auguste, it seems."

"He has no problem with it," he insisted.

"Nonsense," she snapped. "You have a decent bruise and the skin over the knuckles of your right hand is scraped off. The man hit you, that's obvious. Don't take me for a fool."

He shrugged wordlessly.

"You're younger and probably stronger than the guy, but I couldn't find any signs of an injury on him. Why didn't you fight back?"

Marcel Dumont turned away and looked out over the Rance. Sandrine gave him a moment to think.

"I didn't want to get her into trouble," he finally said. "The man is an idiot who's gotten himself fixated on a crazy idea."

"He assumed you were having an affair with his wife?"

"Marie feels lonely in the château. Her husband is always away, and she needed someone to talk to. I'm a decent listener and I find her likable, but there's nothing more between us."

"The Brunels' marriage isn't going well, is it?"

"That's hard to miss. It wasn't a real love match. Marie wanted to leave here, preferably for Paris, and Auguste needed someone to finance him."

"A perfect arrangement, at least for a while," said Sandrine.

"They not only sleep in separate rooms, they live in different worlds. The two have nothing in common."

"Monsieur de Tréchet hired a private detective to monitor Monsieur Brunel. Did you know about that?"

"I heard about it. Marie was upset that her father was once again interfering in her life."

"Can you imagine what the man was supposed to find out? His lifestyle wasn't a secret within the family."

"Marie mentioned a prenuptial agreement. In case her

husband cheated on her, he would get nothing in a divorce. Monsieur de Tréchet insisted on it at the time."

Sandrine whistled softly. That was indeed a solid motive to make the detective's report disappear. Especially now after the death of Alexandre de Tréchet, as Auguste expected significantly higher allowances from the foundation.

"Thank you, that helps me."

"Do you think he's behind the murder?" the young man asked.

"Do you think he's capable of murder?"

Marcel Dumont ran his fingertip over the swelling, which was slowly turning green.

"He certainly doesn't possess any particular self-control. So yes, I wouldn't put it past him."

"We'll find out," Sandrine promised. Adel was surely waiting for her.

She said her goodbyes. It was time to head back to the police station. She was curious about what story Auguste Brunel would serve up once they found him.

* * *

Brigadier Dubois waved them over as they entered the office.

"Did you get our man?" Sandrine asked.

"Monsieur Brunel was exactly where Adel suspected: at the oyster bar at Plage de l'Éventail near the Mairie. As expected, neither he nor his crew were thrilled about having to accompany us."

"Any trouble?" The request to handle the family with kid gloves was still fresh in her mind. The rest of the de Tréchets might find it amusing if she went hard on Auguste, but the relationship between her and de Chezac was already strained enough. She had no intention of doing anything that he might interpret as provocation, at least not if it could be avoided.

"After a serious warning, he became compliant." The older brigadier grinned mischievously. "A bunch of loudmouths whose courage quickly fades when faced with resistance."

"Where is he?"

"In interrogation room one. We brought him a cup of coffee and then left him waiting."

Auguste Brunel looked towards the door as they entered, leaning back in his chair and crossing his arms in front of his chest.

"About time you showed up," he snapped at Sandrine. "Having me picked up by the cops in front of my friends is a bad idea."

"Whether the idea was good or bad remains to be seen." She stayed calm and took a seat opposite him at the table.

Adel switched on the microphone and provided the routine details about the location, time, and attendees of the interrogation. Auguste looked at him grumpily.

"Is this nonsense really necessary?" he asked Sandrine.

"Pure routine. This way, there are no misunderstandings about what was actually said during the questioning."

"I've already given a statement about everything there is to say."

"What was your relationship with Alexandre de Tréchet?" She ignored his objection.

"I didn't like him, which was mutual. The man couldn't get over the fact that his oh-so-beloved daughter couldn't stand being here with him anymore and blamed me for her move to Paris. Even without our marriage, she would have packed her bags and left."

"Doesn't sound like a love marriage." Sandrine hoped to provoke him and get him to reveal more.

"We have a harmonious marriage, where everyone lives as they please." The man remained calm but also very vague.

"So, you sleep on the sofa in the living room?"

"We have different lifestyles. Marie is a morning person, and I wake up in the evening. In Paris, we have separate bedrooms to avoid disturbing each other. Here, I occasionally use the sofa to avoid waking up my wife when I come home."

"Every night?"

"Of course not," he quickly said.

"And on the night your father-in-law was killed?"

"I spent it in bed with my wife. She confirmed it to the police, so why the question?"

"And you didn't notice anything unusual in the house?"

"Absolutely not. I slept like a baby." His grin indicated how much he liked the comparison.

"What reason could your father-in-law have had to hire a detective to watch you?"

"How should I know? He's hardly likely to have informed me about it." Auguste Brunel flattened his hands on the table and leaned towards her. "And what could the snooper have found out? I'm sociable, enjoy going out, and I'm not stingy. None of that would have surprised him. I don't hide my preferences. Everyone knows that, especially Marie."

"Who finances your lifestyle," Sandrine added. "What does she think of your preferences?"

"Don't deceive yourself about her. She didn't marry a stranger. Marie knew exactly what her life with me would be like. It didn't bother her, only Alexandre was obsessed with having to protect her from me. But she doesn't need anyone trying to pull her back into the family fold. She's perfectly happy in Paris."

"Even in your marriage?"

"I'm convinced of it, but no one's stopping you from asking my wife."

"If you're so sure of that, why resort to violence against Marcel Dumont?"

"The little caretaker? Did he file a complaint against me? Are we here because of that trifle?" He tried to appear amused.

"Assault is no joke," she said sternly, to impress upon him the seriousness of the situation.

"The guy tried to hit on Marie. What would you have done in my place?"

"Then you do seem to doubt your wife's fidelity?" Adel asked. Auguste's head jerked towards him, and he stared angrily at the brigadier.

"Absolutely not, but someone had to make it clear to him before he got fresh with Marie or started imagining any romantic nonsense."

"Your self-control isn't particularly strong." Sandrine opened the file in front of her. "You've already been reported for assault."

"The woman tried to extort money with fabricated accusations. That's what happens when you're famous and wealthy."

"So, you didn't hit her?"

"If I had, I'd surely have been convicted, right?" A smug grin appeared on his face. Auguste Brunel knew perfectly well that everyone in the room knew how he had wriggled out of trouble: with a fat cheque.

"Surely you were upset with your father-in-law, trying to interfere in your marriage, perhaps even trying to convince his daughter to divorce you which would have cost you a lot of money. I can understand that you were angry. Did you meet with him to discuss it? The old man remained stubborn, and you lost control again and hit him. Was that it?"

"I didn't exchange a word with him that day. I don't think I even saw the old man. He was busy with this childish drama at the mill and the provincial exhibition at the manor. Xavier was probably following him like a little dog, trying to convince him about his golf project."

"He didn't mention the detective's report to you?" Sandrine asked, watching his facial expressions closely.

"No. As I said, there's nothing the man could have found out." Auguste put his hand to his face and massaged his chin. She didn't need to rely on her gut feeling that he was lying; she had his fingerprints. The question was why he denied it. So far, she couldn't prove anything beyond him being in Patrick Pradel's office. There was no evidence that he had murdered him.

"He was named Pradel and lived in Dinan. Did you know him?"

"Why should I? I don't associate with people like him."

"That doesn't answer the question."

"If I knew him? No, definitely not."

Sandrine slid a photo of the dead detective across the table. Without looking, Auguste Brunel shook his head.

"I had nothing to do with him."

"You're lying," she accused him.

"What do you think you're doing?" he snapped, jumping up. The chair toppled over and fell to the floor. Sandrine and Adel remained seated, watching the man impassively. He barked, but it was clear to them he wouldn't bite. He lacked the courage for it.

"Pick up the chair and sit down!" she ordered him.

The man stared at her wordlessly. The anger drained from his face, replaced by bewilderment. The behaviour of the two police officers puzzled him. By now, Auguste Brunel was probably wondering what they knew and where the trap was that they were trying to lure him into. Yet, with his lie, he had maneuvered himself into it.

Reluctantly, he bent down, picked up the chair and pushed it back to the table, but he didn't sit.

"You can continue to deny it, but it won't do you any good. The forensics team works very efficiently, and your fingerprints were found at the crime scene."

The man's shoulders slumped, and he sank back into the chair.

"Speak up. What did you want from Patrick Pradel?"

He remained silent, avoiding eye contact with Sandrine and instead staring at the tabletop, picking up the empty coffee cup with both hands.

"Denying won't help you anymore," said Adel. "We can prove that you were at the scene of the crime."

"The only question is: what were you doing there?" Sandrine continued.

Auguste let out a deep breath and lowered his head further.

"Alright, I was with the guy," he muttered finally.

"What happened? Did you want the report and did it lead to an argument?"

He raised his head and looked at Sandrine.

"I knew nothing about a detective that my father-in-law had hired. On Sunday, the guy called and tried to blackmail me. I admit, I was quite surprised."

After she and Adel left his office, Patrick Pradel must have picked up the phone directly to call Auguste Brunel and cash in on his knowledge.

"And?" Sandrine urged him to continue.

"At first, I thought he was an inflated big shot, but then he piqued my curiosity, and I agreed to meet him."

"In his office in Dinan?"

"Yes."

"What happened then?"

"I drove there in the late afternoon and met the guy. A pathetic nobody who wanted to make himself important. The amount he had in mind was ridiculously high."

"You couldn't come to an agreement?" Sandrine asked.

"That was unnecessary. That caricature of a detective had nothing that could embarrass me. Like I said, I enjoy going out and perhaps spend too much of my wife's money. But this has been a subject of ridicule in the stuffy family for a long time. Why would I pay for this information?"

"There's a prenuptial agreement." Sandrine played her supposed trump card.

"You know about that?"

"We do our jobs diligently."

"Then you also know what's in it. If we get divorced, I get nothing if I cheat on Marie."

"Did Monsieur Pradel find that out?"

"I like to flirt, I don't deny that, but I've never cheated on my wife with another woman. Whatever that detective claimed, he could never have provided evidence for such slander."

"As you know, he was murdered. In a similar way to Alexandre de Tréchet. I assume it's the same perpetrator."

"Not by me. When I left the guy, he was still alive, albeit bitterly disappointed that we hadn't struck a deal. I lack the motive for murder."

"You claim that. Perhaps you did cheat on your wife, and Pradel found out. You feared soon being cut off from the family's lucrative pots of gold. Your father-in-law was the driving force behind the investigations. You argued with him. Perhaps you didn't intend to kill Alexandre de Tréchet, but your temper got the better of you, and you struck with the first object you could find. To deflect suspicion from yourself, you had to destroy the report. The detective posed a threat. He knew too much, and people like him would continue to blackmail you. What choice did you have but to finally get rid of Patrick Pradel? You have a solid motive, the opportunity, you were demonstrably at the crime scene, and you possessed the weapon you stole from Alain Nebot's forge. Perhaps the murder of your father-in-law was done in the heat of the moment, but the murder of Patrick Pradel was cold-bloodedly planned." She placed a picture of the detective's blood-covered body in front of him, alongside a photo of the murder weapon. "No one brings such a weapon unless they intend to use it."

The blood drained from his face, and he looked at her incredulously.

"I told you, he was still alive when I left him."

"We hear that often here."

"You have to believe me!"

"Do you have a credible alibi for Sunday evening?"

"I want to speak with my lawyer. Until then, I won't say another word."

"Of course. However, we'll keep you here until you remember where you were," she decided.

Sandrine turned off the microphone. The interrogation was over, and she and Adel left the man alone.

She closed the door behind her and instructed a policeman to let Auguste Brunel make a phone call.

"What do you think?" Adel asked on the way to the office.

"The man is our prime suspect at the moment. His motive is clear: he wanted to suppress the detective's report. Adultery could have cost him his financial support. He was undoubtedly in Patrick Pradel's office and had the opportunity to kill both him and Alexandre de Tréchet."

"He's hot-headed," he agreed. "Perhaps you're right and the confrontation with his father-in-law did indeed get out of hand. The man grabbed any weapon in the workshop in his rage and struck. I can believe that, but a cold-blooded planned murder of the detective? I have my doubts."

"When under enough pressure, anyone can become a murderer," Sandrine replied. She had experienced this more than once. "Besides, the battle axes weren't just lying around on a workbench in the forge. They were at the back end against the wall." If Alain Nebot hadn't realised it yet, she would advise him to lock up his weapons better in the future.

The commissaire glanced out of his office and waved to her.

"Do you have a moment for me?"

"I'll be right there," she said to Adel and entered her superior's office.

Matisse took a seat behind his desk and offered her to sit down as well.

"I'm sorry de Chezac gave the impression that we were asking you to spy on your male friend. Of course, you would never do that. I'm aware of that, and I would never ask something like that of you."

"I know. You've had my back during the difficult times. I appreciate it."

"Not necessary. No one here at the station seriously believed you were involved in criminal activities. Absurd idea."

"Well, at least one person assumed or wanted to give the impression." They both knew who Sandrine was talking about. "What's the next step at the station?"

"Brigadier Poutin has admitted to planting drugs on Léon Martinau during the raid. He's currently suspended from duty. An investigation into filing a false report is underway."

"By whom?" Sandrine suspected that the brigadier had either been commissioned by de Chezac or at least believed he had his approval to act. If de Chezac were to lead the investigation, it would become a farce.

"We need to ensure there's no suspicion of a cover-up, so the case is now in the hands of investigators in Rennes."

Sandrine perked up. That was news to her. Was that the real reason for Prosecutor Hermé's detour to Cancale? She had previously considered the man to be objective and possess a deep sense of justice, so he was definitely a good choice.

"Thank you for letting me know."

"It's not a secret. It'll probably be in the newspaper tomorrow. The press office has issued a statement." Commissaire Matisse had thereby given her permission to share the contents of the conversation with Léon.

"Then I'll get back to my case."

"Have you arrested a suspect?"

"We'll keep him here overnight. Perhaps he'll be more talkative tomorrow," she said, although she was doubtful. An experienced lawyer would advise him to keep his mouth shut unless he had a verifiable alibi.

"Do you think he's our guy?"

"He could be. A lot fits together, but I still lack solid evidence of his guilt. Maybe the forensic technicians will find a new lead connecting him to the murders."

"Monsieur Mazet is extremely competent. If anything exists, he'll find it."

"I think so too," she said and left the office.

Sandrine sat in the meeting room. She had pushed her chair in front of the pinboards.

"This will help with thinking." Adel entered and handed her an espresso in one of those delicate cups, whose handle was just enough to hold it. However, sticking a finger through it was impossible.

"Were you at Inès's machine?"

"I lack the technical understanding for that thing; it's too complicated for me. She brewed two cups and sent them with me."

"Very kind of her."

"She knew I'd find you here."

"Did Auguste Brunel call his lawyer?"

"I assume so, he had a phone call."

"I can keep him under provisional arrest for a while."

"For 72 hours, to be exact."

"The man is not some petty criminal. The family is influential and will step on the prosecutor's toes. We need to hurry before de Chezac caves and instructs us to release him."

"That's why you're sitting here staring at the pinboards."

"He lied to us, but that's not a crime. Not even an offense."

"We're lied to left and right every day. Nothing new," Adel said.

"He admitted that Patrick Pradel tried to blackmail him. Auguste Brunel was at the crime scene, is notoriously hot-headed, and had access to the murder weapon. But that's not enough to convict him. Any lawyer will tear the accusation to shreds."

"What else do you need?"

"None of it conclusively proves he's the detective's killer. Not until we can prove he was in the office at the time of the crime. He could get away with the story of meeting the man in the afternoon."

"There's no CCTV in the alley."

She recalled her conversation with the saleswoman at the pastry shop at the entrance of the street leading to Pradel's house.

"The entrance to Rue du Petit Fort is only allowed for residents, which some tourists like to ignore. The woman at the coffee shop told me that the municipal police regularly patrol there."

"Brunel is probably one of those who find it too strenuous to walk up the hill. I'll call the station in Dinan. With any luck, they've given him a ticket, then we'll know if his story checks out."

"Do that. Maybe we'll also get some video footage from the surrounding streets. Brunel must have arrived and left somehow. The red sports car is quite conspicuous."

"Will do."

"Also, we need to examine the man's clothing. The wound on the back of Pradel's head bled heavily. I bet the perpetrator got some of it on them. In any case, he would have walked through the blood at the crime scene."

"So, the shoes and the car's floor mat too." Adel jotted down a note in his pad. "I'll call Jean-Claude; he'll send one of his guys to the château. Brunel's car is still parked in Saint-Malo. We have the keys in custody."

Inès peeked in. "A certain Régis Marceau is waiting at the reception. He wants to speak with you."

"Tell him I'll come to the entrance and fetch him." The man was indeed a lawyer, but specialised in contract law. It was unlikely that Auguste Brunel had chosen him as legal counsel.

"Before that, you're supposed to see Matisse. The prosecutor is with him."

"De Chezac? What could he want?" She didn't expect congratulations for the arrest.

"He looked upset."

"Then I'll go, or my visitor will wait too long." She turned to Adel. "My gut tells me we need to hurry."

"I'll send someone to Brunel's car immediately to look for bloodstains."

"Come in and close the door," Commissaire Matisse instructed her. Sandrine's internal alarm immediately went off. Normally, the door to her superior's office was always open. What could be so sensitive that it needed to remain secret?

"You have Auguste Brunel in the interrogation room?" De Chezac threw the sentence at her before she had even sat down.

"That sounds like an accusation." She sat down, crossed one leg over the other, and leaned back in her chair. She wouldn't let the man intimidate her.

"I instructed to proceed with the utmost discretion in these investigations. What part of that didn't you understand?"

"The man is a prime suspect. Just because he comes from an influential family doesn't mean he gets special treatment."

"On what basis is the provisional arrest founded?" Matisse asked, trying to defuse the conflict between de Chezac and Sandrine.

"Monsieur Brunel has a solid financial motive to eliminate both his father-in-law and the private detective who was on his tail. He could easily obtain the weapons used, and we can prove he was in the detective agency's premises. Usually, that's more than enough to secure a provisional arrest."

"But this is no ordinary case," de Chezac snapped at her. "We're not dealing with petty criminals here, but with a member of a highly respected family. Someone like you should recognise that."

"And so I should let him get away with double murder?" she retorted sharply.

"Can you prove that the man was in Patrick Pradel's office at the time of the crime? As far as I know, he admits to having visited him in the afternoon."

"We're in the process of verifying that."

"That's not enough for a provisional arrest. Release him. Immediately."

She looked to Matisse, who nodded reluctantly. The lifting

of arrests was decided by the responsible prosecutor. The commissaire had no choice but to follow the instructions.

"As you wish." Sandrine stood up and left the office. Only when the door closed behind her did she clench her fists.

She opened the door to the interrogation room and entered. Auguste Brunel's feet were on the table, and he looked at her. The smug smile on his lips was evidence enough that he knew the Tréchets had intervened for him.

"He's here to take me away, isn't he?" He confirmed her suspicion. He hadn't called a lawyer; he had called Régis Marceau, who handled the family's affairs.

"He was very eager to get you out of here."

"That surprises you?" He laughed bitterly. "Me too, if I'm honest. None of that bunch can stand me, and I feel the same about them."

He stood up and walked to the door, which she held open for him. The man stopped in front of her.

"I admit, I've imagined killing him more than once. But I didn't do it."

Without further acknowledgment, he walked through the door. The uniformed officer escorted him, while she returned to her desk. She decided to forego a meeting with Régis Marceau. It was time to go home and get this case out of her head for a while.

* * *

Sandrine took a deep breath and rose onto her tiptoes as the wave splashed against her stomach. Goosebumps raced across her skin. Even in summer, the water felt icy to her. Léon stood behind her, wrapping his arms around her. Grateful for the warmth, she nestled against him.

Kite-surfers shot past them, and she couldn't help but envy

them for their neoprene wet-suits. *Maybe I should get one of those too.*

"How about warming up and then grabbing a bite to eat?" Léon suggested.

"Excellent idea," she replied. She dropped to her knees until the water reached her shoulders. With the next wave, she let herself drift towards the shore.

Two towels lay on the warm sand, and she retrieved another from her beach bag for drying off. After finishing work, she had called Léon, packed her swimwear, and driven with him to Plage de Port Mer. The popular beach lay roughly halfway along her jogging route to Pointe du Grouin. Équinoxe was closed today and tomorrow. She wanted to make the most of the few evenings they could spend together and not dwell on the setbacks in her investigations. The sun hung low over the horizon, its rays barely warming them anymore. Sandrine dried herself off with a towel and wrapped it tightly around her.

"How's your case going?" Léon asked, surprising her.

"Not well. Can you tell?" she replied.

"You seem thoughtful."

"Sorry. I should leave all the unpleasant stuff at the office when I go home in the evenings."

"I struggle with that too, and I only run a club. There's no murder on my plate."

"Kind of you." She leaned against him. "This morning, I thought we had a breakthrough, and then I had to release my main suspect."

"That bad?"

"At least the circle of suspects is narrowing down, which I guess is progress."

"The newspaper is speculating that the two murders are connected."

"You know I can't talk about that."

"But I would like to," he said, surprising her.

"We wanted to keep personal and professional matters separate," she reminded him.

"I like that. So should I call Adel to give him some information, or that journalist? What was her name again?"

"Deborah Binet."

"Right. She reported on the club. I liked the article."

Sandrine did too, though she wasn't surprised that the police department had come off poorly.

"What would you tell Adel?"

Léon had piqued her curiosity, and she cast her concerns aside.

"Since you're investigating the case, it's clear that both murders are connected, otherwise that would be the job of the Gendarmerie in Dinan," he remarked.

Sandrine nodded silently.

"I know the private detective. This Pradel occasionally came to Équinoxe."

"Isn't he a bit old for the club? The man was pushing sixty and didn't seem like someone who'd be drawn to the dance floor."

The image of Patrick Pradel on the dance floor at Équinoxe brought a broad grin to Léon's face.

"Definitely not. He always sat at the bar and hardly ever drank more than one or two beers."

"So he was there for business."

"His specialty was unfaithful husbands. There isn't much else for private detectives to do around here."

"He was hired to monitor Alexandre de Tréchet's son-in-law."

"I know him too. He's been at the club several times lately. He spends a lot of money, but he's stingy with tips. No one will miss him much when he goes back to Paris."

"What did you want to tell me about Pradel?"

"The guy played dirty."

"What does that mean?"

"He occasionally gave his success a boost, if you catch my drift."

"Pradel had women set up on his targets?" She nodded thoughtfully. She easily believed him capable of such tactics. It reduced the workload and increased the chances of coming back with a positive result. She just wondered if his clients knew how he persuaded their husbands to stray.

"Even with Auguste?" The man vehemently denied infidelity, but if Pradel had set him up, the stakes would dramatically increase. With his lifestyle, he could hardly afford a divorce where he came out empty-handed.

"I assume so. He knew two or three women he worked with, and I've seen one of them at Auguste's table with his friends several times. The girl worked hard to win him over."

"Successful?"

"If so, not in my club," Leon laughed. "Équinoxe isn't a swinger club. If someone wants sex, they go home or to a hotel."

She raised her hands defensively. "Sorry, curiosity is an occupational hazard."

"If you're interested, I can give you her phone number."

"You have her number?" Sandrine looked at him surprised.

"Not me, but Simone, my manager. She occasionally helps out as a waitress when too many regulars are missing."

"And where else does she work?"

"Do I hear a hint of jealousy or mistrust in your voice?" Léon teased her.

"Absolutely not. Just professional interest."

"In Saint-Malo, at a gentlemen's club."

Sandrine knew the type of gentlemen who frequented such places all too well from her job in the police force.

"A prostitute?"

"No idea, you're not allowed to ask that in a job interview these days. I don't know how far she had to go in working for Pradel."

"Give me the number," she said after briefly considering it. If Auguste had slept with her and been photographed by the detective, it would strengthen suspicion against him. The question was whether it would be enough for de Chezac to take sharper action. Probably not.

"Was Auguste at the club on Sunday?"

"It was super crowded. But as far as I remember, I saw him. The waitresses will know. Otherwise, I could check the credit card receipts for you."

"Any idea what time he was there?"

"Sometime after midnight. I could find out more precisely. The security camera footage at the entrance is stored."

She waved it off.

"At that time, he could have committed the murder and comfortably returned to Saint-Malo."

"I'll keep the recording just in case. Who knows what else you might come across."

"You're sweet. For that, I'll treat you to dinner later."

"Oh. You want to cook for me?" he teased her.

"Of course. Either scrambled eggs at my place or a three-course meal in Cancale. Your choice."

This time he kissed her. "Preferably at your place," he whispered in her ear. "But only if there's a sophisticated dessert."

"That can be arranged." She knew exactly what kind of dessert he had in mind. It looked like a nice evening ahead. *Hopefully, no one else dies and ruins it for me.*

"Are they trying to pump you for information about whether I'm planning legal action against the department?" He abruptly changed the subject.

"Not Matisse, but the prosecutor. I've made it clear to him that we keep private and professional matters separate and I'm not interested in what you're planning."

"I don't want to cause you any trouble." He sounded apologetic. She turned to him, placed her hands on his cheeks, and kissed his forehead.

"I attract trouble by behaving the way I think is right. You have nothing to do with it. Just make sure you come out of this without any harm, that's what matters most to me."

She could easily imagine his lawyer, Lianne Roche, pushing him towards legal action, which he would hesitate to take out of consideration for her.

"Let's not dwell on it unless you want my advice as your friend. In the role of a police officer, I'm biased."

"We'll talk about it once I'm clear about my course of action."

"I'm here for you. But now I'm getting hungry. Let's head out."

She stood up and carelessly stuffed the towels into the beach bag. From the beach, she could see her black and red Citroën on the parking lot. It was only a few minutes from here to her house. *A hot shower, then I'll see if there's something in the kitchen for dinner.*

Auguste Brunel

Sandrine lay on her back, listening to the rain drumming wildly on the roof. Wind whistled around the corners of the former stable, and she pulled the blanket up to her chin, snuggling close to Léon, who wrapped his arms around her. In truth, she should have been on her way to the police station by now, but she didn't feel in a hurry this morning. She had enough overtime hours in her account to justify a later start. A rainy day like this, she would prefer to spend entirely in bed. Especially after de Chezac had thrown a hefty wrench into her plans yesterday. She groaned softly at the thought of the prosecutor, who was trying to curry favour with the de Tréchets and making her job more difficult. Her phone vibrated on the nightstand.

"Be quiet!" she murmured, snuggling closer to Léon, but the phone ignored her wish.

"Not mine," he mumbled sleepily.

"I know." She cursed softly as she sat up and reached for the phone. The number belonged to the police station.

"They miss you," Léon said, stretching. "Looks like the cosy part of the day is over. I'll make coffee." He got up and put on the trousers lying on the floor by the bed.

"What's up?" she asked, devoid of any friendliness in her tone.

"Am I disturbing?" Inès said.

"Call me back in an hour when I'm ready to face the world."

"I thought you wouldn't be interested, but Adel thought differently. I'll call back later."

"I'm awake now. What's going on?"

"Marie Brunel called to report her husband missing."

"He probably celebrated his victory over the police and got himself drunk somewhere. What surprises me more is that she even noticed his absence." Starting the day with news about that pompous man was a miserable start. Her gut feeling told her it would only go downhill from here. "The man is of legal age and can do as he pleases."

"His car is parked outside the château."

"Send de Chezac there. He was keen on setting him free. He can go search for the unpleasant snob himself. I'm sure they'll get along splendidly."

"Matisse has already informed him."

She sighed in frustration. Nothing would stop the man from immediately heading to the de Tréchet estate to further ingratiate himself with the family.

"Give me time for a proper caffeine shot, then I'll jump in the car and head to the château."

"There are better ways to wake up."

Sandrine paused. She had rarely encountered such frivolity from the young office manager before.

"Such as jogging, for example," Inès quickly added.

"Thanks for the advice. The weather's miserable, so coffee it is." She briefly thought about what de Chezac would promise the family for which she would be held accountable. Then she shrugged. He would arrive at the estate before her, no matter how much she hurried. The ugly duckling wasn't a racing car.

She pulled on a T-shirt and went downstairs to the kitchen. The smell of fresh coffee greeted her. She kissed Léon.

"You're my saviour."

"You have to go?"

She took the cup from his hand and sat down at the table. She skipped the milk. A cube of sugar was enough.

"It can't be avoided. I'm supposed to babysit for a rich and spoiled gang. An adult man, whom I wouldn't put two murders past, has gone missing, and it's up to me to find him." As she complained, she realised how much she was letting her anger about the prosecutor run wild. In the vicinity of the de Tréchets, people had been brutally murdered. It was understandable that Marie Brunel would worry if her husband was unaccounted for.

"Auguste Brunel?"

"Exactly him." She gulped down the small cup in one go, held it out to Léon, and looked at him pleadingly. "Maybe he would have been better off in the cell after all."

She watched as he placed the cup in the coffee machine. "I'd wager he's hiding somewhere to sleep off his bender." Even though she saw this as the most likely scenario, an unpleasant premonition crept over her that there might be more to it than met the eye. Perhaps he sensed that the police were closing in on him and had gone into hiding. But then his car wouldn't be parked outside the estate.

He handed her a piece of paper torn from the notepad hanging in the kitchen. "I talked to Simone yesterday. This is the address of the woman who seduces men for your detective."

"Thanks. I'll talk to her."

"I hope she can contribute something useful, but a look at the guys Auguste was hanging out with might be an eye-opener." He tapped the paper, winked at her, and smiled with amusement. He enjoyed surprising her.

She glanced over the list, which consisted of four names and the brief note he had written beside each one. She raised her eyebrows and scrutinised him.

"Seriously?"

Instead of answering, he placed a full cup in front of her.

"That explains a lot," she muttered.

* * *

The sky had opened its gates, and the puny wipers of Sandrine's Citroën were hopelessly overwhelmed. She was glad to be able to take the asphalted path to the estate. Shortly after, she parked in front of the main entrance. Auguste Brunel's bright red sports car was in the lot. Therefore, he had returned last night. She made a mental note to call Jean-Claude to check if he had found any blood traces in the car.

"Maybe he's shown up sober by now," she murmured, looking up at the cloudy sky through the windshield. No chance it would stop anytime soon. She glanced at the rain jacket lying on the back seat. It hardly seemed worth it to put it on for the few metres to the château. Sandrine jumped out of the car, slammed the door shut and ran to the entrance. The door was unlocked, and she entered. She ran a hard through her wet hair, which clung to her forehead.

"Madame Perrot." Régis Marceau approached her.

"Capitaine Perrot," she corrected him, as she was here on official business.

"Of course." He reached for her cool, wet hand, which he quickly released. "The family is gathered in the salon."

"What happened?" She took the opportunity to speak with the man alone.

"Auguste is missing." The hesitation in his voice indicated to her that he was aware of the impression it made when the prime suspect in a murder case unexpectedly disappeared without telling his wife about his plans. Especially someone whose release he had personally ensured.

"Please, start from the beginning. You picked up Auguste at the police station yesterday. Where did you take him?"

"His car was parked in the lot near the city wall, not far from the casino. I dropped him off there."

"At what time?"

"Right after I picked him up at the police station. We didn't have many common topics of conversation."

"I can imagine. How did he view your position in the foundation?"

The man hesitated briefly. The question had caught him off guard.

"Auguste offered me his full support," he replied, emphasising it.

"What did he demand in return?"

"Why do you think he might have made a demand?"

"Someone like Monsieur Brunel never does anything without expecting something in return – or am I mistaken?"

"No," he said hesitantly, as if unsure whether he should elaborate further.

"Come on, anything could be useful in the search for him," she urged.

"Alright. He asked for my support to represent his wife on the foundation board as her proxy."

"Did you agree to that?"

"I had to deny it, of course. The regulations of the foundation are clear on this point. Only direct descendants are eligible to vote and only in person. Marie cannot be represented."

"He wouldn't have been pleased about that."

The lawyer raised his hands, as if to feign a certain regret.

Sandrine was convinced that Marceau preferred Marie on the foundation board, who seemed more affable and significantly less greedy than her husband. He probably also assumed she would be easier to influence. If he wasn't greatly mistaken in that regard.

"Have you seen him again since then?"

"I stayed overnight at the estate and came down for breakfast. There are still some details to be clarified between the heirs. Then the preparations for Alexandre's funeral. Marie received me with the news of her husband's disappearance. That's all I can contribute."

"Every little bit helps." It was just a platitude, as they both knew. "Let's go join the family."

Antoine de Chezac was sitting in one of the reading chairs. In the second sat Marie, wearing a black sheath dress. Her legs were bent on the cushion, and her pumps lay carelessly on the carpet. She turned her head to Sandrine and straightened up. Interest shimmered in her eyes, which had looked bored a second ago. Fabius had chosen one of the sofas. He helped himself to a plate of cookies on a delicate side table. Xavier posed in front of the fireplace, where a log was burning and spreading the smell of smoke throughout the room.

"There you are, finally. You took your time." De Chezac couldn't help but criticise her in front of those present. It must have been important to him to emphasise that he was her superior. Whether his behaviour cast him in a favourable light, she doubted.

"So, can I assume you've already found Auguste Brunel?" Sandrine knew that wasn't the case, but she couldn't resist the retort.

"No, he hasn't. How could he, when he's only here waiting for you?" The unusual sharpness in Marie's tone caught

Sandrine's attention. Was she genuinely worried about her husband, or did she simply dislike the prosecutor?

"Who among you last saw Auguste Brunel yesterday?" Sandrine asked the group.

"I heard him drive up around ten o'clock," said Fabius de Tréchet. "No one else here drives such a loud car."

Sandrine looked at Marie Brunel questioningly.

"He didn't come into our room. He probably didn't want to wake me and slept downstairs," Marie said.

"How thoughtful," Xavier added sarcastically. "More likely he was too drunk to climb the stairs."

"Stay out of our business," Marie snapped at him. Her brother turned around and adjusted the burning log with an iron hook. He seemed to want to avoid a quarrel with his sister in front of the police. Sandrine wondered what the atmosphere was like at the foundation board meeting.

"Neither Madame Sérian nor Marcel Dumont saw him this morning," Marie said.

"Since his car is here, he can't be far away. Are there any unused rooms? Maybe he found the sofa uncomfortable and decided to sleep somewhere in peace," Sandrine suggested.

"Madame Sérian searched the guest rooms. Without success," said Fabius. "I even checked the car, in case he was drunk and passed out there."

"No one noticed him at the mill either," Marie said, looking at her with concern. "Do you think something happened to him?"

"I can't rule it out," Sandrine replied honestly, glancing at de Chezac, who avoided eye contact with her. If he hadn't released the man from custody, they wouldn't be searching for him this morning.

"Who would harm him?" Xavier asked impatiently.

"Perhaps the same person who killed Father?" Marie's voice cut through the air, and her brother flinched. Sandrine had never seen the woman so present before.

"We don't know why he disappeared," Sandrine interjected. "Most missing persons reappear on their own after a while."

"As a precaution, the police will thoroughly search the château and the surrounding areas," de Chezac said decisively. "If he's here, we'll surely find him."

"A tempest in a teacup. I'm sure he's just sleeping off his hangover somewhere." Xavier didn't mince words when it came to his opinion of his brother-in-law.

Marie sat up straight and stretched her legs out. "I need some fresh air," she said, looking at Sandrine. "Would you do me the honour of accompanying me for a bit?"

"Of course." Sandrine suspected that the woman intended to share something with her that she didn't want the rest of the family to hear.

In the hallway, Marie retrieved a pair of rubber boots and a green raincoat from a cupboard and put them on. "We're not going to a fashion show. We'll likely only see a lost sheep or a cow." Marie buttoned up her jacket and stepped outside. Sandrine followed the increasingly surprising woman. Although the rain had stopped, the sun remained hidden behind thick clouds.

"We should hurry before it starts raining again," Sandrine suggested.

"I'm not made of sugar," the woman replied.

Sandrine went to the car and retrieved her jacket. She noticed smoke rising from the forge's chimney. Alain must be working.

"Come on, before someone else decides to join us," Marie Brunel urged.

"I doubt anyone will," Sandrine muttered, following the

woman towards a narrow path leading to the banks of the Rance.

"You don't really believe that Auguste killed my father and that person from Dinan, do you?"

"He had a motive."

"He didn't," she insisted.

"Your father disapproved of your marriage."

"That's putting it mildly."

"That's why he hired a private detective to catch your husband cheating. As far as I know, the prenuptial agreement stipulates that he would get nothing in the event of a divorce."

"That's correct."

"The detective was a sleazy man who hired women to seduce husbands."

Marie Brunel's laughter was bright and genuine. "They couldn't touch Auguste."

"Of course not, but you knew that."

The laughter died abruptly. "You know?"

"It depends on what you're referring to. That Auguste is gay? Yes." At least, she had assumed so, as Léon had written it beside each of Monsieur Brunel's companions' names.

"I don't know the details of your arrangement, but I suspect you married him to get away from here. In return, you provided for his livelihood."

Marie Brunel stopped and scrutinised Sandrine intently, then nodded in agreement.

"You figured that out remarkably quickly."

"A friend of mine knows your husband's companions, so it wasn't a particularly clever feat on my part."

"Nevertheless." She turned her head and looked back at the estate. "None of them would have even thought that Auguste might be interested in men."

"He made extraordinary efforts to hide it, and the marriage with you was an excellent façade."

"You see, he has no motive to kill my father. Besides, I would never have divorced him; our arrangement was too advantageous, and jealousy played no role in it whatsoever."

"If jealousy didn't play a role, I don't understand why he hit Marcel Dumont."

"Out of vanity. He can't stand the thought that other people see him as a betrayed husband. So, he believed he had to intervene."

"I understand. But there's still the fact that he lived off the allowances you received from the foundation."

"That's not a crime. I was well aware of what kind of person he was when I married him, and it doesn't bother me. It's just money, and there's plenty of it. In return, I can live my life as I please. He doesn't interfere, and I enjoy my freedom. Something I never had here. I was constantly under observation." Marie Brunel continued walking, but slower than before.

"With your father's death, you became a voting member of the foundation and could significantly increase your financial allowances. Something that suited your husband."

"For an outsider, that looks like a solid motive, I must admit. However, it's also the case for us children."

"But?"

"Fabius and Xavier may consider me somewhat idealistic and naive, but that's mainly because the three of us don't live in the same world. Fabius is an epicurean and aesthete. Money is a means to an end for him. He only sees the small pleasures he can afford: excellent restaurants, fine wines, rare books and such luxuries. I don't think he fully exploits the budget available to him."

Sandrine nodded. That aligned with how Fabius de Tréchet had described himself.

"And Xavier is a concrete man."

"A what?"

"He invests his money in concrete and stones: shopping centres, office buildings, and so on. Oh, and in a golf course that Father would have never allowed on his land."

"And you?" Sandrine asked. "How do you invest your fortune, besides in your husband?"

"I prefer people and their ideas."

"Meaning?"

"I support original business ideas, mostly from women, and I'm a silent partner in at least a dozen cafés, some boutiques and galleries, sports studios, design firms, a premium goat cheese manufacturer, and other crazy projects. You wouldn't believe how well vegan chocolates sell. A journalist calls it the new Paris: young people with innovative ideas or creative products. Success requires very little: passion, dedication, some money, business experience, lots of encouragement, flattery and a bit of luck."

"Is that lucrative or more of a hobby?"

"If the foundation were to cut off my funding, our lifestyle wouldn't change."

"Then why the charade with Auguste?"

"I'm his façade, and he's mine. It's quite simple; I'm unknown but successful. Few people see more in me than Madame Brunel. I can roam Paris in peace. The marriage not only keeps the family off my back but also anyone else interested in a wealthy heiress, without Auguste demanding marital duties." Marie laughed again, and Sandrine admitted to herself that she had completely misjudged the woman. Something that didn't happen to her often.

"Will the foundation increase the allowances?"

"Fabius is doing quite well, and so am I, so we've left everything as it is."

"And Xavier?" She remembered Sébastian Hermé's hints that Xavier's business was only moderately successful.

"Privately, he doesn't receive more than the rest of us, but we agreed that the foundation would invest in his company and improve his liquidity. The meeting went extremely smoothly."

"Except for his golf course project?"

"He'll manage." She took a step closer to Sandrine. "I'm convinced he only wanted to see it through to prove something to Father about what he could achieve. In fact, Xavier is a terrible golfer. I suspect he's secretly relieved to be rid of it."

"He accused Alain."

"Because he neither read nor understood the will."

"What do you mean?"

"Alain hasn't inherited anything that could give him significant benefits. The farmhouse can only be used for one purpose. Alain can't sell it or make any other profit from it. Essentially, my father tricked him and burdened him with an elaborate project without getting his consent beforehand. Would anyone kill for that? Not me."

"There's one thing I don't understand," said Sandrine.

"And what's that?"

"The decoy the detective set on your husband was a failure. Why did Auguste visit him in his office? We found his fingerprints, and he admitted to being there. However, he claims the man tried to blackmail him. From what I've heard from you, that doesn't make sense."

"I'm sorry; I can't help with that. He didn't mention anything about a detective or blackmail in my presence. This is the first time I've heard of it."

"Then I'll go back to the house now and let you continue your walk in peace."

"I have my phone with me. If you find him, please call me."

"Of course." Marie nodded farewell and continued along the

narrow path. It was only when she disappeared among the trees that Sandrine made her way back.

The rain started again as she reached the château. She took off her jacket at the entrance and shook off the water.

"May I take it from you?" Madame Sérian, the housekeeper, stood behind her and reached for the raincoat before she could respond. She hung it in a closet in the entrance hall.

"We're looking for Monsieur Brunel. When did you last see him?"

"Come with me!" Madame Sérian turned and walked away. Sandrine followed her down a narrow corridor that led to the kitchen. The room must have been one of the more modern ones in the château. The countertops were made of shiny stainless steel, and the appliances looked new. Only the massive wooden table in the middle looked like it had been around for centuries.

"Have a seat!" The woman gestured to a chair, and Sandrine followed her order curiously.

"You're too thin." The housekeeper placed a plate, cutlery, a basket of baguette, butter, jam, cornichons and mustard, as well as a pot of game pâté in front of her. "I'm sure you didn't have a proper breakfast this morning."

"Thank you." In fact, her breakfast had consisted of just two cups of coffee, and her stomach grumbled at the sight of the food.

"Are you also looking for that raggedy fellow now?"

"When did you last see him?" Sandrine repeated her question.

"Yesterday at breakfast. After that, he disappeared to Saint-Malo, as he does almost every day."

She poured coffee into Sandrine's cup. "Milk?"

"Yes, please."

Madame Sérian lit the gas stove, placed a small pot on it,

and filled it with milk. "Cold milk is unhealthy." This theory was unknown to Sandrine, but she didn't question it.

"You already had Monsieur Brunel in the cell. Why did you let him out again? I would have thrown away the key instead."

"Do you think he could have killed Monsieur de Tréchet?"

The housekeeper shook the pot slightly, nodded satisfactorily, and poured the steaming milk into a white porcelain jug, which she placed next to Sandrine's bowl before sitting opposite her at the table.

"The man is loud and boastful, but I would be surprised if he had the guts to kill someone. A few days in a cell wouldn't have hurt him, though."

"Then the question remains, where is he?"

"Maybe the same person got him, the one who's responsible for Monsieur de Tréchet's and that man from Dinan's deaths."

"I find that unlikely, but nothing is impossible." Sandrine sliced a baguette and spread lightly salted butter and the fragrant pâté onto it. Finally, she added some cornichons.

"It goes perfectly with this: traditional Dijon mustard in a stoneware pot. My cousin brings it when she visits."

Sandrine looked at the white-grey pot and took a small amount, spreading it on the front end of the baguette and taking a bite. "Delicious," she mumbled with a full mouth.

"Monsieur de Tréchet valued good food. Otherwise, he was rather frugal."

"What was he like as a boss?"

"Better than most. He cared little about my area and didn't interfere as long as I stayed within budget, the house was clean and the food was served on time."

"He was stricter with his children."

"I think he only wanted the best for the three of them.

Perhaps he went a bit overboard with control here and there, especially with his daughter. Marie married that loudmouth to get away from here. In the end, Alexandre de Tréchet lived alone in the big estate." She smoothed her dress with both hands as if embarrassed to share these family matters with a stranger.

"Has Auguste Brunel been sleeping on the sofa in the salon every night?"

"Mostly. Occasionally, he stays in one of the free guest rooms. He never stays with his wife. Strange marriage, if you ask me."

"Who has a perfect marriage?" Sandrine answered vaguely. "On the night Monsieur de Tréchet was murdered, did Auguste Brunel sleep on the sofa?"

"I didn't see him sleeping on the sofa. But the blanket he uses was sloppily folded and the room smelled of cigarette smoke."

"Is that his habit?" Sandrine asked.

"Oh, where did you hear that? Usually, he leaves his things in an utter mess; after all there's staff to tidy up for him."

"That's how I see him as well." *But why not that night? Was he trying to hide where he had slept? There must be a good reason for that.*

"The man either stays in the château, mostly in the salon, or he's out driving in his car. Since his sports car is parked outside, he can't be far," Madame Sérian said.

"Does he never accompany his wife on her walks?"

"The guy hates fresh air like the devil hates holy water."

Sandrine continued eating in peace. The pâté was excellent, and she wouldn't let de Chezac or the family spoil her belated breakfast. Besides, she had learned quite a bit in the past hour, which she needed to ponder over.

Marcel Dumont burst into the kitchen, snapping Sandrine out of her thoughts. He leaned forward, panting heavily and rested his hands on his thighs. His cheeks were red, and sweat glistened on his forehead. He must have run a considerable distance.

"I found him," he exclaimed, breathless.

"Where?" Sandrine jumped up and approached him.

"There." He pointed to the window leading to the Rance. "At the mill."

"Is he alive?" she asked urgently, but the young man just shook his head.

"I pulled him out of the water."

"Take me there!"

"Of course." He straightened up and walked to the door. Sandrine briefly considered whether she should inform the prosecutor but decided against it. First, she needed to see if it was indeed the person they were looking for, and then she needed to secure the location until the forensics team arrived. She trusted de Chezac to handle the crime scene cautiously, but not the members of the family who would undoubtedly join him.

With quick strides, they marched towards the mill. Even from a distance, Sandrine noticed Alain Nebot standing next to a human body. She cursed quietly. It was Auguste Brunel, still wearing the same clothes as the day before.

"Hello, Alain," she greeted the man, who kept his distance from the deceased.

"I seem to have a real knack for guarding corpses," he replied with a mix of bitterness and sarcasm.

"Did you touch him?"

"No, it wasn't necessary. Marcel found him, floating face down in the millpond, and pulled him out of the water. I only came out of the forge when he started shouting for help. I didn't get any closer to the body than I am now."

Sandrine nodded in satisfaction and crouched beside the

body. Auguste lay on his back, his open eyes staring lifelessly at the cloudy sky. Algae was tangled in his hair, and water dripped from his clothes.

He would have been better off in the holding cell.

Slipping on her gloves, she inspected the body. She lifted his head slightly. Rigor mortis was setting in, but the muscles still moved. There were no open wounds on the man. She found no traces of blood anywhere. He must have drowned. The question was whether someone had helped him along.

"Do you think he took his own life?" Alain asked. Sandrine's gaze followed the wall leading away from the mill in a semicircle. The millpond operated on the same principle as the tidal pool at Plage de Bon-Secours. The tide filled the pool, and the wall prevented it from emptying at low tide. The only outlet was the mill wheel, which was currently still. Auguste Brunel could have drowned here at any time, whether at low or high tide. Or somebody could have drowned him.

She pulled out her phone and called Adel. He would coordinate the operation at the police station. As always, she relied on her assistant.

"What should I do?" Marcel Dumont's breathing had calmed. He stood behind her, doing his best not to look at the body. "I had nothing to do with this," he blurted out. "I just found the man and pulled him out. But I was too slow. If only I had checked here earlier, then..."

His hand went to his eye, and his fingertips brushed the bruise he owed to Auguste Brunel.

"No one is accusing you. There was nothing more to be done for him; he's been in the water for several hours already. Do me a favour and inform his wife. She's out for a walk along the Rance."

She could have easily made the call herself, but it seemed

more appropriate to have the news delivered by someone closer to her. She assumed that the caretaker knew her phone number.

The mill pond was an ideal place to take one's own life. Currently, there was no evidence of foul play, but she would leave that determination to Dr Hervé. She looked out over the Rance. If she had wanted to kill him, it would have been downstream. With the current, the body would have drifted out to sea by now and likely never been found.

She gently felt over the body and felt the wallet, which she left untouched. A corner of a note peeked out from a side pocket. Between her thumb and forefinger, she pulled it out and placed the paper on the dead man's chest.

"I can't live with the guilt anymore. Please forgive me, Marie."

The handwriting was shaky, as if he had scribbled the few words hastily. The ink was smudged and barely legible. She took out her phone and photographed his farewell letter. Perhaps it would bring Marie some comfort that his final thoughts had been of her.

"As soon as you reach Madame Brunel, please go to the château and fetch the prosecutor. He should be with the family in the salon. But make sure the others present don't catch wind of it."

"Right away." He turned and ran off. Sandrine took a plastic bag from her pocket and slipped the note inside. Only then did she stand up and approach Alain.

"First, someone kills Alexandre in my forge, later this detective with one of my weapons, and now Auguste is in my pond." The justified fear of being suspected again flickered clearly in his eyes.

"No one will accuse you of Auguste Brunel's death." She recalled her conversation with Marie, which had revealed some surprising insights into the family. "In essence, even the de

Tréchets don't believe you could be a murderer. Grieving people often like to blame someone else for their loss."

"Or distract themselves from their own guilt."

"Do you suspect someone from the family is behind the murders?" Sandrine asked.

"The number of suspects is rapidly dwindling," he replied, glancing at the corpse.

She handed him the plastic envelope containing the farewell letter.

"Perhaps your investigations have just become unnecessary," he said, returning the letter.

"Maybe," she agreed half-heartedly. Much indicated that Auguste Brunel was behind the murders. But was he someone who would take responsibility for his actions and muster the courage to pass judgment on himself? Not the courage, perhaps, but the desperation. *We were closing in on him. Without the influence of his family, he would still be sitting in a cell in Saint-Malo.*

De Chezac arrived from the château, his long raincoat tightly wrapped around him and one hand on his hat to prevent the gusting wind from blowing it away. He stopped next to Sandrine and looked down at the body. His lips pressed so tightly together that only a thin line was visible. He had assured that the man was released despite her objections. She was unsure which affected him more, the dead body or appearing bad in front of her.

"Damn," was his only comment.

She handed him the farewell letter, which the prosecutor stared at for a long time without a word. She didn't expect an apology; none would come, just as there would be no expression of regret for the death of Auguste Brunel.

"It seems the case is solved," he finally said. "I'd better speak to the family."

"Go ahead. I'll wait for Adel and the forensic team."

He left her and went back to the château. He didn't hurry. She knew how much he hated delivering unpleasant news. Some of the mess always stuck to the messenger.

Twenty minutes later, the dark official car of the commissioner arrived. The black van of the forensics team followed closely. Adel and Jean Matisse got out and approached her.

"*Merde.*" The brigadier stared at the pale face of the dead man. His superior nodded in agreement.

"It was a mistake not to resist his release more strongly," Sandrine said.

"Nonsense. You know very well that you couldn't have prevented it," the commissioner contradicted her. "Any more than I could."

She greeted Jean-Claude Mazet with a nod. He had already put on a blue disposable overall and joined them.

"Murder or suicide?" he asked, rubbing his finger thoughtfully along his thick moustache.

"That's for Dr Hervé to determine. At first glance, I can't see any external signs indicating violence. There are no open wounds like with the two previous deaths, nor are there any signs of strangulation or pressure marks, as I would expect if he had been forcibly held underwater."

"The doctor is on his way; he should arrive soon, as well as the van to take the body to the morgue." The forensic technician knelt beside the body and examined it closely. "Perhaps he was drunk or under the influence of drugs."

"This was in his jacket pocket." She handed him the farewell letter to be examined for any traces. However, after several hours in the water, there was unlikely to be much left to find. Even a handwriting comparison would be challenging; fortunately the message had been written with a durable ballpoint pen, but the paper had been soaked by the river water, and the writing looked blurred.

"Then let's get to work." A polite but firm way of dismissing her from the crime scene, which he now claimed for himself and his team. One of his colleagues took photos of Auguste Brunel before covering him with a dark blue blanket.

Alain Nebot said his goodbyes and headed back to the forge. His steps were heavy, his shoulders slumped as if carrying a tremendous burden. The accusations Xavier de Tréchet had levelled against him obviously weighed heavily. He probably wished he hadn't been mentioned in the will.

A gust of wind tugged at Sandrine's jacket, prompting her to glance at the sky, where grey clouds were gathering once again. On the horizon, the first veils of rain appeared, and the increasing wind caused the moored sailboats to rock in the river's waves. It wouldn't be long before the downpour began. The forensic team needed to hurry before the rain made their work impossible.

"You didn't pick a good day, weather-wise," she remarked to her boss.

"Believe me, I'd rather be in the office," he replied, pulling up the collar of his raincoat and buttoning the top button.

"Would you take statements from the caretaker and Alain?" she asked Adel. Normally, she would have done it herself, but she didn't want to delay the meeting with the family. Above all, she was curious about what de Chezac would report to them. She wondered if Matisse had come to the crime scene to defend her against unjust accusations.

"He'll try to pin the release of Mr Brunel on me," she said, testing her theory.

"Perhaps not if I'm present," the commissioner replied. "After all, I was there when he asked you to release the man."

She found the family members in the salon, where she had

left them. Marie had returned from her walk, her dress hem damp and splattered with mud. Her cheeks were slightly rosy, perhaps from exertion or perhaps from the shock of her husband's death. Marcel Dumont must have told her everything.

Meanwhile, Fabius had finished the cookies and placed the plate on the side table. Xavier was posing again in front of the fireplace, where a second log was burning.

"What has happened exactly? Monsieur de Chezac could only tell us that Auguste was found dead in the mill's basin. He couldn't tell us exactly how my husband died." Marie stared at her questioningly.

"I'm very sorry," Sandrine said. "We have to wait for the autopsy before we can say anything more precise."

Marie burst into tears, as if only now acknowledging his death as a fact. Fabius stared at the floor, and Xavier shook his head in disbelief.

"It's hard to imagine Auguste as a murderer," the older brother said. Apparently, de Chezac couldn't contain himself and had informed them about the farewell letter. It was information she would have preferred to keep under wraps for a while longer.

"He's not. He could never kill anyone," Marie snapped at him. "That's complete nonsense."

"I'm sincerely sorry," de Chezac addressed her, "but all indications suggest that he chose to take his own life to avoid punishment by the justice system. His written confession can't be interpreted any other way."

"If you were convinced of his guilt, why was he not in custody but released?" Marie's words shot through the room, choppy yet sharp as a razor blade.

"I understand that it's hard for you to see your husband as a criminal. Many things pointed to his guilt in recent days, but his arrest by the police turned out to be premature. Unfortunately, not all evidence was adequately examined, and we had no choice but to release him. The farewell letter dramatically changes everything," de Chezac explained.

Matisse gave her a brief glance that spoke volumes. The man was trying to shift the blame for the release onto her. At least he had refrained from mentioning her by name. Perhaps he was saving that for the inevitable press conference.

"The man had many faults," Xavier interjected. "But I never would have thought him capable of murder."

"We found the confession in his jacket pocket. There's no doubt about his guilt," de Chezac said gravely, scanning the room.

Marie straightened up and looked at Sandrine. "Show me the letter."

"It reads as if your husband confessed to the murders. Once it's examined forensically, we'll hand you his letter," the prosecutor decided. Sandrine wondered why the man was still keeping the hastily scribbled note under wraps after blurting out its contents without a second thought.

De Chezac stood up. "I'm afraid I must excuse myself. There's a lot of work to be done, but I assure you, I'll personally keep you informed of the investigation."

"Of course." Régis Marceau, who had been sitting silently in a chair in a corner, also stood up. "I'll accompany you out."

She, Adel and the commissioner joined him. Sandrine took her time retrieving her raincoat from the closet in the entrance hall.

"I'll take Brigadier Azarou back to the office," she offered to her boss. "There's no reason for you to wait here." She preferred him to be at the police station in Saint-Malo, keeping an eye on what de Chezac would do next.

"As you wish." He bid farewell and went out into the rain.

Sandrine stood in the shelter of the heavy front door and watched as he got into his car and drove away.

Behind her, footsteps echoed on the stone floor of the entrance hall, and Marie approached her, as Sandrine had expected she might.

"Is the man right about the farewell letter, in which Auguste confessed to my father's murder?"

The sharpness with which she had confronted de Chezac in the salon was gone. Instead, grief for a husband whom she may not have loved but evidently had liked, was clear in her features.

Sandrine pulled out her phone and loaded the photo she had taken of the letter.

"This stays between us." The demand wasn't necessary, but it fostered the woman's trust, assuming Sandrine would take risks for her.

Marie looked at the image, her lips moving silently as she read the text.

"Is this your husband's handwriting?"

"It's scribbled, as if it were hastily written, and the writing is smudged." She glanced at it again. "It could be."

"Would you provide me with a sample of your husband's handwriting for comparison?"

"Of course, but that won't be necessary."

"Do you believe the letter is genuine?"

"Absolutely not. Auguste would never have written that. It's a forgery." She hesitated, her hand covering her mouth. She realised what she had just implied. If someone had forged the letter and then put it in his pocket, it meant that Auguste had been murdered.

"How do you know?" Sandrine didn't doubt the woman's conviction, but needed clear evidence pointing to forgery.

Marie stepped closer and lowered her voice. "Auguste was dyslexic, which for inexplicable reasons was unspeakably embarrassing to him. Therefore, he hardly ever wrote by hand. Judging by the writing, the letter was scribbled hastily, as if he were desperate. In that state, he would never have written those two sentences without a single spelling mistake."

Sandrine nodded thoughtfully. The woman's argument was compelling. Of course, she would need to verify it, even though she had no doubt about its accuracy. Someone was trying to pin the murders on Auguste Brunel, and she feared the prosecutor would be all too eager to go along with it to close the case.

"Wait here." Marie quickly went up the stairs. It only took a few minutes for her to return. In her hand, she held a postcard.

"Auguste wrote this to me recently. It was still in my travel bag."

Sandrine glanced at it briefly. An expansive beach. Cap d'Agde on the Mediterranean. A transposed letter in the first line immediately caught her eye.

"Thank you very much. I'll return it to you once we've compared the handwriting."

"He wasn't the most exemplary person, but he was certainly not a murderer. The one who killed my father and husband is still at large."

"We'll do everything to bring them to justice," Sandrine promised. A sense of having overlooked an important clue crept over her.

Adel emerged from the mill. He had finished questioning Alain Nebot. Sandrine bid farewell to the woman and went to meet him. The return journey to the police station would have to wait a while; first, a trip to Dinan was on her agenda.

Sandrine parked the 2CV in front of Patrick Pradel's house.

"Major Albert is on his way," Adel said, pocketing his phone again.

"Let's make use of the time and talk to the shop owner," she suggested, getting out of the car.

A two-step, worn stone staircase led to the entrance of the pottery shop. The bell above the door rang brightly as they entered. Sandrine looked around. Plates, bowls, vases, cups and cute animal and fantasy creature figurines in various colours and shapes were stacked on shelves and wooden tables. The artist seemed to have a particular fondness for blue pottery.

"Can I help you?"

A thin man, whom she guessed to be no more than twenty, emerged from a back room. His hair hung well past his shoulders, and what kept his trousers on his narrow hips was a mystery to her. His slightly bulging eyes surveyed them curiously. He didn't seem to consider them potential customers. To confirm his suspicion, she flipped open her badge.

"You're surely here because of Monsieur Pradel."

"That's correct. Are you the owner?"

"No," he deflected. "The shop belongs to the pottery. I just sell the items."

"Were you here over the weekend?"

"Of course. Those are the best selling days. The tourist buses bring in a bunch of people to Dinan who like to take home a few souvenirs. Our frogs and the little elves sell particularly well." He picked up a green porcelain frog from the table and placed it in his palm. "Very cute. My girlfriend makes these." He offered it to her. "You'll get a special price."

"I'm afraid it doesn't quite fit with my decor."

She saw Adel smirk out of the corner of her eye. The brigadier knew her apartment and her aversion to such dust collectors.

"Too bad." He put it back and adjusted the frog group until the arrangement pleased him.

"Sunday morning, I unlocked the shop." He rolled his eyes

and audibly sighed. "The blood had seeped through the floorboards and dripped onto this." He tapped on the table crowded
with plates, bowls and vases. "Of course, everything was already
dried up. Charles, the owner, was pissed that we couldn't open
the shop until the cops were gone." He looked at Adel. "We don't
have a dishwasher. I had to wash the mess by hand. Revolting."
To confirm, he made a disgusted face and emitted a gagging
sound.

"I can imagine," Adel nodded sympathetically.

"Did anything catch your attention the day before?"
Sandrine asked.

"On Saturday?"

"Yes."

"No. It was a day like any other. Business was good."

"Did a red sports car park on the street in front of the shop at
any point?"

"Red sports car," he repeated slowly. Suddenly, his face
brightened up. "Oh, yeah. It was right in front of the entrance. A
couple from Germany bought a complete set of tableware and
couldn't park in front of the shop because the guy had taken up
two parking spaces."

That sounded like Auguste Brunel.

"When was that?"

"Late afternoon, I'd say. I can't remember exactly."

"How did the couple pay for their purchases?" Adel asked.

"With a card, of course. Who carries around that much
cash?"

"Can you check when the payment was made?"

"Sure." He pulled up his trousers and disappeared into the
back room.

"So Brunel was indeed here in the afternoon," Adel said.
"That explains the fingerprint."

"That's for sure. But it by no means rules out that he didn't come back. Brunel probably needed some time to get the cash. ATMs all have a daily limit, and the banks are closed on Saturdays."

"That's a plausible scenario, considering he confessed to the murder."

"Or someone slipped the letter to him." She told Adel about her conversation with Marie, who doubted that the note was written by her husband.

The seller returned and handed her a credit card receipt. "You're lucky the owner hasn't picked up the receipts yet."

So, Auguste Brunel had parked in the alley just before four o'clock. So far, everything corroborated his statement.

"Did you see Monsieur Pradel after that?"

"He came downstairs later, waved at me, and then marched up the alley. He usually goes to Crêperie du Roy for dinner on Saturdays."

"Did you see when he came back?"

"Around eight, I'd guess. I usually close the shop at seven, but that evening Charles came with the van and brought a few crates of dishes that I unpacked and sorted onto the shelves."

"Was he alone?"

"I didn't see anyone else."

"And the man with the sports car – did he reappear?"

"Not while I was here. I closed up at nine and rode home. My bike is behind the house."

So, Patrick Pradel had likely still been alive at nine, at least according to the coroner's report. The murderer must have visited him later.

"Thank you very much, you've been very helpful."

"Always happy to help the police. Maybe you can return the favour sometime if I get a parking ticket or something."

At that moment, she remembered the saleswoman from the pastry shop.

"I've heard the police frequently check drivers in the alley," she said.

"Sometimes there's trouble with customers who buy heavy or unwieldy items and come by car to load them in. But that's not really because of the cops."

"Then what?"

"Come." He walked between the tables, opened the door, and stepped outside. Sandrine followed him. She was curious as to what he wanted to show her.

"Do you see the house diagonally across?"

"Of course."

"The woman looking out the window is Madame Servant." He waved to her, and she responded with a brisk nod. "Since her husband passed away, her entire life has revolved around reporting illegal parking to the cops. Really sad."

"Even on weekends?"

"Especially on weekends," the seller confirmed.

"Thank you. We'll talk to the woman."

"Best to bring Major Albert with us," Adel suggested, glancing toward the Porte du Jerzual, through which the man was currently walking.

"I need to get back to work." The seller quickly disappeared into the shop, as if trying to avoid the policeman.

"Bonjour, Major Albert," she greeted the major from Dinan.

"Bonjour. I didn't expect to see you again so soon. I heard there's been another death."

The grapevine worked exceptionally well in this region. The prominence of the de Tréchet family surely contributed to that.

"Unfortunately, yes. Auguste Brunel, the son-in-law of the first victim. We found his body in the Rance this morning."

"An accident or another violent end to a life?"

"That's still unclear. I'm hoping the results from the coroner will shed some light."

"You want to revisit the victim's apartment? What do you think you'll find there that the forensics team might have overlooked?"

"The forensics team examined the rooms as the crime scene and collected evidence of the murder. Monsieur Mazet, the head of forensics in Saint-Malo, assured me that your people did excellent work."

"I'm glad to hear that, but you haven't answered my question."

"Monsieur Pradel lied to us. There were documents he used for blackmail, which likely cost him his life."

"The safe was open and emptied," the major replied. "The documents you're referring to are missing."

"Do you think an ex-police officer like Pradel would rely solely on the presumed security of a safe? That's the first thing burglars look for. I suspect the man was cunning enough to have set up alternative hiding places. Even I have a few spots in my apartment for small items I don't want found."

"The forensics team is trained to find such things." The confidence in his voice wavered. Doubts seemed to be creeping in for him as well.

"And an ex-police officer like Pradel knows where the forensics team looks first."

"Very well. It's your time to spend here. I wish you good luck." Major Albert handed the key to Adel.

"First, I'd like to speak with the lady across the street," Sandrine said, looking at the neighbour who had placed a cushion on the windowsill and was leaning on it with her forearms, attentively watching them.

"Madame Servant?" Major Albert rested a hand on the round fender of the Citroën. "Has the woman reported you for parking violations? She likes to do that, especially since you're not one of the obvious residents."

"Did she report anyone to the police on Saturday?"

"Several cars. After the brigadier inquired, I obtained the day's logs from the municipal police. Your red sports car was among them. I forwarded the information to the Saint-Malo precinct. However, it was parked in front of the pottery shop in the afternoon, so we initially overlooked it. At the time of the crime, she didn't report anyone."

"I'd like to question her. Come with me, it'll be easier."

"I doubt that. But I'll accompany you, even if she doesn't particularly appreciate me."

They crossed the street and stopped below the window. The woman, whom Sandrine presumed to be in her late seventies, looked down at them curiously from the second floor.

"Can we speak with you, Madame Servant?" the policeman asked.

"Wait, I'll come down."

The woman disappeared, and shortly after, someone descended the stairs. Sandrine approached the door, but to her surprise, a window on the ground floor opened. Madame Servant evidently had no intention of inviting them in.

"What can I do for you, Major Albert?"

"It's about the red sports car that was parked here on Saturday," he began, but she interrupted him quickly.

"Now it suddenly matters, after they bashed Pradel's skull in? Otherwise, I'm just the annoying old lady stealing police time. Why don't you just take down the no-parking sign if nobody cares about the drivers blocking the street for the residents?"

"Nobody claimed that about you," he defended himself against her accusation.

"Oh, really?"

"A red sports car parked in front of the pottery shop on Saturday afternoon, around four," Sandrine interjected. Their arguments could be settled by them after she'd left.

The woman reached into her apron pocket and pulled out a small notebook, the kind one could buy in any stationery store. She quickly flipped to the last pages.

"It arrived at a quarter to four and didn't leave until five past. Twenty minutes. But do you think a cop would come by to restore order? No. Nobody bothered."

She leaned on the windowsill with her hands, shooting an annoyed glance at Albert.

"We've filed the report, and the driver will soon receive a ticket," Albert assured her.

Madame Servant emitted a short, gruff sound and turned to Sandrine again. She clearly didn't think much of the municipal police in Dinan.

"Did the car return that evening?"

"No."

"After 10 pm?"

"I told you, no. I'm not so old that I go to bed as soon as it gets dark."

"One doesn't always have the street in sight," the major interjected.

"I don't need to. That red car made a devilish racket that could have woken the dead. I guess the exhaust was broken. You couldn't miss it."

She nodded rapidly like a chicken pecking at grains. The woman was convinced she hadn't seen or heard Auguste Brunel's car in the evening, and Sandrine believed her. Another piece of evidence speaking against the man's guilt. She tended to believe he was innocent.

"Thank you very much, that's been very helpful."

"And you're not interested in the other car?"

Sandrine had already turned away but abruptly returned. "What other car?"

"A small one. Also red, but not such a showy one."

"When was it here?" Sandrine pressed.

"Right in front of the pottery shop. A man got out and rang Pradel's doorbell. That was around ten, I'm sure."

"Can you describe him?"

"No. It was already dark, and he stayed in the shadows. Wait... maybe it wasn't even a man."

"What now?" Major Albert urged.

The woman flipped through her notebook.

"737," she muttered. "Starting with an F, but I couldn't make out the rest of the letters. The license plate was pretty dirty. That's why I didn't report it. Should I have?"

She directed the last sentence directly at Major Albert, who couldn't ignore the irony.

"A murder occurred across the street. This information would have been helpful in solving the crime." The policeman fell silent and shook his head disapprovingly. Sandrine was convinced he would have liked to say much more about it. The woman reported parking violations daily, and the one time she witnessed something truly crucial, she kept it to herself. The man's frustration was easily understandable.

Sandrine noted down the number. Brigadier Dubois could check the suspects' license plates.

"Thank you very much. If you remember anything else, please call Major Albert."

She left her own business card. She wouldn't put it past the woman to report parking violators to the Criminal Police in Saint-Malo as well. Best to reach out to her personally.

. . .

The staircase ran alongside the old stone house to the second floor. She placed a hand on the masonry. The house had seen several centuries pass by, and she wondered what it had experienced. Pradel's murder might not have been the only one to occur here. Life in the Middle Ages was harsher, and the chances of a violent death were much higher than nowadays.

"Come in." The major pulled her out of her thoughts. The paper seal was cut, and he held the door open with one hand.

Sandrine entered the office where they had questioned Patrick Pradel. Since her last visit, hardly anything changed. The safe was still open, grey speckles from the powder used for fingerprinting dotted the white windowsills, documents were scattered on the desk and the wooden floor. A bottle of Cognac had rolled under the worn-out sofa and still lay there. Nobody had bothered to tidy up. The dried bloodstain on the floor caught her attention for a moment. It would hardly be possible to remove the stains completely; they had already penetrated too deep into the cracked wood.

"Pradel didn't leave any heirs, only an ex-wife." The policeman seemed to have guessed her thoughts. "She hasn't contacted us yet, if she even cares about her ex-husband and such an old building."

"When will you release the apartment?"

"In essence, it should have happened already. Now I'm glad it didn't, even though I'm sceptical about finding anything here that the forensics experts overlooked."

"Let's sit down," Sandrine invited him, and went to the sofa. She tapped the upholstery, and a cloud of dust rose, which she blew away before sitting down.

"A peculiar way to search – sitting." Major Albert stretched his legs and found the most comfortable position on the sofa, whose cushions sank under him.

Sandrine let her gaze wander around the room, memorising every tiny detail. She was convinced that a man like Pradel kept his secrets – especially those that could bring him money – close to himself. In case he had to disappear quickly, which an extortionist always had to anticipate; every second counted.

"He had a safe," the policeman said after a while. "Shouldn't that be enough to store his valuables?"

"Pradel was a pro. People like him have easily detectable safes for two reasons: so that inexperienced burglars struggle with them and leave empty-handed, or professionals spend precious time opening them, only to find just enough to make a quick getaway without further searching the apartment. A safe draws attention to itself like a Tarte aux Pommes attracts wasps on a hot summer day."

"You mean he leaves enough money in the safe to satisfy a thief and hoards his savings elsewhere?"

"More or less. A burglar has to consider whether they're content with the loot from the safe or take the risk of spending more time, during which they could be discovered, searching for other hiding places. My choice would be simple."

"You'd pocket the loot and disappear?"

"In fact, I'd ignore the safe and immediately look for the lucrative hiding spot," she said, smiling. At least, that's what her uncle had taught her.

She disregarded obvious places like the desk, hollowed-out books, or the toilet tank. None of those would have escaped the forensics team.

Eventually, she stood up and knelt on the floor. Using the knuckles of her right hand, she tapped on the creaky boards. A floor safe seemed to her the most probable hiding spot in this old house.

Adel entered the office and paused at the sight of his colleague sliding across the wooden floor and tapping against it at regular intervals. She noticed his grin and the amused glance he exchanged with Major Albert from the corner of her eye.

"Make a corny joke, and you'll be crawling through the rest of the apartment," she threatened him.

He raised his hands defensively and sat down on the sofa next to the policeman. From experience, he knew his boss didn't need any help, especially not from him. He would only distract her.

After a while, she sat back.

"The floor is clean. There's nothing under the shabby rug even."

"And now?" Major Albert asked.

"Now, we go up a floor." She stretched out her left arm and rested it on the broad baseboard.

"At this rate, it could take all day," the man remarked, looking at the door leading to the private apartment.

"I hope to find something sooner. But even if it takes that long, it might be worth it."

She ran her fingers along the baseboard and tapped against it at regular intervals.

"Can you turn on the floor lamp?" she asked the brigadier. "It's pretty dark in the corner."

Sandrine heard the click of the switch, but nothing happened.

"The bulb must be out." Adel tilted the lamp, which was taller than him, and checked the light bulb.

Her gaze followed the cord. "In any case, the plug is in the socket."

He returned the lamp to its place and switched on the ceiling light. Sandrine turned her head, searching for other power outlets. Next to the desk, she noticed one, and a second one by the door.

"Take a closer look," she instructed the brigadier.

"They look pretty normal."

"Could you pass me the desk lamp, please?" Adel turned it on and off before unplugging it from the outlet and placing it next to Sandrine. "It's working."

"Let's take a look then," she muttered, plugging in the lamp. She flicked the switch, but nothing happened.

"The wiring must be faulty. That happens in these old houses sometimes," said Major Albert.

Sandrine took a pocket knife out of her trousers and opened it. Carefully, she slid the blade behind the socket frame and levered it away from the wall.

"Actually, only the frame should come off," she muttered.

She grasped the edge of the socket and pulled on it. With a crunching sound, it completely detached from the masonry. Behind the facade was a metal box, often used in rental apartments as a key box.

"What the hell..." Major Albert stood up and leaned over her.

"No wonder the lamp didn't turn on. There's definitely no electricity coming out of here." Sandrine handed him the box.

"A small safe." Surprise, but also admiration, filled the major's voice. "Who would have expected that?"

Sandrine refrained from pointing out that she had been crawling through the apartment for a while now to find exactly this.

"Can you open it?" Adel asked.

She ran her fingers over the keypad on the top of the box.

"Maybe. But it'll definitely be quicker if Jean-Claude cuts it open in the workshop."

"We were looking for a report, this box is too small for that." Adel took the safe that Major Albert handed him.

"Probably a USB stick. The man wasn't as technologically clueless as he pretended to be."

"Hopefully, it's not encrypted."

"That would be advantageous." She stood up and brushed the dust off her trousers. "I think we're done here."

"Shall we head to the police station?"

"Can you stop at this address first?" She handed him the note Léon had given her.

"Sure. What are we doing there?"

"Meeting the woman who worked as bait for Pradel."

They pulled up in front of a dreary three-storey apartment block on the outskirts of Saint-Malo. Sandrine found the name on the doorbell.

"Hello," responded a woman's voice as Sandrine approached the intercom.

"Madame Isabelle Mornier?"

"Yes. What do you want?"

"Captaine Perrot from the Police Nationale. I need to speak with you."

There was silence for a few breaths.

"Madame Mornier," Sandrine repeated clearly.

"At the moment, it's not very convenient for me. Could you come back tomorrow?"

"Unfortunately not. It needs to be now."

Another pause. Sandrine was about to leave when the door buzzer hummed.

She climbed the stairs to the second floor. A woman, perhaps in her mid-twenties, in a bathrobe, with casually brushed brown hair and the imprint of a pillow on her face, stood in the doorway.

"Did I wake you?"

"Night shift," she said vaguely. "I have to go back to work soon."

Sandrine knew what occupation the woman pursued. She was quite pretty; she would still be in demand for a few more years before the customers dwindled and the prices for her services dropped.

"You're from the police?"

A brief glance at the badge was all the woman needed. It certainly wasn't the first one she had seen.

"May I come in?"

"I haven't tidied up. What's this about?"

"You work for Monsieur Pradel?"

She shook her head, but the slight twitch of her lips had given her away.

"The man is dead."

"Dead?" Her eyes widened in shock. Clearly, she didn't read the newspapers.

"He was murdered. Someone bludgeoned him, quite a bloody affair." Sandrine wanted to surprise the woman and throw her off balance before she decided it was better not to say anything without a lawyer present.

"My God. Who would do such a thing?"

"He told us what work he paid you for," she lied.

The woman stepped forward and looked into the stairwell to see if any nosy neighbours were listening. Then she opened the door.

"Come in, the neighbours don't need to hear everything." Madame Mornier went into the tiny kitchen and sat at a narrow table that barely accommodated two people.

"Who did this to him?" She interlocked her fingers, but Sandrine noticed the trembling of her hands.

"That's what we're trying to find out."

"I have nothing to do with it."

"At least not directly."

"Am I in danger?" She leaned forward, her gaze almost glued to Sandrine. Probably she was mentally going through the list of men she had been involved with on the detective's behalf.

"I can't assess that yet. Tell me exactly what you did for Monsieur Pradel."

Madame Mornier seemed to be struggling with herself. She was almost certainly aware that the private detective hadn't always been on the right side of the law, and she was probably wondering if she could be held accountable for a crime.

"He wanted me to help him with his job. Nothing illegal," she said hesitantly.

"What exactly?" Sandrine had no intention of putting words in her mouth. She needed to come clean on her own.

"To flirt with men. Patrick was paid by women to catch their husbands cheating."

"And you were the bait?"

She looked down and nodded almost imperceptibly.

"How far did you have to go?"

"I never slept with any of them, Patrick always showed up beforehand."

"And did he hand over the photos to the wives?" she asked, following a hunch.

"Most of the time, as far as I know," she admitted. So the man was skilled in blackmail. He just misjudged his last victim, which cost him his life.

"What about this one?" Sandrine showed the woman a photo of Auguste Brunel. "Was he part of it too?"

"Yes," she admitted. "But nothing happened there. The guy brushed me off cold." Anger at the rejection and wounded pride crept into her tone as she crossed her arms over her chest.

"I can imagine."

"Why?"

"Monsieur Pradel must have been upset." Sandrine ignored the question.

"I thought he would be too, but he was in a great mood and gave me my money without complaint. He even bought me a bottle of champagne."

"Remarkable. Then he must have had something to celebrate."

"He followed the guy in the photo for a week without finding out anything. He must have made good money for that."

"And he didn't drop any comments? Think carefully. Something about this surveillance cost him his life."

"He had quite a bit to drink on the last evening and talked a lot. All ancient stories that bored me. But he paid well, so I stayed," Madame Mornier confirmed.

"There must have been something. Even if you don't know what he was talking about."

"He rambled a lot about the casinos, Rennes, and French Tech, acting pretty mysteriously. And there was an acronym he often muttered to himself and chuckled. CSR or something. I have no idea what he meant, but he believed he could really cash in with it. Maybe he wanted to buy stocks. Who knows?"

"French Tech," Sandrine repeated. She hadn't heard of that in her investigations yet. No one in the family had mentioned the term. Patrick Pradel must have stumbled upon something that someone wanted to keep secret and was willing to kill for.

"Now, I'd like to get dressed so I can get to work on time." The woman urged Sandrine to leave.

"You need to stop by the police station to give your statement."

"Really?"

"Unfortunately, yes."

"Then I'll come by in the next few days."

Sandrine left Madame Mornier sitting in the kitchen and exited the apartment.

* * *

Sandrine sat on a chair in the meeting room, one leg crossed over another, and studied the pinboards. In her mind, she rearranged the various pieces of information into new constellations, but so far, no theory completely convinced her. Only Auguste Brunel had been definitively crossed off her list of suspects.

There were Alexandre's children, possibly Régis Marceau, though she still puzzled over his motive. Alain Nebot and Lilou Lanvers, maybe even Marcel Dumont, seeking revenge against Auguste. Madame Sérian, who knew about the expected inheritance, was ruled out. Sandrine couldn't imagine the elderly lady as a murderer wielding a morning star. That was absurd.

Commissaire Matisse, the prosecutor and Adel entered the meeting room. The brigadier handed her the obligatory cup of coffee and sat down next to her. De Chezac took the seat at the head of the elongated table.

"With the confession we have, we can close the case," he said. It didn't sound like a suggestion, more like a demand, just like the day before when she had to release Auguste Brunel. Even though she bore no guilt for his death, she wouldn't allow murders to be pinned on him that he hadn't committed.

"I've scheduled a press conference for tomorrow," the prosecutor announced.

"He didn't do it," she said in a tone that sounded calmer than she felt.

"The man confessed in writing and committed suicide. What more do you want?"

"At the very least, wait to see if the forensics results support this theory."

"It's more than just a theory," he retorted.

"Dr Hervé called me on the way here. Auguste Brunel had a blood alcohol level of over two per mille. It's a miracle he could still walk," Adel said, giving her an apologetic glance.

"Did he drink voluntarily?"

"That was my first question, but there's no indication he was forced. No injuries to his lips, teeth, or gums. Unfortunately, we can't prove if someone held a gun to his head," Adel said.

"It's no surprise that the handwriting comparison was inconclusive. The man was too drunk to write properly." De Chezac sounded satisfied. He wanted to close the case, and without a trial whose outcome might be uncertain.

"Where do you think we stand?" the commissaire asked.

"Not completely at the beginning anymore, but still far from a resolution. We have Brunel's fingerprints at the detective agency. His claim to have been there in the afternoon is confirmed by the seller at the pottery shop on the ground floor of the building and a neighbour who has nothing better to do than monitor the street. So the fingerprints don't help us further."

"He must have planned the murder on his second visit and worn gloves."

"That's possible. He would have also had to change the car. A red compact car was seen outside the house. Unfortunately, we only have fragments of the license plate. Brigadier Dubois is currently checking them."

"And the suicide note?"

"As I said, the handwriting comparison was inconclusive. But his wife is convinced he couldn't have written those lines."

"Wives tend to not believe their husbands capable of murder," said de Chezac.

"I got the impression Marie Brunel sees her deceased husband quite objectively. It wasn't a love match, more like a business alliance. She wanted to get away from here and lead her own life, so she married him."

"What did he get out of it?" Matisse asked.

"Besides money? His wife confirmed my suspicion that he was homosexual. For some reason that eludes me, it was important to Auguste Brunel to hide that and continue to be seen as a playboy and ladies' man. The marriage was a perfect cover."

"Back to the confession," said Matisse. "Why does she believe he couldn't have written it?"

"Auguste Brunel was dyslexic. However, the letter was error-free, something he would have found very difficult to accomplish, especially if he was drunk and in a hurry."

"Has anyone verified this?"

"Inès called his family in Paris. His mother confirmed it," Adel said.

"Alexandre de Tréchet pressured his daughter to divorce him, and Patrick Pradel might have found something incriminating about him. Would that be impossible?" Matisse asked.

"Madame Brunel's statement, that she wanted to hold on to the marriage under any circumstances, seems very credible to me. So the man didn't have a sufficient motive to get rid of his father-in-law," Sandrine replied.

Adel retrieved several sheets of paper from a file folder in front of him and pushed them across the table to his superior.

"The technicians were able to open the hidden safe. There was a USB stick inside. Along with photos of at least a dozen more men and some women, it also contained the report he made for Alexandre de Tréchet. It doesn't contain any information that the family or his wife weren't aware of. Monsieur Brunel plays, drinks, and spends a lot of money. He couldn't pin an affair on him. There's nothing he could use to blackmail Auguste Brunel."

"Perhaps he threatened to reveal his homosexuality publicly?" Matisse speculated.

"The man comes from a wealthy and snobbish family, he's married, and he lives in Paris. How much damage could that do to his image? We're not living in the last century anymore." She looked to the commissaire, who nodded hesitantly.

"It also wouldn't explain the murder of Alexandre de Tréchet. The man didn't have anything he could use to push his daughter towards a divorce." Matisse seemed to agree with her again.

"Marie Brunel has assured me that under no circumstances would she divorce him, as the arrangement was too perfect for her," said Sandrine.

"Very well. Who else could be considered?" De Chezac leaned back as if he were now merely an observer leaving it to his subordinates to solve the case.

"I would rule out Alain Nebot and Lilou Lanvers."

"Why? Out of personal friendship?" He couldn't resist the dig.

"They legally bought and renovated the mill from Alexandre de Tréchet. No matter how much Xavier de Tréchet may want it back, he has no legal recourse to reclaim it."

"And the inheritance?"

"There is no evidence that they knew about the will. Also, they haven't inherited anything they could turn into money. All income from the lands goes into the development and maintenance of the museum and cultural centre to be built in the farmhouse. Not a cent will land in their pockets," she explained.

"In essence, the old de Tréchet burdened them with an unpaid honorary position," said Matisse. "In their place, I wouldn't accept this inheritance."

Sandrine perked up. *How foolish of me.* She hadn't thought of this possibility. Who would then maintain the estate: the foundation or Xavier de Tréchet? Perhaps he insisted on his accusations to pressure Alain into relinquishing the inheritance.

"I also don't see a concrete motive for Régis Marceau. He had nothing to gain from Alexandre de Tréchet's death. At most, his position as manager became more uncertain," she continued.

"Then there's the caretaker," interjected de Chezac, who was still trying to protect the family. "He had a physical altercation with Auguste Brunel and seemed quite close to his wife. Maybe the motive lies in an affair between them, which her father discovered and wanted to suppress. First, he got rid of him, and then the husband and rival."

It wasn't easy for her to agree with the prosecutor, but this theory couldn't be dismissed out of hand. Love and jealousy were always strong motives.

"He doesn't have an alibi for the murders, and he discovered Auguste's body," said Sandrine.

Adel stood up and pinned his index card to the centre of the bulletin board.

"By the way, what does La French Tech have to do with this?" de Chezac asked abruptly, looking at the card she had pinned earlier.

"Do you know what it is?"

"Of course. It's a program of the French government to support startups in the technology sector. Most of the supported companies are based in Paris, but there are some activities in this area, mainly in Brest and Rennes. What does this have to do with the investigation?"

"Patrick Pradel, the private detective, was talkative with a witness and mentioned La French Tech and Rennes in connection with the possibility of scamming someone out of a lot of money. Does the abbreviation CSR also mean anything to you?" Sandrine asked.

"Perhaps a company that is being supported. We need to find out."

She looked at Adel.

"It's being taken care of."

"Xavier is a real estate developer, and in Rennes, a technology centre is being built as part of the program. Perhaps he's involved," said Matisse. "And Patrick Pradel found out something about him that would bring him so much trouble that he killed for it. Corruption would be one possibility."

"And Alexandre de Tréchet?" she asked.

"After all, he was the client. The detective might have informed him about the misbehaviour of his eldest son," Adel added, pinning Xavier's photo to the centre of the wall as well. "The man cared a lot about the family's reputation. He might have threatened to report or disinherit Xavier. That's why he killed him, possibly in a fit of rage."

"Pradel blackmailed him, knowing that only he could be the murderer. He also paid with his life for that," Sandrine concluded the brigadier's theory.

"And Brunel?" Matisse looked at her curiously, but she had to disappoint him. "For what reason did he get rid of him?"

"I can't say yet. Maybe he saw something he shouldn't have, or the detective divulged too much during their meeting, so he could figure out who killed his father-in-law. We'll only find out when we've caught the murderer."

"What about the other two children?" Matisse brought up the missing family members.

"I don't see a sufficient motive with them. Although they gained a say in the foundation through their father's death, Marie has her own fortune, and Fabius never exhausted the financial resources available to him in recent years. We've verified both," she pre-empted de Chezac's question.

"Then we're left with two very different suspects." The prosecutor rubbed his hands. The cracking of his knuckles echoed in the now silent room, a sign of how nervous the man was.

"Check out the technology centre in Rennes and Xavier de Tréchet's financial relationships," he finally agreed. "But don't forget about this caretaker."

"We'll keep an eye on him," she assured him. "But not today. It's getting late, and I have plans."

"Then we'll see each other again tomorrow," Commissaire Matisse concluded the meeting. He and de Chezac left the conference room.

"A rendezvous?" Adel looked at her with a smirk. "Since when do you have a private life alongside the investigations?"

"Sometimes you can pleasantly combine both."

In fact, there was no appointment, at least not yet. She would call Léon, maybe he had time for an evening together. It was Tuesday, and the Équinoxe wouldn't open again until tomorrow.

* * *

Sandrine waited at the entrance of the casino in Saint-Malo for Léon.

"I didn't know you had become a gambler." He embraced her and tried to kiss her, but she put her index finger on his lips.

"Later."

"So, you're still on duty?"

"Just a few minutes, then I'm off."

She linked her arm with his, and they entered the casino. She introduced herself to the lady at the reception and showed her badge.

"I have an appointment with the manager."

The receptionist made a brief call.

"Monsieur Dechelle is expecting you in the bar."

"I wouldn't want to keep him waiting then."

A man in an elegant dark suit approached her.

"Bertrand Dechelle," he introduced himself.

"Capitaine Perrot."

"How can I assist the police?"

Léon left her alone and sat down at the bar a few metres away. She was here on official business, and he didn't want to disturb her.

Sandrine showed the man the group photo taken on Friday at the de Tréchet estate and zoomed in on Auguste Brunel on her phone. She tapped on him briefly.

"I just want to know if this person was here on Saturday evening, and if so, was he with anyone?"

"Monsieur Brunel? No. Not on the weekend. He visited our establishment on the days before. But he was here." He pointed to another man.

"Are you sure?" she asked, surprised. She hadn't expected that.

"Absolutely, he's one of our regulars," the manager assured her.

"That surprises me."

"We have a wide range of guests."

"One question: does he usually win or lose? If so, how much?"

"You know I can't disclose that information to you. Come with a court order, and I'll hand over all the documents we have to the police."

"It's urgent. It's about a murder case."

"Business information is subject to confidentiality." The man looked around. There was no one nearby who could eavesdrop on them. "He doesn't have much luck at blackjack, I can tell you that much. For anything else, you'll need a court order."

"I think that's enough for now. Be prepared to see me again in a few days."

"With the greatest pleasure."

"End of the workday," she said to Léon. "Now there's nothing stopping us from a kiss."

"Not in a casino," he replied, standing up. "They say 'luck in love, bad luck in gambling,' after all. I don't want to ruin my chances at the roulette table."

She laughed, took his hand, and they left the casino together. The information was surprising, and she needed to think about its implications on her theory, but that could wait until tomorrow morning. Right now, she was off duty and determined to enjoy a pleasant evening with Léon.

"A little stroll along Plage de Rochebonne and a nice dinner on the way?" Sandrine suggested.

"Sounds perfect."

They walked down the promenade together. The investigation could wait. Tomorrow, she would apprehend a triple murderer, she was sure of it.

La French Tech

Her shirt clung wet against her back, the muscles in her legs burned and her heart beat at a rapid pace. Sandrine had set out for a jog just before sunrise. From her house, down the stairs to Zöllnerweg, past Port Mer to Pointe du Grouin on the northern tip of the peninsula. Barely five kilometres, but today she ran faster than usual. The frustration over the conflict with de Chezac and the murders she couldn't prevent drove her along the narrow hiking trail. The day would be crucial for the investigation. She was optimistic about apprehending the culprit, but it would only succeed if she remained focused and didn't let herself be distracted.

The house came into view, and she slowed her pace. In a leisurely trot, she ran up the stairs leading from Zöllnerweg to her garden. Behind her, the waves rolled foaming against the rocks of the cliffs, and the rays of the low sun broke through the branches of the trees. The rain clouds that had darkened the sky yesterday had given way to a radiant blue day. Sandrine took it as a good omen.

The table in the garden was set, and Léon brought out a fresh baguette and two pains au chocolat from the house.

"Back already? You were quick," he greeted her.

"I needed to blow off some steam to keep my composure for the rest of the day."

He tried to kiss her, but she ducked away.

"No way. I'm sweaty, sticky and smell bad."

"I don't mind."

"But I do," she replied and walked past him into the house. She needed a hot shower and dry clothes.

Léon sat at the table, drinking his coffee from a bowl. A second one was ready for her. The milk froth was firm enough for the spoon to stand upright in it.

"You got a fresh baguette?"

"I went shopping while you were out. The nearest bakery isn't far."

"Thanks, I'd be lost without you." She ran her fingers through his short hair and kissed him.

"That's nonsense. You're a confident and smart woman who can easily call for takeout."

"I can cook," she protested.

"You just don't want to." She looked at Léon, noticing how hard it was for him to suppress a grin. It didn't take an interrogation specialist to see that.

"Next weekend, I'll cook us a multi-course meal," she said firmly.

"You don't have to. It's enough if one of us knows their way around the kitchen. I'm happy to do it, and you hate being at the stove."

"That's out of the question. We'll invite Rosalie and a few friends," she impulsively decided, regretting it shortly after. The bar was set pretty high with Léon and Rosalie, two enthusiastic cooks. Adel's parents owned a North African restaurant, and one of his sisters was fighting for her first Michelin star. *Why did I have to open my big mouth?*

"They'll be delighted," Léon said, turning his head slightly to the side so she couldn't see his expression.

Her phone rang, and she was glad to be distracted.

"Perrot," she answered.

"Sebastian Hermé here."

"Up and about so early?"

"The pursuit of justice knows no rest," he joked.

"Thank you for returning my call."

"I'm happy to help. Fortunately, I know someone from the organisation of the technology centre being built in Rennes."

"Am I right with my assumption?" She held her breath. His answer could easily collapse her theory.

"Unfortunately not. Xavier de Tréchet did submit a bid for the construction and operation of the technology centre, but he didn't get the contract."

She suppressed a curse. That was it. The next suspect was out of the picture.

"I guess I was way off with my assumption."

"Even Capitaine Perrot can't always hit the bullseye." The prosecutor from Rennes sounded unusually upbeat.

"Apparently not."

"But no reason for excessive sadness," he replied. "You're on the right track."

"What do you mean by that?"

"The contract for the construction and operation of the technology centre went to a company owned by the de Tréchet Foundation."

Sandrine let out a low whistle. She hadn't expected that. Had Alexandre de Tréchet outmanoeuvred his own son? What an interesting family.

"Do you need any further information?"

"Thank you very much, what you've found out is enough for me for now."

"We'll be in touch," said the prosecutor, ending the call.

Sandrine wondered what he meant by that, but didn't dwell on it for long and placed the phone on the garden table.

Léon had chosen the spot for the table carefully. The trees were spaced far enough apart that they barely obstructed the view over the bay. She watched a dinghy heading towards one of the sailboats moored off the coast. Several people disembarked and spread out on the deck. She wondered where the outing would take them. *Perhaps I should learn to sail too, since I live in Brittany.*

The bowl of café au lait warmed her hands pleasantly. She blew thoughtfully over the milk froth and took a sip.

"Bad news?" Léon asked.

"I can't assess that yet. It's confusing."

"You'll figure it out."

She placed her hand on his and squeezed it tenderly. His confidence in her abilities was reassuring. Sandrine had resisted getting into a serious relationship for a long time, but now she loved spending her days with Léon. He provided her with a secure anchor in her otherwise chaotic life.

"I'm glad you're here." She set the bowl down, leaned towards him and kissed him, this time not on the cheek.

* * *

"Good morning, Madame Perrot."

A stylishly dressed woman in her fifties, with dark red curls only a gifted hairdresser could create, and matching glasses and lipstick, greeted her with a radiant smile.

"Thank you for taking the time, Madame Lomi."

"For the police, anytime, especially for a fellow female." She winked cheerfully. "We have to stick together, after all. Call me Madeleine, it's less formal."

"Of course."

"This way." The accountant led her into her office. Some small decorative items and a framed Monet poster gave the otherwise functional room a personal touch.

"Have a seat." Madame Lomi pushed a chair towards Sandrine, which looked more like a bar stool and lightly swayed under her.

"It's good for your back and takes up little space," she explained. Space was surely scarce in the small office, but the workspace looked perfectly organised.

"You're responsible for the accounting of the de Tréchet family foundation?"

"The foundation is by far our most important client. I'm in charge of the technology centre in Rennes that you mentioned."

"It came up in an investigation, and I'm interested in some details. I hope there's no confidentiality agreement."

"I've checked with my boss. As long as we're discussing matters that aren't subject to secrecy or data protection, there's no issue."

"The abbreviation CSR came up in the investigations. Does that mean anything to you?"

"It could mean anything, but in this case, I'd guess it stands for Cyber-Security-Rennes. A company that provides services for the operation of the technology centre. I assume the name speaks for itself. Nowadays, these hackers try to get into everything. We also work with a similar company, but on a much smaller scale."

"Have you noticed any discrepancies with CSR?"

"No. The foundation works with the company on various projects. There have been no problems so far. The bills are high, but the foundation has approved all of them without complaint." She tapped the end of a pen lightly on the desk and ran several tables on her computer monitor. "The annual costs amount to a mid-six-figure sum."

"I'd call that expensive."

"The damage hackers can cause these days is much higher. Plus, some insurance companies require special security measures. In the end, safety comes first."

"Do you know anyone from CSR personally?"

"Céline Ballard, the CEO. She lives in Rennes but also owns an apartment in Saint-Malo. She can afford it." The woman wrote down Céline's address in elegant handwriting on a pink notepad.

"Thank you very much. You've been very helpful, Madeleine." Sandrine bid farewell to the accountant.

"It was my pleasure. I hope you catch Alexandre's murderer. He was a pleasant person and always friendly."

"We're doing our best."

In the car, she called Brigadier Dubois.

"Any progress with the license plate?"

"Unfortunately, not yet. The number combination doesn't appear in the de Tréchet's circle, nor with Marceau or the mill owners. Dumont drives a similar car, but the license plate doesn't match."

"Thanks. Keep at it. In the meantime, could you do me a favour?"

"What is it?"

"Find out everything about a certain Céline Ballard. She's the CEO of the company CSR in Rennes, responsible for the security of the technology centre. She owns an apartment in Saint-Malo, on Rue Guy Louvel."

"By when do you need the info?"

"As soon as possible."

"I'll get on it right away."

"Thanks."

She texted Adel to meet her at the château. He'd likely arrive before her if he hurried.

* * *

Sandrine met Madame Sérian in the entrance hall.

"Where can I find the family?"

"They're currently having breakfast. Afterwards, the first ones will leave. Only Madame Brunel will stay here until her husband's body is released by the police."

"Then I've come just in time."

The housekeeper took her coat, leading her to the dining room. It was part of her job at the château, although she could have found her way there easily.

Marie was the first to look up as Sandrine entered the room.

"Have you found out anything?" she asked.

"Perhaps." Sandrine remained vague. At that moment, her phone vibrated. A message from Dubois. She quickly skimmed the short text and nodded in satisfaction. He had worked quickly, and she seemed to be on the right track.

"What do you mean by 'perhaps'?" Xavier de Tréchet's tone was harsh and pressing.

Adel entered through the door behind her, bringing Marcel Dumont with him.

"Have a seat," she instructed the caretaker, and he sat down hesitantly. Either he felt uncomfortable among the family members, or he feared they might have found something incriminating.

"We're getting ready to head home. Unfortunately, the police didn't cover themselves in glory. They failed to solve my father's murder. If Auguste hadn't confessed..."

"He's not a murderer," Marie snapped at her brother, who merely shrugged. For him, the case was closed.

"Since you're on the way home, and I'll keep the questioning brief," she promised. Xavier de Tréchet sat at the head of the table, already occupying the position of family patriarch, and he seemed quite comfortable with it.

"When will our father's body be released by the forensics examiner?" Fabius asked. "We need to prepare for the funeral."

"The foundation will take care of the formalities," Monsieur Marceau said from a corner, as if he preferred to remain unnoticed.

"I expect we'll release the body within the next few days."

"What brings you here today?" Xavier de Tréchet pressed impatiently. "We're in a hurry."

"There are some points to clarify before we can apprehend the murderer."

"The murderer is already known." The man repeated his viewpoint impatiently.

"We found a witness who convinced us that Auguste Brunel did meet with Patrick Pradel, but several hours before the time of the crime. It's unlikely he had anything to do with the murder. The confession didn't come from him. Someone planted it in your brother-in-law's pocket."

"I told you so." Marie gave Xavier a triumphant look. Sandrine could imagine what she had endured from her siblings as the wife of the suspected murderer of their father.

"The three deaths are closely linked, that's undeniable," Sandrine observed.

"Who killed my husband?"

"We will find out."

"The only person who had a dispute with Auguste was Marcel." Fabius de Tréchet glanced at the caretaker. "After all, they had a physical altercation. In such situations, one thing can lead to another."

"He had no reason to be jealous at all," Marcel snapped at

him. "There was nothing inappropriate between Madame Brunel and me."

Marie cast a contemptuous glance at Fabius. "I've never been unfaithful to my husband."

"Do you drive a red compact car?" Sandrine asked the caretaker.

"Yes. An old Mini Cooper."

"Such a car was observed outside the detective agency at the time of the murder."

"I haven't been to Dinan for weeks," he said in defence against the unspoken accusation.

"Love and jealousy are powerful motives."

"I have nothing to do with that," he interrupted impatiently.

"I believe you," she replied.

The young man seemed taken aback. Apparently he hadn't expected her support.

"Then I lack the imagination to envision someone who hates our family enough to kill my father and my brother-in-law." Xavier de Tréchet looked at her expectantly.

Sandrine glanced over the attendees. She couldn't imagine any of them loving anyone enough, except perhaps themselves, to commit such a crime.

"Get to the point." The man glanced pointedly at his Rolex.

"I am convinced that following the money trail will lead us to the murderer of Alexandre de Tréchet. The two subsequent murders were solely committed to protect the perpetrator from being discovered."

"Was Auguste an innocent victim?" Marie sat up, challenging her brothers. If she expected an apology or sympathy, she was disappointed.

However, Sandrine didn't consider the man entirely innocent. With a little less self-interest and more honesty towards the police, he might still be among the living.

"Patrick Pradel was hired by your father to surveil Auguste Brunel. He stumbled upon something more lucrative than uncovering a simple affair."

"What are you suggesting?" Xavier de Tréchet had taken on the role of the family spokesperson and looked at her grumpily.

"I suspect the detective earned a substantial part of his income through blackmail."

"And now you believe he might have blackmailed a family member or someone from our circle?"

"That's my assumption."

"With what?"

"The focus is on the construction and operation of the new technology centre in Rennes. You bid on that project, Monsieur de Tréchet. Or am I mistaken?"

"I did. Unfortunately, I wasn't successful. Where are you going with this?"

"You weren't selected, but a company owned by the foundation was awarded the contract."

"What?" Xavier de Tréchet turned to Régis Marceau, staring at him. "Is there any truth to this story?"

"What can I say? Alexandre was enthusiastic about the project."

"I showed both of you my calculations. And you used them for your own bid? That's despicable."

"I have nothing to do with it. It was your father's decision. I advised against it, but he ignored my advice."

"What a bunch of miserable cheats." The man leaned back in his chair, taking a deep breath. The supposed betrayal by his father had clearly affected him.

"When did you find out about it?" Sandrine asked.

"Just now. I was completely unaware."

"To be betrayed by one's own family makes one angry, doesn't it?"

"You can say that again." He turned to Régis Marceau. "We need to talk about this," he threatened.

"Perhaps Patrick Pradel had already informed you of this betrayal? You were upset and confronted your father. Your anger boiled over, and you grabbed one of the weapons hanging on the wall, striking out in your rage."

The colour drained from his cheeks, and he stared at Sandrine with widened eyes. "I wouldn't kill my father," the usually arrogant man stammered.

"We will find out." She wasn't ready to let him off the hook yet. His inflated ego would only interfere otherwise.

"Did you know about it?" asked Fabius de Tréchet. He had remained silent until now, but his question hung heavily in the air. His brother simply shook his head wordlessly.

"The whole tragic story began with the surveillance of Auguste. Patrick Pradel discovered a lead that took him to the construction project in Rennes. One of the companies involved caught his attention: CSR. Cyber-Security-Rennes. At least, he mentioned the company several times to a witness."

"A company that frequently works for us. There have been no complaints," Régis Marceau interjected.

"They invoice you a considerable sum annually," Sandrine added.

"Normal costs associated with all technology projects. There's nothing unusual about it. I fail to see where this is leading."

"I was curious why Pradel was interested in this company. At this point, things got interesting, and everything began to make sense."

"Shouldn't you be focusing on solving Alexandre's murder?" the CEO interjected.

"Monsieur Hermé, a prosecutor from Rennes, was kind enough to pay CSR a visit. Unfortunately, he didn't find a bustling IT company but merely a secretary in a shared office, taking and redirecting calls. It's a shell company."

"You think we're being swindled?" Régis Marceau leaned forward in his chair, looking around as if trying to guess the thoughts of the family members.

"The question is rather, who is this 'we'? Without the knowledge of someone within the foundation who signed the contracts and approved the invoices, such a sophisticated fraud that has been going on for years could never have occurred."

"Are you suggesting I had something to do with it?" the man exclaimed. "Why would I?"

"During the surveillance of Auguste Brunel, the private detective took note of you. When I checked Monsieur Brunel's alibi, I also came across you. You're a regular at the Saint-Malo casino, with, as I've been told, a rather unfortunate hand at blackjack."

"That's a lie." He jumped up, shooting an angry glance at Sandrine. Adel took a step to the side, blocking the exit.

"A court order is on its way. I'm convinced the casino manager won't hesitate to answer some questions for us." Although not entirely true, she had no doubt that de Chezac would cooperate. Though finding a culprit outside the family would better suit him.

"I haven't done anything illegal," the man retorted in an unusually defiant tone.

"You needed money to finance your gambling addiction, hence the deal with Madame Mornier, who played the role of the CEO of CSR on your behalf."

"You can't prove any of these baseless accusations. I'll sue you and the entire Saint-Malo police force."

"You're welcome to," Sandrine replied before continuing. "I imagine the sequence of events roughly like this: Patrick Pradel hit a dead-end in the surveillance of Auguste Brunel. None of his usual tricks worked on him." She saw Marie smirk out of the corner of her eye. "Alexandre was a shrewd businessman, and I assume he lured Pradel with a hefty bonus. The hope for that quickly faded, but Pradel had stumbled upon another piece of information about a corruption case within the foundation that seemed valuable enough to extort a tidy sum. He certainly didn't reveal who was involved until he had the money in hand. But whatever he told Alexandre de Tréchet was enough for him to seek a confrontation with you. Alexandre probably didn't suspect his longtime CEO. But you knew your scam was on the verge of being exposed. Several years in prison and financial ruin were imminent. I suspect you suggested a meeting at the smithy, where you wouldn't be disturbed. Had you already planned to kill your boss, or did the act happen in a fit of rage when you saw no way out?"

"These are just fairy tales you're spinning to deflect from your incompetence."

"When Patrick Pradel learned of the murder, he immediately realised that only one person could be responsible: the one who defrauded the foundation. He couldn't expect any more money from his employer, but he knew too much about you. Extortion was nothing unusual for him. When did he contact you? Before or after our visit to him in Dinan?"

"I've never heard of this detective."

"Marie Brunel convinced me that her husband had nothing to do with Patrick Pradel's murder, so we meticulously retraced his steps. While he did visit the victim, it was several hours before his death. At the time of the murder, another car was observed outside the house in Dinan: a red compact. Unfortunately, the witness could only remember parts of the license plate. A comparison with the vehicles of the family or other suspects yielded no results. It wasn't until we looked into the project in Rennes that we identified the car: it belongs to Madame Mornier, the CEO."

"Then she must have killed the man," Régis Marceau exclaimed angrily. "She wanted to conceal her fraud."

"Or she lent the car to a friend. Someone she shares an apartment with in Saint-Malo. Perhaps she didn't know the car was used for a crime."

"A rather far-fetched theory."

"The car has already been retrieved and is currently undergoing forensic analysis. I'm confident we'll find your fingerprints on it, probably even blood stains on the floor mat. What will Madame Mornier say when she finds out you're denying your affair with her?"

"You can't possibly believe this." He turned to the victim's children.

"It seems quite plausible to me," Marie Brunel replied. Régis Marceau avoided looking at her and sank into the chair, which creaked under his weight.

"You paid Patrick Pradel and demanded the documents," Sandrine continued. "The man made his first and most serious mistake: he underestimated you. In the briefcase you always carry, there was plenty of room for the morning star you had stolen from the smithy beforehand. As soon as he turned his back on you, you struck. A single powerful blow was enough to solve your problem. At least, that's what you thought. But a stroke of bad luck thwarted your plans."

The man glared at her with hostility and clenched his jaws tightly. It dawned on him that denying it wouldn't save him anymore.

"Unfortunately, Madame Brunel gave her husband a false alibi, otherwise I might have figured it out sooner. Auguste had made it a habit to sleep on a sofa in the salon when he returned from his late night excursions. He must have seen you leaving the house with his father-in-law on the night of the murder and returning alone later."

"The damned drunkard," Régis Marceau cursed. "Who could have known that the marriage was in such a mess that he preferred to sleep on the sofa rather than with his wife?"

"When did he confront you?" Sandrine didn't give him time to think. The man had started confessing; now she needed to keep him talking.

"On the day he was arrested. At first, he didn't realise the significance of what he had observed in his drunken state. It wasn't until he heard from you that the detective who was shadowing him had also been killed that he managed to put two and two together. The idiot."

"You killed Auguste!" Marie shouted at him.

"Be glad to be rid of him," he retorted.

"Hardly had you gotten rid of one blackmailer, the next one showed up." The banter with Marie couldn't distract him from his confession. "What did he want?"

"The fool wanted a seat on the foundation's board. That was impossible; not even Alexandre could have arranged it. The statutes were clear. I offered him money, but he was too greedy."

"You must have panicked when we arrested and interrogated him."

"His greed prevented him from turning me in to the police. That was a grave mistake."

"So you pulled out all the stops to get him released."

"It was easier than I thought."

"And then?"

"He started drinking in my car right away. One interrogation and those few hours in the station had shaken the wimp. I knew another interrogation would break him, and he would rat me out."

"So you gave him more to drink."

"I didn't need to force the man. He crawled into his flashy car almost on all fours and sped off. Honestly, I hoped he would kill himself on the road, but he actually made it here. What choice did I have?"

"A few more deep swigs from the bottle, a walk to discuss his demands, and a shove off the wall into the mill's tidal pool. Was he too drunk to make it back to land, or did you have to help him?"

He lowered his head and fell silent. He wouldn't say anything more. But that was no longer necessary. A court would decide what would happen to him. She signalled Adel to take him away. Régis Marceau looked up at him, stood up heavily, and let himself be taken away without resistance.

Xavier de Tréchet watched him go. Disbelief etched his features. The realisation that the man he had known for many years had killed his father was clearly seeping slowly into his consciousness. Sandrine looked around; the others seemed to feel the same, except Marie, who shot the man a hateful look.

Now it was up to the family to speak amongst themselves. She wasn't needed here anymore and bid farewell. No one objected, and she left the dining room.

Madame Sérian handed her coat in the entrance hall. "I knew I could count on you."

"Thank you for your trust." She had doubted several times whether she would track down the murderer.

Adel was waiting for her on the outside stairs. Régis Marceau was already sitting in a patrol car, which drove off.

"Let's treat ourselves to an early lunch," she suggested. "I was at Le Sillon recently. I'd like to try it out."

"I'm in. There's something I want to discuss with you."

"And what would that be?"

"Inès was with me. She needs an intern for the office and hopes that Jamila might be interested."

"A good choice. She'll have my support."

"I'm not sure if Jamila is interested in an internship at the police. We're not particularly popular among her friends."

"I could talk to her sometime," she suggested. "If you're okay with that."

"As long as it's just a position in the office, that's fine." He looked at Sandrine and chuckled. "She doesn't have to turn out just like you, after all."

"Why would she want to? But I'll do my best not to be a bad influence on her," she promised.

"There's no danger of that since Jamila will work exclusively in administration."

We'll see how long it takes before she gets bored there.

They circled around the château and headed back to their cars parked at the rear. On the way back, she wanted to stop by a bookstore and buy a cookbook. Léon would remember her bold promise to cook a meal for him and some friends.

"Your sister is a chef, isn't she?"

"The absolute best in all of Saint-Malo."

"I heard she gives cooking classes."

A wide grin spread across his face.

"You want to learn to cook?" he asked incredulously.

"I've been thinking about it."

"She organises an ongoing course and would be happy to teach you something."

"Not a word to Léon or Rosalie, understood?"

"Of course not, otherwise you'll have me directing traffic in uniform for a year."

They looked at each other and smiled.

At that moment, her phone vibrated. A text message had arrived.

"Something unpleasant?" he asked.

"Sébastian Hermé wants to speak with me." The message sounded unusually formal for the man.

"Our case involves a company from Rennes. He'll want to know the details."

"You're probably right."

She pocketed the phone. If the prosecutor was merely curious, he would have called her personally. A text message indicated that he had formally contacted her. She couldn't shake the feeling that something ominous was brewing.

I'll worry about that when it arrives.

She got into her car and left the château behind.

Directory of persons

- Sandrine Perrot: Headstrong detective in Saint-Malo
- Adel Azarou: Brigadier with a penchant for fashion extravagance
- Jean Matisse: Chief of Police in Saint-Malo
- Jean-Claude Mazet: An often underestimated forensic technician
- Inès Boni: Office manager and invaluable source of local information
- Doctor Hervé: Meticulous forensic pathologist from Saint-Malo
- Renard Dubois and Luc Poutin: Police sergeants
- Antoine de Chezac: Ambitious Prosecutor
- Geneviève Drouet: Historian, love interest of Adel Azarou
- Marcel Dumont : Jack-of-all-trades at the Château de Tréchet
- Sébastian Hermé: Prosecutor from Rennes
- Bertrand Barais: Farmer and tenant

- Rosalie Simonas: Successful crime writer and friend of Sandrine
- Deborah Binet: Ambitious journalist always hoping for insider tips
- Léon Martinau: Club owner and ove interest of Sandrine
- Alain Nebot: Blacksmith and owner of the Tide Mill
- Lilou Lanvers: Martial arts fighter and friend of Sandrine
- Alexandre de Tréchet: Owner of the Château de Tréchet
- Xavier de Tréchet: Eldest son of Alexandre
- Fabius de Tréchet: Youngest son of Alexandre
- Marie Brunel: Daughter of Alexandre
- Auguste Brunel: Marie's husband
- Régis Marceau: Manager of the family foundation
- Patrick Pradel: A dubious private investigator

Thanks

I am delighted that you joined Sandrine Perrot and Adel Azarou in their investigation in Brittany. Feedback from my readers is very important to me. Critique, praise and ideas are always welcome, and I am happy to answer any questions.

My email address is: Author@Christophe-Villain.com

Newsletter: To not miss any new publications you can sign up to the newsletter and get the free novella: Death in Paris - The prequel to the Brittany Mystery Series.

Free Novella

Subscribe to the newsletter and receive a free eBook: Death in Paris.
Sandrine Perrot's back story, her last case in Paris.

Sandrine held the warm coffee cup in her hands and looked out through the café window. The gusty wind drove dark clouds across the sky and swirled leaves along the boulevard. Pedestrians zipped up their jackets and scrambled to keep dry before the impending rain. She wasn't particularly excited about the prospect of having to take her motorbike on the road. Sandrine forgot to shop most of the time and hated to cook. Café Central was her salvation so she wouldn't turn up at work with her stomach growling.

"Would you like anything else to drink?" asked the waitress, who regularly saw Sandrine during her morning shift. She bet the young girl was a student who worked here to earn a few euros. Judging by her distinct accent, she was probably from Provence.

"Thank you but I have to get on the road pretty soon."

"Not a nice day." The young woman took a peek outside and picked up the used plate on

which the remains of scrambled eggs and baguette crumbs lay.

"That's why I hold on to my coffee cup for a while and enjoy the warmth in the café before I have to go to work." A bad feeling swept over her that she couldn't pin down to any specific event, but it nagged at her, as if the day could only get worse. The case she was investigating was stuck in her head and she couldn't shake it, which she usually could.

"No hurry," said the waitress, looking around the half-empty café. "It doesn't get crowded again until lunchtime, so until then I don't have much to do."

Sandrine's cell phone, which was lying on the table in front of her, vibrated and she glanced at the display.

"I'm afraid I have to take this call."

The waitress took the hint and took the dirty dishes into the kitchen. "Hello, Martin, what's up?"

She listened to her colleague in silence for a while.

"On the Richard Lenoir Boulevard? I'll be there in fifteen minutes."

Sandrine ended the call and cursed under her breath. Her gut feeling had proved to be right; the day lived up to its promise. She put money on the table, pulled on the waterproof motorcycle jacket and picked up the helmet that was lying on a chair.

She quickly drank the rest of the coffee. The waitress gave her a friendly wave as she left.

Her motorcycle was parked on the wide sidewalk between two trees. She wiped the wet seat with her sleeve before climbing on and pulling on her gloves. She took a deep breath and started the engine. Shortly thereafter, she merged into traffic.

Half a dozen patrol cars and an ambulance were parked by the Saint-Martin Canal. The paramedics were hunkered down in the car and puffs of smoke rose through their slightly ajar windows. They were more comfortable than their police colleagues, who had to go out to cordon off the area. The first onlookers were already gathering on one of the narrow bridges that spanned the watercourse. Sandrine drove through a gap in the metal fence separating the canal from the boulevard and parked the motorcycle on the wide pedestrian promenade. Bollards – stocky vertical posts – were set at regular intervals, but today no boats were moored here and the lock gate was closed.

"Good morning, Sandrine," a grey-haired man with angular features greeted her. His badge identified him as Major de Police. "Kind of shitty weather to be out on a motorcycle."

"Hello, Martin. It's still a lot quicker than driving a car. Not to mention parking." She stuffed her gloves and scarf into her helmet and stuffed it into one of the panniers. "Is it our guy?"

"The Necktie Killer? Looks like it."

"Is that what they call him now?" She shook her head in disgust. "Far too friendly sounding. He's a sadistic murderer and should be considered and referred to as such."

"I didn't invent it. We owe that to the journalists who needed punchy headlines." He held up his hands defensively.

"I'm sorry. I was thinking of the victims."

"That's all right. Whenever things like that don't get to you anymore, it's time to change careers."

"In there?" she asked, looking toward the entrance to the Saint-Martin Canal, which ran underground for the next few miles. Even on sunny days, this gloomy place seemed ominous to her. "Who from our team is here?"

"Brossault, the medical examiner with the forensic guys and some cops cordoning off the area. The big boys are on their way, it was probably too early in the morning for them."

Sandrine laughed softly. The chief of homicide and the juge d'instruction, the prosecutor in charge of the investigation, would not be long in coming. They were forced to demonstrate that

the police were doing everything they could to take the perpetrator off the street since the series of murders was dominating the front pages of the newspapers. However, they hadn't even come an inch closer to him since they'd found the first victim in the summer. It was now February and two more dead women had joined the list of victims.

"Let's go then," she said, walking towards the scene of the crime.

The rain started, pattering on the dark water of the canal. Major Martin Alary pulled up the collar of his raincoat and walked faster across the slippery pavement. A uniformed cop stepped aside and waved them through the barricade.

"Was it closed?" Sandrine asked, looking at the lock where the water was damming up. The Saint-Martin Canal was just under two-and-a-half-miles long, and connected the Bassin de la Villette in the north with the Seine in the south. It had a total of five locks – enclosures with gates at each end where the water level could be raised or lowered.

"Most people only use the exposed area: a few tourist boats, but mostly paddle boats and small motorboats used for family outings in the Bassin de la Villette. Hardly more than a dozen boats a day traverse the entire length of the canal."

"The less water traffic, the more noticeable things are. Let's hope someone noticed something."

They entered the tunnel through an open metal door guarded by another police officer. Martin Alary wiped raindrops from his shoulders and adjusted his gun holster. A brick path, on which two people could comfortably walk side by side, ran along the length of the canal. The dim light of the rainy day reached only a few feet deep into the tunnel, and the antique-looking lamps that hung at regular intervals on the wall allowed one to see the way, but were useless for forensic

work. The forensics team had already set up blazingly bright spotlights so they wouldn't miss a thing.

A thin man with a pointed beard and a bald head walked towards them.

"Ah. Capitaine Perrot and Major Alary. Already here?" Marcel Carron, the forensics manager, patted Sandrine's companion on the shoulder and gave him a wink before turning to face her. He refrained from giving her a chummy pat on the back.

"How far along are you with securing the crime scene?"

"Almost done. However, there was hardly anything to secure."

"What can you tell me?"

"An employee of the city building department discovered the body during a routine examination. She was floating in the water. He informed us immediately and left the site. Very prudent."

"Is this also the scene of the crime?" the major asked.

"There's no evidence thus far," Carron replied. "We've searched the path for evidence of a struggle, but to no avail. The corpse is unclothed, but we couldn't find clothes anywhere."

"Not surprising."

"I concur."

"Any idea how the body got here?" Alary asked.

"There aren't many options left. There is no current in the canal sufficient enough to move a human body. She would have been spotted within one of the locks."

"Then she was put here," said Sandrine.

"The question is how." The forensic scientist pointed to the metal door at the entrance to the tunnel. "Entry is forbidden and the door is normally locked. However, there's no problem climbing over the door but dragging a corpse of an adult person up and over would be almost impossible without risking being discovered."

"Then there's only one option left," Sandrine said, stepping up to the railing that was too dirty to touch. "The perpetrator threw her off a boat at this point."

"An ideal location," the major agreed. "Nobody would notice since people seldom come in here."

"I'm assuming there's no security camera in the tunnel." Despite saying this, Sandrine looked around.

"Maybe the doctor can tell us more." She wasn't particularly hopeful. So far, the killer had left no usable evidence.

"Good luck."

Sandrine pulled a pair of disposable gloves and shoe covers out of her jacket pocket and put them on. Even though the forensic scientist assumed there wouldn't be anything of interest here, she played it safe.

A few feet away, she found Doctor Brossault standing next to the victim, a blue blanket spread over it.

"Bonjour," she greeted the older man in a dark suit, bow tie and handkerchief in his breast pocket. He turned to face her and used his forefinger to push his rimless glasses up the bridge of his nose. "An ideal place to dump a body, isn't it?"

"Absolutely." He nodded enthusiastically. "The murderer has a soft spot for historical places. You have to give him that."

"The canal dates back from the early 19th century, from what I remember from my history class." "1825 if you want to be exact, but who cares about that anyway?"

Sandrine suppressed a grin. The medical examiner was the type of person who always wanted to be as precise as possible and didn't withhold his knowledge.

"The canal, anyway. The structure built over the canal did not take place until much later: in 1860. At first, it was designed by Haussmann to improve traffic in the city."

"At first?" Sandrine asked. The man loved sharing his knowledge of history and enlightening those around him. It made him happy, so she let him have his fun.

"Naturally. Napoleon III was not exactly a popular head of state. Resistance to his rule simmered particularly in the revolutionary neighbourhoods such as Faubourg-Montmartre and Ménilmontant. So the plan to build over the canal came in handy. A wide swath through the city along which to send cavalry to maintain law and order."

"Interesting," said Major Alary, who Sandrine heard come up behind her. "But it didn't do him any good in the end."

"Fortunately," the doctor agreed.

Sandrine knelt down next to the body and looked inquisitively at the medical examiner. Only when he nodded did she lift the blanket under which the victim lay. A young woman's bloodless face stared at her with lifeless blue eyes. Blonde hair clung damply to pale skin. She wore a silk tie around her neck, where strangulation marks could be seen.

"She was strangled," Sandrine murmured, more to herself than to Doctor Brossault. "Just like the previous two victims," he confirmed.

"What can you tell me?"

"I'd put the woman in her mid-twenties, blonde and attractive like the other victims. She was strangled with the necktie. There are cuts on her wrists. Without wanting to commit myself, I would conclude that plastic restraints were used. The police use those things, too."

"Any other signs that she fought back?"

"I can't imagine that she didn't, but she had no chance of surviving. Not with her hands tied. Of course we are also looking for narcotics."

"Maybe the tie will get us further."

"A silk tie. Quite expensive and downright exclusive. Forensics will confirm that, although I can't imagine Monsieur Carron being an expert on the subject."

She looked up at him probingly.

"Have you ever seen the man properly dressed before?" His brow furrowed as if surprised at her lack of awareness.

"What's so special about these ties?"

"The quality of the silk is impeccable. In terms of design, I would guess mid-century. In addition, our killer is able to tie a perfect Windsor knot, something that is becoming increasingly rare these days. People either forgo a tie completely or fasten it sloppily. I would narrow the circle of perpetrators down to people with style and money."

He finished the sentence and straightened his bow tie.

Sandrine put the blanket back over the woman's face. She would see her again in the medical examiner's office. She'd seen enough for now.

To subscribe to the newsletter, please use the QR code.

Other Books

Emerald Coast Murder

Sandrine Perrot's investigation takes her from the picturesque fishing towns to the rural hinterland of Brittany's Emerald Coast.

Police Lieutenant Sandrine Perrot is on leave from her post in Paris and has settled in Cancale, the oyster capital of Brittany. She is temporarily assigned to the Saint-Malo police station for this case. The body of an unidentified woman is discovered on the Brittany coast path along the bay of Mont- Saint-Michel.

With her new assistant, Adel Azarou, she takes on the investigation, which leads them to a cold case from Paris, but also deep into the tragic history of a venerable hotelier family.

Saint-Malo Murder

Christophe Villain
Translated by Terry Laster

Saint-Malo Murder

Sandrine Perrot - The Brittany Mystery Series

Death of an influencer

The tranquillity of the picturesque old town of Saint-Malo is shattered by a gruesome murder. The dead woman is a well-known influencer and radio presenter who has made many enemies in the region with her controversial opinions and themes. The killer has not only professionally staged the body and crime scene, but also meticulously recorded the crime.

Will she find the perpetrator in the dead woman's private surroundings, or will she have to dig deep into the victim's past?

Deadly Tides at Mont-Saint-Michel

A dead woman loved by all.

Instead of spending a pleasant day with Léon on the coast and at Le Mont-Saint-Michel, Sandrine Perrot is called to a fatal accident in the Saint-Malo marina. The driver's death touches her personally, as she had just met the woman. In the course of the forensic investigation, she discovers that there is more to the alleged accident than she first suspected.

Her investigation leads her into the world of a well-known family in Le Mont-Saint-Michel, a family marked by antiquated traditions but also by conflicts between siblings.

Another person soon disappears without a trace. Was he trying to evade interrogation, or was an unwelcome witness being silenced?

Booklover's Death

A dead book collector

A new case takes Sandrine Perrot to Bécherel, the Cité du Livre of Brittany. A place where life revolves around books. The president of a well-known book club has been found murdered in his private library. Did contempt and rivalry among the book lovers lead to murder or does she have to look elsewhere for the motive?

While Sandrine investigates in the city of books, the prosecutor de Chezac builds a case against her. From the sidelines, she has to watch as the situation in Saint-Malo escalates.